Praise for

Maxine Unleashes Doomsday

"Take one of Richard Stark's Parker novels and throw it in the blender with DVDs of *Mad Max* and *The Warriors*. Guess what? You just broke your blender. Find solace in this book, which is what you should have done in the first place."

—Rob Hart, author of *The Warehouse*

"*Maxine Unleashes Doomsday* rolls in with bang-up premise and keeps on punching. This is a trip into the far future and then the near future, where the oceans have swallowed up the coasts, the United States has fractured, and people like Maxine are left in the dust. But Maxine is tough and she's got no patience for any crap and she will survive...one way or another. Filled with a terrific carnival cast of characters, cracker-jack scenes, and Kolakowski's witty prose, *Maxine* is a fantastic read and definitely well worth your time."

—Jen Conley, author of
Seven Ways to Get Rid of Harry

"Loaded with savvy world-building, memorable characters and precise, sharp plotting, I devoured Nick Kolakowski's latest. The post-apocalyptic and wonderfully bonkers *Maxine* will keep you turning pages at a breakneck pace."

—Alex Segura, author of *Dangerous Ends*

"I don't know which is more terrifying: how wildly inventive this book is, or how close this fractured world is to ours. In *Maxine*, Kolakowski gives us the hero we need for the apocalypse we deserve."

—Nik Korpon, author of
Wear Your Home Like a Scar

"White hot words and images of a crumbling society leap off the page giving the reader a scary look at a future which, in light of what's going on today, is not so far-fetched. Kolakowski is a master at creating fascinating, horrifying characters fighting for existence in a world gone wild."

—Charles Salzberg, author of
Swann's Last Song and *Second Story Man*

Praise for the Books by
Nick Kolakowski

"Bounty hunters, a Monkey Man and Zombie Bill, explosions, sharp violence and even laughs. Kolakowski brings the goods with this one!"

—Dave White, author of the Jackson Donne series,
for *Boise Longpig Hunting Club*

"It's no surprise that Nick Kolakowski brought the heat with his latest novel *Main Bad Guy*. The surprise is that you won't know which landed harder: His stripped-down, hard-boiled prose, the explosive dialogue, or the wickedly insane and diabolical humor. Grab hold of this one with both hands and hold on tight."

—Eryk Pruitt, author of *Townies*
and *What We Reckon*

"Dark, bleak and in-your-face, take-no-prisoners prose, everything you want in crime fiction."

—Frank Bill author of *Donnybrook* and
Crimes in Southern Indiana, for *Slaughterhouse Blues*

MAXINE UNLEASHES DOOMSDAY

OTHER TITLES BY NICK KOLAKOWSKI

Boise Longpig Hunting Club
Somebody's Trying to Kill Me (and Other Stories)

The Love & Bullets Series
A Brutal Bunch of Heartbroken Saps
Slaughterhouse Blues
Main Bad Guy

NICK KOLAKOWSKI

MAXINE UNLEASHES DOOMSDAY

Down & Out Books
3959 Van Dyke Road, Suite 265
Lutz, FL 33558
DownAndOutBooks.com

Cover design by Zach McCain

ISBN: 1-64396-049-0
ISBN-13: 978-1-64396-049-4

To Mom + Dad

File 2.78.93821.2
Date: 5/29/2110

Recovered from the hard drive of a Winpple Laptop Series 5, the last generation of that device line to enter the consumer market. Although the drive was heavily damaged (REF: Midtown EMP, "Big Guy War," Final Stage), our machine-learning algorithms managed to extrapolate most of the missing text using contextual data. Nonetheless, there are still some breaks, which are clearly delineated for your researching pleasure.

This document is particularly interesting as it provides a glimpse into conditions in Manhattan immediately following the Collapse. Those scholars of the life of Maxine Hardwater will find some brief observations of her character during her "terminal" stage.

[Begin Recovered Text]

Baby, I crashed the sailboat.

Its gleaming white bow crunched into the new oyster reefs off Governors Island, the ones planted by the Revival Brigade to blunt the higher tides, and splintered like a cheap toy. Two months of sanding and painting and caulking and then puzzling out how to rig a sail, reduced in three minutes to fiberglass chunks and slithering nylon rope and bits of foam bobbing in the harbor's toxic stew.

By the way, the Revival Brigade's motto is "The Big Apple! Glorious Once Again!" They believe the first Flood was Special Delivery from the Almighty himself. And with enough prayer and repair work on our part, they think He might deign to spare us a second bath. Good luck with that one, I say.

I strapped on my life preserver, offered the dying ship a quick middle-finger salute, and leapt overboard. It took an hour to kick my way back to shore, where I swallowed two handfuls of antibiotics to kill any of those newfangled super-bugs in my bloodstream. The pills went down easy with my weekly ration of Jim Beam.

Do you remember a book on my shelf in the home office, J. G. Ballard's *The Drowned World*? It turned out to be a remarkably prescient novel: global warming, rising water levels, a little bit of social chaos to keep things interesting. Its hero, a scientist named Keran, ends up wandering south ("Like a second Adam") into the blooming jungles.

I was taking the opposite path: due north, toward you. By sailing, I would have avoided the crumbling highways, the dead towns and ports stripped of food and gasoline, and New England's warring clans: the New Iroquois, the Battling Irish, and—just when you think the human race has exhausted its capacity for corny nicknames—King Tut and the Beatdown Seven.

"Love you," was the last thing you said over the phone, from Halifax, before the connection went dead. I want to believe that Nova Scotia fared better than everything south. Given the rising temperatures, they say, Canada will soon become the breadbasket of the world. Once that happens, they'll likely demand a stop to any jokes about moose and ending sentences with "Eh."

Lower Manhattan now looks like Venice with a couple added skyscrapers. Half of Brooklyn is out to sea on a tide of PBR cans and fake hipster moustaches. The latter case demonstrates, yet again, that every bad situation has a silver lining.

In the first hours of our watery doom, when the tide rushed in and the news screamed about the barriers and floodgates finally giving way, I splashed my way uptown past bellowing cops and tiny skiffs from which street capitalists, who only a month before had been shilling Gucci knockoffs, hawked everything from swim trunks to scuba gear. The Bluetooth in my ear connected to the broker in Shanghai.

Don't roll your eyes: For once, I wasn't just working the numbers. Remember that Shanghai survived its own deluge, at great cost: thousands of casualties before they erected those concrete barriers and flood channels.

"How did you make it through?" I asked the broker, whose clipped and pleasant voice bore the faintest trace of an Oxford accent. By this time, I had huddled in the vestibule of an apartment building on Park, after slipping the excitable doorman a crisp fifty and waving him away. Screaming crowds and water churned past.

"I stayed in my condo, near the top of a skyscraper," she said. "I drank beer for weeks, because it was cleaner than the water from the taps. The ones with money survived. The ones with money always survive."

Considering our three-story brownstone in Brooklyn, the advice about skyscrapers helped me not one bit. "Thanks so much. Let's short my entire U.S. stock portfolio," I said, then tapped my jaw three times to end the call.

[NOTE: Missing text]

I start off every morning with a watery cup of instant coffee and three painkillers. Depending on the weekly rations, lunch and dinner are some combination of energy bars, noodles, and jerky. People around here would massacre a dozen nuns for a bag of fresh apples, but nobody dares touch the fish eating our wreckage.

I call it the "End of the World Diet," and let me tell you, there is no better way to erase those love handles.

Two weeks after I crashed the sailboat, I awoke and rose and swiped the moisture from the bedroom window and stared out at a world of gray water needled by soft rain. The tide seemed higher than ever, the roofs of parked cars like flat pond stones. Above the white-noise hiss of weather, I could hear Brooklyn settling on its rotted joints: the low growl of crumbling concrete, broken by the occasional shriek of steel on steel. In a few thousand years they might whisper legends about this place, the same way Victorian people once wondered about Atlantis.

"Jake!"

The voice sliced sharp and high through the rain. On instinct, I ducked back and flattened myself against the wall, then peeked around the windowsill. But I knew the figure rowing down my street: skin red and craggy as something left in a smokehouse for a month, the face of a pugilist with no knack for defense. He wore an enormous tri-corner hat, a knee-length brown coat splattered with paint, and a truly impressive cutlass on his belt.

I walked downstairs and unbolted the seven locks on my steel-reinforced door and stepped onto the stoop that now doubled as a small dock. I had my double-barreled shotgun in my hand, out of habit. I said, "How goes it, Walter?"

The burnt man stood in his tiny rowboat and doffed his hat, revealing hair dry and tangled as a bird's nest. "Dear me, that's an impressive phallic symbol in your grip. Yet, as the Martians say, I come in peace." He bowed. "I'm sorry about your sailboat."

"You saw that?"

"A few uncharitable souls laughed. Not me, I hasten to add." Walter rocked on his heels, almost stumbling. Bottles clinked along the rowboat's bottom. "I come with a tale of woe, involving none other but our fearless leaders. Cheats and liars all, but what did we expect of democracy, where any moron can become a king, provided he purchases enough television ads in swing states..."

"You know you talk like a pirate when you're trashed, right?" Walter served as the gopher for Brooklyn's Operating Committee, and I suspect they paid him in top-shelf liquor. It seemed like he needed a quart of scotch a day to kill the demons from his tours in Afghanistan and Egypt.

"Doing my best to preserve the King's." He shook himself like a dog, scattering rainwater in a wide fan. "Listen, it's the shipment."

Ah, I knew it. Every Monday, twenty trucks rolled across the Brooklyn Bridge from Manhattan, loaded with everything from instant noodles to my good friend Jim Beam. For the first two months following the Flood, those supply boxes had "Property of U.S. Government" stamped on their sides—until a federal transport oh-so-mysteriously exploded in the harbor.

I always suspected The Big Guy had ordered that little escapade, from his Midtown skyscraper. If he wanted to keep outsiders away from his island kingdom, it worked. Now our supplies came courtesy of the Sovereign Nation of Manhattan, which in exchange wanted Brooklyn's brains: our engineers, electricians, horticulturalists, gunsmiths, and the occasional pastry chef.

Investment bankers rank pretty low on that list, and for that I'm grateful: Rumors abound that The Big Guy likes hanging people for middling infractions. Such as speaking your mind.

You see why I want out of this whole mess?

This past Monday, though, the trucks had rumbled halfway across the Brooklyn Bridge—and stopped. *Surrounded by men with guns,* my buddy Marv told me over chess that afternoon. *Add in some snipers on their side of the river. They're taunting our little City-State here.*

I stared at Walter floating off the coast of my front steps, like Blackbeard arriving to the party three centuries late, and wondered anew about the situation. "Last I heard, it was still on the bridge," I said.

"Yes, yes," Walter said, "and we need you to get it back for us."

"Yeah? And how'll I do that?" Manhattan's fighters outnumbered ours by a ratio of three-to-one, thanks to its Jersey refugees, and while I can blast decent-sized holes in things with my trusty shotgun, I am not exactly Mad Max reincarnate.

"Because a former acquaintance of yours, one Charles Teague, is apparently The Big Guy's Bridge Man." Walter sighed. "We need to know what he wants."

Teague had been a senior vice president at Goldman, the sort of plus-sized jackass who commissions a self-portrait and hangs it in the living room of his Park Avenue apartment. "He probably wants bottle service," I said. "You know there's only one reason The Big Guy put him in that position, right? What are you prepared to offer me for my help?"

Walter moaned. "How about civic duty, cur?"

"Teague likes thirty-year-old Scotch and his strippers blonde," I said.

"Huh?"

"I mean, I know how the man thinks." Back when I did

6

mergers and acquisitions, my firm and Teague's targeted the same companies. He once mailed me a gutted trout wrapped in newspaper after I snatched a particularly rich biotech firm from his grasp. Sadly, that was not an unusual occurrence in my former line of work. "They probably have a couple RPGs aimed right at those trucks, you try and launch a raid or something."

"Aye, we suspect so."

I thought it over as Walter swayed like a metronome ticking off the seconds. "I'll do it," I said, "under one condition." And I named it.

He shook his head. "Impossible."

"Then good luck to you." I turned for my door. From behind me came a furious splashing as Walter tried to dock with the front steps. That sort of action constitutes justifiable homicide these days, but I kept the twelve-gauge lowered as I spun around again.

"We got sick people in the hospital," Walter said, in his panic dropping the stupid pirate affectation. "Some sort of water parasite. Kids are getting it the worst. The drugs we need are on those trucks. How heartless can you be, man? Come on. We'll work something out."

[NOTE: Missing text]

I left my shotgun behind.

As I passed through the crowd on our side of the Brooklyn Bridge, hands reached out to shake mine. Others slapped me on the back. Funny how much people start loving you when they need something. It was three minutes to noon and the rainclouds had burned away, revealing a nuclear sun that glinted and sparked on the span's suspension wires and the water below.

Before I stepped onto the Bridge, I turned to Walter, who had rowed us from my house to Brooklyn Heights' drier land. "We have a deal," I told him.

He nodded, and I started up the slope toward Manhattan.

The crowd applauded, a tiny sound against the vastness of the East River, the towers of ruined steel and concrete. After a few moments, it stopped. Nobody wants to celebrate at a funeral.

The sunlight glared off the windshields of twenty battered trucks, parked midway down the Bridge's three Brooklyn-bound lanes. Dozens of men stood atop their roofs, bulky and spiny with weapons: AK-47s, riot pump-actions, antique rifles, machetes, and a few long spears.

I stopped fifteen yards from the first truck, climbed atop a convenient pile of rubble, and yelled: "I'm here for my buddy Teague."

I never saw the meteor. It rocketed out of the throbbing blue sky and smashed into my chest, hurling me backward—

No still alive still alive it's only pain stop screaming—

I blinked. Coughing blood, yes, but alive. On the pavement near my twitching hand, a stubby blue beanbag round, loved by riot cops the world over for its crowd-suppression abilities. *That's okay,* I thought. *I came with a little weaponry of my own.*

The sun went dark, eclipsed by a man. "Small world, huh?" The square-jawed face, once moisturized and exfoliated to a polished sheen, seemed gaunt as a skull. The gray-speckled beard hacked in a ragged line below the chin. He wore a pair of brown coveralls dusted white at the elbows and knees.

"What?" I gasped. "No tailored suit?"

"Real workers don't wear suits." Teague glanced toward the trucks and waved. A guard by the outer rail waggled a stubby black launcher, probably the very one whose beanbag destroyed my ribs. "You're a little far from the boardroom, kid."

"Remember...DynMed?" My strength was returning, along with my voice.

He cocked his head, confused. "Um, yeah. You lying bastards stole that one from us. Little backroom dealing."

"What we did," I said, "was save you...a twenty-million-dollar bath when their HIV vaccine didn't pan out. Well, it's... payback time."

8

"You're a funny guy." Teague knelt on cracking knees, and his scabbed hands circled my wrists, patted my hips and legs, felt along my spine for any weapons. He rifled through my pockets, removing my battered wallet and a silver pen and tossing them on the concrete. "You know why these trucks haven't moved? Your masters forgot to send our tribute."

"Teague. Don't be a douche," I said. "Those trucks are carrying medicine."

"You think I don't know that? Spare me the do-gooder crap," he said. "They're giving you something to do this, aren't they? Maybe if you cut me in, we can do some business."

"What's The Big Guy want?"

"Oh, every one of your mechanical engineers." Teague jabbed a thumb over his shoulder, toward Manhattan shimmering in the heat. "We lost a whole bunch the other night—maybe you saw the smoke? Big accident. I'm surprised Penn Station's still standing after that, frankly."

"And if I say no?" I anticipated the creative litany of threats: pulled apart by revving motorboats, perhaps, or fed piece by quivering piece to the fishes.

"Simple. Your sick people die. We shoot you."

Ah, that golden oldie: a bullet through the frontal lobe.

"I have an alternate proposal." Reaching out very carefully, I took the pen and lifted it so Teague could see the hinge beneath the clip. "How about your men drive those trucks over to our side of the bridge while I go on my merry way?"

I pressed the hinge, flipping it open to reveal a bright red button.

Teague chuckled, his eyes wary. "What's that, some kind of toy?"

"It's a bomb," I said. "Six ounces of C-4, enough to turn both you and me into a red jelly with bone bits mixed in." Walter may have pickled his brains in single malt, but I suspect you never really forget how to rig ways to vaporize people.

To his infinite credit, Teague managed some outward cool.

"Liar, there's no bomb on you," he said slowly. His knees cracked again as he leaned backward. "You always were a bad bluff."

"Plastic capsule, filled with explosive." I lifted my left leg, making what my younger brother once called the Universal Fart Gesture. "Too bad you were never a prison guard. You would've remembered to check me in that one very special place. Hurt shoving it up there, but it was so very worth it to see the look on your face."

I tried not to laugh, waggling that pen back and forth like an old-style hypnotist with a pendulum—and for the first time since you left on that business trip to the Great White North, I felt a little bit good. Nothing beats sticking it to a longtime rival, especially in the name of sick kids.

Teague's eyes darted from mine to the pen. I struggled not to blink. My scalp itched with sweat, my stomach sizzling with acid. I was not ready to die. But if I learned anything in my years on Wall Street, it's that you sell your story to the bitter end.

"Three trucks," Teague licked his dry lips. "And I let you live."

I shook my head. "No. All."

"Ten. And you bring your own drivers here. We're not doing it."

I placed my thumb on the red button.

"We're going to kill you," Teague growled, very low. "Maybe not now, maybe not next week. Someday, we're coming across this bridge."

"Too bad you won't see it," I said, totally calm. We could have been negotiating over deal points, before taking our respective teams to dinner at a walnut-paneled steakhouse.

Teague blinked. I had him then. He knew it, and he knew I knew it. You can take away a man's Kobe beef and in-office foot massages, but his outsized ego will still demand he pays any price—surrender principle, toss a baby to the alligators—so his precious self can survive to hump another day.

"Your funeral," he said, raising a fist above his head. The

first truck rumbled to life, spewing gritty black smoke, and the guard atop its roof leapt to the pavement. The second truck added its own roar, followed by the third and the fourth. The convoy inched forward, tires crunching gravel and glass, gaining speed as it climbed the grade toward Brooklyn.

I took a burning lungful of air, held it, and stumbled upright on quaking legs. The world reeled and tilted, its edges graying. *You will not vomit,* my inner drill sergeant yelled deep in my brain. *You will not vomit, and you will not die. Take another breath.*

I did, and my vision cleared. "You're coming with me," I told Teague, raising the pen, "as our very special guest. Or our future bargaining chip. Whichever term suits you best."

He paled. "You're sorely mistaken."

"No, I'm not. You're my hostage now, buddy."

He gestured over his shoulder, toward the guards beginning to realize something was seriously amiss: questioning cries, stamping feet, the dry snap of a clip into a rifle. "What makes you think these men won't just attack?" he asked. "Kill me along with you?"

"Maybe the fact The Big Guy's your loving uncle, for starters."

Teague said nothing. I took a slow step, and he matched it. We retreated across the Bridge—lagging too far behind the convoy for my taste—as Manhattan's warriors circled behind us, wary as hyenas. The shoreline passed beneath our feet, the span sloping into the shadowy canyon of riverfront condos. Our own people had advanced to the exit lanes and pedestrian ramp, their rifles and blades at the ready, closing ranks in the wake of the last truck. My spine tingled, right where I expected the first spear tip or bullet to hit.

"Back in the day, we weren't good people," I told Teague. The words rolled out nice and strong, despite the deep throbbing in my chest. "But we were better than this. Call them off."

Teague had no interest in dying in a crossfire hurricane, either. Turning in mid-stride, he raised his hands to his people, palms outward. They stopped; a few yelled incoherent threats in my direction. If you closed your eyes, they sounded like dogs. "Tell me something," he said. "Were you bluffing?"

I stared at the exit ramp at the bottom of the Bridge (*Welcome to Brooklyn*, proclaimed the rusty sign above the turnoff to Middagh Street. *How Sweet It Is!*), and what seemed like half of Brooklyn swarming the stopped trucks: boxes torn apart, food and bottles disappearing among a forest of hands and heads.

"You'll never know." I smiled with bloody teeth.

I could only hope the medicine really made it to those kids.

[NOTE: Missing text]

That night, they came for Teague. Say what you will about The Big Guy, he obviously cared about his family. We knew something was wrong when the sentries on the bridge failed to radio their usual check-ins. By that point, of course, it was far too late. The only reason I'm alive to write this stupid letter (which, let's admit it, you'll likely never read) is because of Maxine.

If I'd been smart, I would have returned to my flooded abode immediately after saving the convoy. Instead, I stuck around for a drink—or five, if I'm being honest—with Walter and some other folks. I'd decided to give sociability a try. Not my smartest move.

Walter lived in this little hut in the shadow of the marble monstrosity that had once housed the Kings County Supreme Court. It was little more than four walls made of aluminum siding and pink-foam insulation, topped with a solar-panel roof, but it was warm and had electric light. Walter had invited the Stray brothers, a pair of twins you could tell apart only by their fading tattoos. We drained one bottle of only-mildly-awful plonk, and Walter was opening another when a peculiar sound came from outside, in the shanty that filled the higher elevations of downtown Brooklyn.

It sounded like a loud, metallic sneeze.

Walter sobered up. Leaping from the table, he tore away a ratty blanket from a battered steel chest in one corner, which he opened to reveal an old-style assault weapon, bolted together from chipped metal and 3D-printed polymer. "Come on," he said, snapping a magazine into the weapon, and disappeared through the door.

The Stray brothers nodded and, in perfect sync, drew wicked knives from their jackets. They ducked after Walter, leaving me alone at the table with four empty glasses and an unopened bottle. As the shack seemed to lack any other weaponry, I took the bottle with me. Maybe I could confuse an enemy by offering him a drink.

I stepped outside in time to see the first warning flares rocketing into the sky, from the shanties closest to the bridge. The dead buildings around us flickered white and red. I heard that metallic sneeze again, followed by the harsh chatter of automatic rifles. Our friends from Manhattan weren't even trying for stealth.

The Stray brothers had disappeared, but Walter had taken a position behind a lamppost that someone had refashioned as an art piece, its steel sprayed in bright whorls of neon, topped with a thicket of colored wires and springs. "Look sharp," he growled. "The ruffians are upon us."

Indeed they were. As I crouched, holding the bottle like a club and feeling thoroughly absurd, I saw The Big Guy's men break through the closest line of shanty. It must have been a special team: They wore bulky armor studded with blunt stumps, built from material designed to thwart all kinds of detection gear down to infrared. It was expensive stuff and made them look like porcupines. Their eyes were glowing red circles, courtesy of their night-vision helmets.

They raised their battle rifles, and I cringed back, ready for oblivion.

Then one of the soldiers dropped his weapon, slapped his

hands against the sides of his helmet, and screamed. The others turned to watch as he hopped from foot to foot in a madcap jig. One of them cursed—muffled by layers of armor and electronics—before his own rifle fell from his loose hands, and he launched into the same weird dance. The rest turned to run, only to be seized by the same compulsion: the world's most heavily armed chorus line, jerking and leaping in front of the shanty.

Walter looked at me and shrugged, as if this sort of thing happened every night.

Before I could say anything, the soldiers joined in a collective shriek that rose higher and higher, like dogs on helium, before they collapsed in a still heap. I could sense people in the shanty around us, watching from their peepholes and cracks, waiting to see what happened next.

A woman stepped from the darkness to our right.

She was old, her face etched with wrinkles and battle scars, her left eye covered with a black patch. As she paused to examine the fallen soldiers, I saw the faint light glint off the plastic and steel encasing her left arm. No, it wasn't armor: It was a prosthetic, a high-tech one that nobody around here could afford. The glow illuminated a faint pattern of purple lines along the top of her brow, which disappeared beneath her chopped gray hair. A small bud in her right ear blinked blue.

"Denied my chance to die in battle," Walter said, lowering his weapon.

"Trust us, that's just stupid," the old woman called out, turning to us. "Who are you?"

Walter swept into an old buccaneer's bow. "At your service."

The woman snorted and turned to me. "And who are you?"

"Someone who wants to get out of here," I said.

"You know this area?" She strode toward us, and I fell back a few steps. I wondered what she had done to the soldiers. If I gave her the wrong answer, she might afflict me in the same way.

"A bit," I said. Why lie?

"Good." She tapped her ear. "We are Maxine. We're here to

help. But in order for us to do that, you're going to have to tell us the best way to get into Manhattan."

We? *Us?* I looked around for some companion, but the only figures emerging from the shanty were the local residents, who began stripping armor and weapons from the soldiers. No, she meant whoever was on the other side of her earbud, no doubt feeding her intel.

[NOTE: Missing text]

This woman and the Pig are going to liberate us all.

[END FILE]

File 2.81.10000.3
Date: 6/01/2110

cResearchers should take care with the following document, as it is not a "pure" primary source. Rather, it has been "blended" together from several sources, including memory files from Maxine Hardwater during her "merging" with the Intelligence General. Although scholars (the few of those who are left) may argue stridently against these machine-learning methods, we are trapped by the circumstances of recent history.

Seventy years ago, a growing proportion of the human race relied on digital production and storage; uploading video, text, and images to the so-called "cloud" seemed like the safest way to archive material. Nobody anticipated the widespread rise of EMP weapons, not to mention the renewed use of nuclear bombs. A single EMP blast over the Eastern Seaboard circa 2025, for example, eliminated decades of government records, as well as two social networks' combined data holdings. In order to make sense of the remaining fragments, we have resorted to these alternative techniques, which at least give us the "flavor" of history and our subjects' mindsets, even if the veracity is occasionally suspect.

Another note: Although scholars may denigrate the following as "too narrative-driven" or "breathless in its prose; not scholarly" (early comments from Dr. Chad Perkins of New Harvard—

16

sorry, Chad!), the A.I. insisted on structuring the information in this way. "It needs to be readable," *the machine insisted. "Who wants to grind through that academic garbage?"*

Forgive us, but the machine might have a point.

I.

The year Maxine turned fourteen, she found her true calling, at the cost of two lives.

Maxine spent her childhood mornings at the front window of the crumbling farmhouse where she lived with her brother, Brad, her mother, Joan, and her mother's big bastard of a synthetic-heroin monkey, watching for cars on the road. Whenever one passed, she imagined herself behind its wheel, zooming out of her life with glorious speed, and her heart ached with need.

Maxine knew that, without her, life in the house would fall apart. She needed to feed and clean Brad, kill as many cockroaches and rats as possible, keep the phones powered, stop her mother from choking on her own vomit during the bad highs, and throw rocks at the junkies who lurked in the weedy driveway. That was a typical list of tasks before she left for school. Every two weeks or so, her uncle Preacher came down from the hills and, living his nickname to the fullest, spent hours yelling at her mother to clean up her act. Her mother would groan and shake her head and agree to go straight, only to break that promise once he disappeared back into hiding.

Maxine liked to play the No Crying Game, which goes like this: You run into a wall so hard it knocks you backward, leaving your nerves humming like guitar strings and your mouth salty with blood, but you never cry. If you slam yourself hard enough to chip a tooth or bruise your face, and not a single tear rolls down your cheek, you can stop doing it for a week.

On the fifth of every month, their benefits came, and Maxine's mother would pile them into the family's rattling wreck of a van for the fifteen-minute trip to Red Junction, where the big grocery store gladly accepted EBT. Maxine loved the store's bright lights, the aisles lined with shiny packaging, the sleekness and color that reminded her of the cars zipping down the road: signs that someone out there cared enough to do a good job, to make something perfect. Maxine chose not to see how some of the shoppers looked at them with horrified pity, as if they were roadkill.

Maxine's mother always acted happy in the store. She whistled and told knock-knock jokes as she filled their cart with cereal and the cheapest kelp-meat, which Maxine could stretch far if she mixed it with herbs and roots pulled from the small yard behind the house. When she was sober, her mother was very good at calculating everything down to the cent, in order to prevent the embarrassment of having to leave food on the cashier's conveyor belt. That had happened once, and Maxine's mother yelled, and someone called security, and it was only because Maxine acted so cute with the manager that they were ever allowed to come back.

Maxine's father was in prison forever, thanks to a drug deal gone wrong, and all their relatives were dead except for Preacher, who needed to stay in the hills because the police wanted him in a cell or a coffin, preferably the latter.

Maxine hated the police, especially the two who came around to stand in the weedy yard and call her a waste of life, dangling candy bars as they asked where her uncle was hiding, as if she were stupid enough to give up a blood relative for a sugar rush. Maxine would hiss at them and bare her teeth, but she knew to go no further. A friend of hers, Monica Miller from down the road, once bit a cop on the ankle during a scuffle, and they hit her in the head hard enough to put her in a coma. Sometimes stuff just happens. It's a mean world.

The cops called her family rednecks and trash and hillbillies. "You gonna be just like your mama," one of them liked to tell Maxine, "and your kids gonna be just like you. How you feel about that?"

Maxine always stuck out her tongue at that cop, whose name was Dwight and who rocked a blond caterpillar of a moustache. Dwight liked to take out his club and run at Maxine as if he intended to bash her brains all over the porch, but she knew to hold her ground.

"You never getting out of here," Dwight usually said. "You're just another waste of breath, you ask me."

Maxine thought of Dwight as an angry possum in a tent, anxious to bite anything trapped in there with it. But deep in her heart, she feared the cop was right. She had no idea of a life other than this one. On the cracked screen of her cheap-ass phone, she watched shows where beautiful people in sleek dresses and suits marched through gleaming spires of steel and glass, scenes from New York City that might as well have taken place on a planet far from this one. Her own eyes had never seen anyone in clothes so shiny, nor buildings so magical.

When the cops came by, Maxine imagined Preacher watching them from the black trees along the top of the ridge. When the roof collapsed, or some man in a suit threatened to kick them out of the house for good, or mother's EBT card no longer worked at the store, Maxine sent up a silent cry for Preacher to save them, knowing that he would never appear, not until the danger had passed. So she learned to do everything herself.

Maxine was very good around cops until she turned fourteen, and then everything went to hell.

II.

To celebrate her birthday, Maxine took a little joyride.

She had skipped school that morning, choosing instead to hang out on the porch of The Tony Eight with her best friend, Michelle. The Tony Eight was a hard bar but its owner, Tony the Third, kept a counter by the front door stocked with goodies such as candy and burner phones. He let kids use his porch as a chill-out zone ("Better they stay here than go in the woods. They don't all come back from the woods," is how he defended that choice) from eight in the morning until five in the evening, when the number of drunks inside reached critical mass. He only had two rules: no cursing within his earshot, and none of that boy-band crap on the throwback jukebox he kept in one corner.

That Tuesday afternoon, Maxine and Michelle had already spent two hours on the wooden steps, smoking cheap Beijing Blue cigarettes and talking dreams.

"Someday I want to go to California," Michelle told Maxine. "Did you know it used to be a state?"

"Duh." Maxine rolled her eyes. "But good luck getting across their border. I heard it's total lockdown. Like, they shoot anyone that even tries to come close."

Michelle groaned. "Why?"

Maxine prided herself on reading the news every day, even though her mother liked to call it fake. "There was this thing called the Water Wars. We tried to cut off their supply, so they started shooting back. I'm not trying to be mean, but you really got to study."

Before Michelle could reply, a red Mustang screeched into the bar's gravel lot. They both tensed, knowing it was Ricky, a local weed dealer who liked his girls a little too young.

Ricky lurched from the car, creepy smile in place, and paused to check his phone before sauntering toward them. Maxine reached into the left pocket of her jeans jacket, palming the small knife she kept there. Without looking up, she could feel Ricky's gaze slithering over her legs, and shuddered. Please God, she begged, just make him go away.

God declined to answer, but someone else did. Ricky made it ten yards across the lot when a big black car slithered into view behind him, its lithium-ion motor silent but its tires squealing on the slick road, its passenger window zipping down to reveal a hand with a pistol—pop, pop, pop, and Ricky collapsed, his purple jumpsuit puffing as the bullets punched through his flesh. The black car zipped past the bar before disappearing around the far curve.

Through the open door behind her, Maxine heard Tony the Third curse. Michelle clutched her knees and rocked back and forth, tears rolling down her cheeks. Maxine felt curiously numb, her breathing nice and regular as she stood and walked over to Ricky just as he managed, with a loud grunt, to roll onto his back, his front stained black from moist gravel and probably a quart of spilled blood.

Maxine pulled out her phone and dialed 911. Those calls were free, which was good, because she was running low on minutes this month (again) and didn't like the idea of burning a few on a piece of crap like Ricky. As she held the phone to her ear, she knelt and rifled through the pockets of the jumpsuit, removing a wad of pleasingly retro twenty-dollar bills in a gaudy money clip (bloody), a key fob attached to a silver dog's head (ugly), and a brand-new phone (bonus!) with one of those cool bendable screens.

"Some of your dealer friends tracked you down, huh?" she asked Ricky.

"Help..." The sides of Ricky's mouth bubbled with pink froth. "Help..."

"Nine-one-one's on hold," she said, popping open the money clip and flicking through the stained bills. "Like, what else is new, right?"

Maxine handling his cash shocked a bit of life back into Ricky. His cold hand gripped her wrist and squeezed as he rasped, "Don't...take...bitch..."

She smacked him on the forehead with the money clip. "Hold on, the phone's ringing." The operator clicked to life, asking about her distress, and Maxine cheerfully told her all the gory details about a drive-by shooting at The Tony Eight. That task complete, she called over her shoulder, "Michelle, go inside. Tony's got a med-kit."

Michelle obeyed without backtalk. She was one of those types: prickly as a porcupine on a mega-dose of Heisenberg Blue most days, but a total lamb in a crisis. Maxine knew that Tony kept a fully loaded med-kit behind the bar, next to the shotgun. While she waited for Michelle to return, she helped herself to Ricky's car keys.

Ricky hissed, "Don't...take..."

"Look," she said. "You got shot, but you're gonna make it." That was definitely a lie, given the amount of blood pumping out Ricky's holes. "Tony got a good kit. Ambulance be here in a minute. We going through all this trouble for you, means you owe us a favor. So I'm taking a spin in your sweet car over there. Don't worry, you'll get it back."

Ricky tried to spit blood at her and missed.

She slid behind the Mustang's wheel, unsurprised at Ricky's choices in tricking out the interior: a blue glow from LEDs beneath the front seats, oversized speakers that probably cost three times more than the engine, and a steering wheel wrapped in the finest imitation leather. Maxine wrinkled her nose at the near-overpowering stench of cheap cologne and spilled beer as she popped the key fob into the slot on the dashboard, the gas engine awakening with a roar, the stereo booming vintage rap-rock (classy, Ricky, classy) loud enough to rattle the substandard fillings in her teeth.

Maxine smacked dashboard buttons until the music went quiet, spun the wheel, and gunned the Mustang out of the lot. In the rearview mirror, she saw the Tony rip Ricky's jumpsuit open and squirt something from a can into the wounds, but not before giving Maxine a big thumbs-up. What more pseudo-parental approval did she need?

Her first joyride almost went wrong ten seconds in, as she tried to muscle the Mustang's fat ass into the first sharp turn and almost skidded out, nearly ramming into a truck in the oncoming lane, spinning the wheel to correct and overcompensating, clipping a rusty traffic sign, shrieking in fear and joy as she finally pointed the car's nose in the right direction and slammed the gas pedal to the floor. The Mustang snarled its pleasure. It was her first time driving and she was a natural, powering into each curve, feathering the brake at the intersections.

The black car appeared just ahead, and her jubilation curdled into unease. From Preacher, she'd learned the first rule of doing crime: you hide after the crime's been done. So why were they still on the road? She needed to get out of here before they noticed Ricky's car in their rearview mirror, but they were on a straight-away: no turnoffs, no side roads.

The black car tapped its brakes. She slowed to keep distance, her dread igniting into outright fear as the car's front-passenger window buzzed down and the hand with the pistol emerged. She veered the Mustang left just as the gun spat fire, a bullet snapping off her roof.

If she stayed back, the next bullet might smash through the windshield and her forehead. If she stopped, they would turn around and hunt her down. That left her with one choice.

Punching the gas, she rammed her fender into the other car's trunk, bumping it forward and to the right. The shooter's head and shoulders appeared above the car roof, silhouetted by the sun, the gun waving as he tried to aim, and she accelerated again until her front tires came parallel with the other car's rear door and she swung the wheel hard right. With a crunch of metal, the other car left the road—a faint scream from the shooter above the boom of two tons of metal rolling into a deep ditch. The wheel slithered hot in Maxine's hands as she fought for control, finally skewing to a stop in her own lane.

You need to drive away, she thought. Get out of here.

An inner voice interrupted. It sounded like an adult, not some scared kid: *You need to see if anyone survived.*

What if they're still alive?

The voice declined to answer—maybe because the answer was obvious. Her hands shook as she searched the junk in the passenger footwell. Beneath a pile of soggy bills, she discovered a short pry bar, its tip a sharp point. Despite her fear, it felt good in her hand.

Before she climbed out of the Mustang, she wiped her shirttail on the steering wheel and anything else she might have touched. Her sweaty palms made it hard to grip the pry bar as she tiptoed into the weeds.

The black car had entered the ditch on its side, landing in three feet of oily water. A broken tree stump jutted through the crumpled steel of the hood. The windshield had cracked but not shattered, and through the webbed glass (Maxine snuck close now, breathing hard, ready for the bullet) she could see the body hunched in the driver's seat, limp hand on the steering wheel.

She leapt onto the far side of the ditch and discovered the top of the shooter's head in the water, blond hair streaming like kelp. No bubbles meant no breathing meant it was safe to come closer, which she did, recognizing the face just beneath the muddy surface.

It was her good friend Officer Dwight, his torso pinned

beneath the car's frame.

Maxine's fear deepened into nausea. She sank to her knees on the wet grass and vomited a neon spray of half-digested junk food.

Now you can get out of here.

Yes, that was the best idea. Wiping her mouth, she stood and walked across the field beyond the ditch, toward the distant band of forest that would give her cover from anyone driving past on the road. Her boots sank into the muck, slowing her progress. Maxine pulled out her phone and made another call.

III.

The inside of the diner was a time capsule, from the fading Trump 2020 poster on the wall above the old-fashioned cash register to the deep-fat fryer sizzling away in complete defiance of all state health laws. Behind the register leaned Johnny Oates, whose burning hatred of everything politically correct had led him to create this temple to a fantasy America where everybody enjoyed a God-given right to clogged arteries and blackened lungs.

Maxine entered, checking out the three regulars sitting at the counter, all working doggedly on their eggs and butter-soaked carbohydrates: reddened men, their middle-aged muscles dissolving into fat, their knuckles beaten into scar tissue.

"Hunting's for wimps," Oates was telling them, engaging in his favorite pastime of goading customers into an argument. "You're just killing something can't shoot back. If I'm going to head out into the woods after something, it's gonna be a human being."

At the far end of the counter, Oates' biggest customer at two hundred ninety pounds, the one and only Perry Parks, trembled and purpled, primed to explode in a fury of grease-fried rage. "You got no idea how difficult it is. The skill it takes. Even for deer."

"Why don't you wire a machine gun to a deer's horns? I

27

mean, that's a fair fight. Give it the chance to take a few of you with it," Oates smacked a few buttons on the register. "Jane, you agree with that?"

The waitress in the far booth, eighteen going on forty, e-cigarette clenched between pillow-puff lips the shade of a ripe plum, lowered her phone and said, in the flattest possible tone, "Whatever."

Maxine took a seat in the booth furthest away from the action, wondering if Oates and the rest of them could see her sweat. It was an hour after the crash, and her hands still shook, so she placed them underneath the table where nobody could see. Oates wandered over, a smile unzipping his face. For all his attempts to sink barbs into his customers' psychic meat, he was a decent human being. "How's it going?" he asked her.

"Okay," she said.

"I'm sorry, darling, but I gotta ask before you order: You got cash?" Oates dropped his voice a few decibels, even though everybody in the diner could still hear him. As Maxine reached into her pocket and tugged out a few bills from Ricky's wad, she felt her face flush with familiar shame.

From the way his eyebrows arched, she knew Oates wanted to ask where she'd earned that money, before deciding any answer would only lead to grief on someone's part. "Okay," he said. "Good. Sorry about that. What can I get you?"

"Coffee," she said. "Toast is awesome, too." More than any-thing else, she wanted to step into a shower and crouch under its hot drool and stare at the drain cover as if she could some-how shrink and slide down the sewer into a better life. Barring that, she needed some food in her belly, for the energy to deal with whatever was coming next. After vomiting her stomach into a ditch, all she could handle was something plain.

Oates nodded and headed for the kitchen, returning a few minutes later with coffee. She dumped roughly half the sugar dispenser into the steaming liquid, not caring whether the sweetener was the real deal (unlikely in a place as cheap as this) or one of those synthetics that provided half the taste and all the diabetes and cancer. She drank it boiling-hot, barely noticing how it scorched her tongue, eyes focused on the screen above the counter, where a talk-show host cracked bleak jokes about the latest round of suicide bombings in Seattle.

The food arrived, and Maxine found herself surprisingly hungry. She was chewing the last bit of crust when the bells above the front door tinkled. Preacher walked in like John Wayne in those old movies that Oates loved—only Preacher was more John Wayne than John Wayne, who had been a mirage, a Hollywood actor named Marion Morrison who discovered that, if he held his hips right and aimed a rifle, people would start calling him "sir." Preacher came through the door looking solid as stone, bringing his own weather with him. Everybody in the place fell silent.

First, Preacher flicked the thumb lock behind him and flipped the old-fashioned sign on the door so it read "Closed." Next, he pulled a plastic bag out of his pocket and walked along the counter and back into the kitchen, collecting phones from everybody. After he tossed the phone bag to Maxine in the booth, he reached into his pocket and pulled out a thick wad of bills and distributed them to all customers and Oates and Jane and the short-order chef.

With those tasks completed, he helped himself to a cup from the ancient coffeemaker behind the register and sat across from Maxine, taking his first sip with a handful of pills from his jacket pocket. His love of medication stemmed from his three years in the military: red painkillers to ease the burning in his shoulders, from the shrapnel embedded in the muscle, always followed by two or three blue gel caps that kept his mind crackling. The Army fed you a steady diet of chemicals that helped you deal with cognitive load, think your way lightning-quick through firefights. The downside came after they discharged you, when you missed that sharpness to your thoughts, even if it came with side effects such as sweaty nervousness, paranoia, and the occasional burst of epic flatulence. Preacher kept his prescription filled through a backchannel to the local VA.

Maxine finished chewing, admiring Preacher's gunslinger gait, smiling at how everybody in the diner resumed their conversations a little too loudly, anxious to show their new guest how they could play it as cool as him.

"You making some trouble on your birthday, kiddo?" Preacher asked.

"I didn't start nothing."

"It's okay. I'm not mad. Just tell me everything."

"So I'm down at The Tony Eight..."

"Wait, why weren't you in school?" His cheeks reddened, his hand tightening on the cup.

Maxine rolled her eyes. "Thought you said you weren't mad."

"You need to be in school. One of my big regrets is not making it past fourth grade. Now, I like to think I'm smart, but I sometimes wish I learned more math or engineering. Moved to a city or something. Gotten a job where people aren't shooting at me." His voice trailed off.

Maxine sighed. "You know school sucks. The teachers don't care, the place is falling apart, half my classmates are on friggin' pills. I learn more reading on my own."

"You're not thinking like a gangster, darling." Preacher offered a slab-toothed grin. "You don't show up to school, the so-called authorities notice, they start getting up in your business. You go to school—even if you just sit there and read—it gives you leeway to do whatever else you want in your life. Does that make sense? Am I getting through to you?"

Maxine didn't like people correcting her. "Yeah, yeah, yeah."

"Yeah, yeah, yeah, okay." Preacher leaned forward and gently pinched her chin. "So tell me what happened."

"I took a joyride, ran into a couple of cops. They're dead."

"So my guy said, when you called him. How'd you get his phone number?"

"You gave it to me, remember? Told me use it in an emergency.

If you actually owned a phone, I would have called you direct."

"Yeah, well, he's got one of those special phones, it's harder to trace. I can't figure out how those work." In Preacher's world, nobody carried hardware connected to the internet or went online without hiding behind lots of electronic voodoo. "My guy, he said it was Ricky's Mustang ran those dirty boys off the road?"

"Yeah, it was Ricky's car."

Preacher looked concerned. "You shoot Ricky?"

"No, the cops did that. I was just hanging out. You ask me, he had a deal with them that went bad, or something."

"Who knows? Ricky bled out before they made the hospital." Preacher washed down another pill with his coffee, his eyes humming electric. "I'm going to clear this up. You don't need to do anything. Hang tight, don't say anything to anyone, okay?"

She sighed. "I'm sorry. It's trouble you don't need."

Preacher's giant paw settled on her small one. "When I was your age, I got in scrapes like this a lot. It's part of growing up."

"This'll sound kinda psycho." She smiled a little. "But I liked the driving part."

"See? Silver lining," he said. "And here's the other good thing: no more cop to sniff his little pig snout around your house. Five-oh knows one of their own was crooked, they'll be glad to see him disappear. In exchange for all this, though, you owe me a favor."

She nodded. "Name it."

"Finish high school, try to go to college, the whole run. You can read your books there. You keep a low profile, you graduate, and if you still want, you can come work for me. We'll have some fun together. Deal?"

"I go to college, who'll watch Brad? Or my mom?"

"I will." Preacher held up a hand, anticipating her argument. "I know I haven't been great about sticking around. But I've started paying the right people, and I got some good folks on my side. I'll be around more, I swear. So, do we have a deal?

Low profile from here on out?"

Maxine laughed. "Okay, you got a deal."

Preacher departed after handing the bag of phones to Oates behind the counter. Maxine finished her coffee and left. Nobody ever found the wreckage of the black car, or Dwight and his partner in crime. No cop ever swung by her family's little house again.

File 3.41.10003.5
Date: 6/05/2110

The debate about Maxine Hardwater's motives has gone on for years. During the so-called "Night Mayor" period, many contemporary pundits and analysts assumed that she was a "basic" thief, motivated by lust for money. Following the Liberation of Buffalo, however, some began to ascribe a more political motive to her actions. But without delving too much into "armchair psychology," those explanations are a little broad: People are rarely creatures of pure greed or socialism.

For this next file, which gives insight into the formation of her true character, our algorithms relied on two sources: cognitive files from Maxine Hardwater herself, recovered from her "merge," and some heretofore undiscovered interview transcripts of her uncle "Preacher" Hardwater. These transcripts were discovered in the basement collection of the New York City Public Library during a postwar sweep, filed in a subsection devoted to criminal justice. They have been uploaded and scanned, and the information was incorporated into the machine narrative.

P.S. We informed the A.I. of some scholars' complaints about these narratives' tone and structure. The A.I. responded by quoting 20th-century writer Salman Rushdie: "We challenge *fears. Literature is unafraid."* We will ask the Supervisory Intelligence to consider some tweaks to the underlying code.

P.P.S. The Supervisory Intelligence says: "This is how revolutions are made." (!?)

I.

When Maxine was seventeen, they came for the house.

On a warm spring afternoon, she returned from school to find her mother on the porch, dancing across the creaking boards on bare, calloused feet. Her mother hummed a classic tune from last century as she strung a clothesline between the porch supports. Maxine noted a pile of wet laundry on a towel draped over the railing, and her stomach clenched in fear. These days, her mother only did chores during the manic times, when she also burned herself with cigarettes and spent all their money on useless trinkets.

Maxine stopped at the bottom of the porch steps, far enough away to dodge anything thrown at her. "Hi," she said, shifting her backpack from her shoulder to her left hand in case she needed to use it as a shield. Her mood shirt, a cheap knockoff of an expensive brand, flared from blue to a nervous pink.

"Why, hello," her mother burbled, holding up a handful of bright plastic clothespins.

Maxine flinched. "You're cheerful," she said, steeling herself for the next revelation: the last of the living room furniture sold, or their state benefits spent on lottery tickets. Not that many benefits came in these days. The current governor, deciding that poor people didn't already have things hard enough, had shredded welfare payouts. If you wanted your unemployment check, you had to give the bureaucrats full login access to your social networking profiles so they could pick through your photos to check you weren't using taxpayer dollars for drugs. Good thing Maxine had deleted her mother's accounts a year ago.

"We are about to make some money. A whole lot of money." Her mother pinched clothespins onto the line. "Mama's going to make everything good again, you'll see. We'll get rid of our debts. We'll get some real nice clothes instead of those ratty old ones. Maybe we can even go on vacation somewhere special."

"That'll be a first." For most of our family, Maxine thought, the only vacation is the time between busting the cuffs and when the law catches us again. I just want to go upstairs and do my homework, except now I have to deal with whatever sad crap you've just pulled. "How are we making money?"

"We're selling the house!" Maxine's mother exclaimed, grabbing two handfuls of wet clothes and swirling them in the air like a pair of pom-poms, swaying her hips as she did so, water and soap spattering the porch. "For a lot of money! A lot!"

"That's great," Maxine said, suddenly exhausted. Of course it was a lie. Who would buy their piece of crap? There was no working plumbing most months, the heat barely managed to keep the bedrooms above freezing in the winter, and the first floor always stank like something had died under the floor-boards. "I'm happy for us. So where are we going to live?"

Her mother caught the tone in her voice. The colors stopped spinning. She stood there with a sour frown, the limp clothes dripping onto her rough feet. Maxine could feel the anger crackling the air, hard and nasty as the ozone after a lightning strike, and decided to retreat as fast as possible. Running up the steps, she shoved open the porch door and ducked inside, forcing herself to ignore the low sound coming from her mother's throat.

In the kitchen, she found her younger brother, Brad at the rickety table by the back windows, doing his best with his math homework. Brad had a buzzcut and a long, angry scar on his forehead, the latter courtesy of a schoolyard fight against a kid four years older and two feet taller. Her brother never backed down from a brawl, a fact that made Maxine feel equal parts pride and terror.

"Hey," Maxine said, dropping her backpack on the floor before opening the fridge in search of food. The otherwise empty shelves held a single piece of fake cheese, its plastic wrapper smeared with the beginnings of some horrible super-mold capable of surviving extreme temperatures and zero oxygen. Ugh.

"Hey," Brad said.

Refusing to give up her quest for calories, Maxine tried the freezer, finding a single can of energy drink half-buried in the icy wasteland. "Mom sold the house?" she asked, prying the can free and popping the ring-tab.

"Yeah, some guy showed up." Brad shrugged. "Told mom she wouldn't have to pay no more bills or nothing."

"What did I tell you about double negatives?"

"No more bills or anything."

"Good. What did this guy look like?"

Brad shrugged again, staring at the problem sheet in front of him. Unlike kids in the suburbs, who had cheap tablets for lessons and homework, the classes at their local idiot-factory still relied on paper. Blame that one on the mayor, who decided that taxes needed to go to the police department instead of education. Maxine, who liked to doodle fantastic vehicles in the margins of her work, sort of preferred notebooks and printed worksheets. But seeing her brother slowly scratch out the answers to simple addition problems, instead of swiping and tapping his way to a better future, made her quake with rage.

"Tell me," Maxine said.

Brad kept his gaze fixed on the table. "He had a fancy suit on."

"What else he say?"

"He told mom he would get rid of the mort-i-gage. Mom got real excited about that. She tried to play it cool for, like, a minute, but then she started jumping around."

"It's pronounced 'mortgage.' I don't even know if we got

one." She slugged the energy drink, hoping its caffeine would ramp up her courage. "You remember what I told you?"

"'Never trust anyone in a suit.'"

"That's right. Anyone in a suit is out to screw us, no exceptions. They're worse than regular robbers. Did you see mom sign anything?"

Brad nodded. In the gray light filtering through the dirty window, a tear glistened on his cheek. Despite his capacity for fury (Maxine had once seen him sink a wooden stick, sharpened into a spear, a full inch between another kid's ribs), Brad had a heart too big for this crappy place.

The screen door crashed open behind them, their mother booming loud. Gritting her teeth, Maxine picked up her backpack and marched into the front hallway. "Mom, what did you sign?" she nearly yelled. Her mood shirt flashed a fearsome shade of crimson, hotter by the second.

The question slammed her mother to a cold stop beside the front door, one foot off the floor, her hands raised to her shoulders, like some weird dance move. "Nothing," she said, arms falling, sullen in an instant. "Besides, it's my house. Don't you tell me my business."

Without answering, Maxine veered left, through the doorway that led to the living room, kicking through the mountain of debris that sprouted over the couch and coffee table and mismatched chairs. On the hunt for any sort of contract or official-looking paper. She spied a bright red folder atop a dusty tower of unopened bills, opened it to find a thin stack of documents bound with an irritatingly cheerful yellow paperclip, its paragraphs sprinkled with legal-sounding terms that made zero sense to her. What the hell was 'deed transferred to LLC'? The business card pinned under the paperclip had a phone number, an address, an email, and a name: Alex Smith. Who knew if any of that information was real?

Standing in the doorway, Maxine's mother squawked like a startled bird. As Maxine brushed past her, folder in hand, she reached to grab her daughter's shoulder—her fingers frozen an inch away by the fury in Maxine's eyes.

"I bet you screwed us," Maxine said before slamming through the screen door, her phone already in her hand.

She dialed the number on the business card, unsurprised when a robot directed her to voicemail. Standing in the yard with its yellowing weeds, its rusting fence, the gray dirt that smelled like diesel whenever it rained, the dead car engine on cinder blocks sprouting red flowers from its popped piston heads, she wondered: Why would anyone want to buy any of this? Why would mom let herself get hustled? She knows not to trust folks who come around.

People want to hope, Preacher whispered in her head. And they're willing to overlook anything, even things that'll hurt them, if they can live in hope for just a second or two. That feeling, it's better than weed, better than junk.

The screen door creaked open behind her. Quiet footsteps on the boards. "I'm sorry?" her mother said, voice quavering on the edge of tears.

"Whatever," Maxine said, stuffing the folder into her pack. "Now I got to put all my own crap aside, try and fix this." She had parked her bike at the end of the driveway, behind the rotted frame of the garage, its rear wheel locked with a massive clamp scarred from more than one theft attempt. Unlocking and heaving the clamp aside, she straddled the bike, twisted the electric motor to life, and purred onto the main road, her shirt blazing like a falling comet, never looking back at her mother.

The bike's old motor, capable of maybe twenty miles an hour on a steep downhill with a hard wind at your back, nonetheless carried her to town in a few minutes. When her mother was a child, you smelled the place before you reached it, courtesy of the working slaughterhouse on the outskirts. The killing floor had long closed, taking a hundred jobs with it, and the only thing Maxine could smell was faint smoke from the forest fire troubling the western edge of the county, leaving hills of gray ash in its wake.

By the time she reached the traffic light that marked the beginning of Main Street, her rage seethed on the edge of nuclear, and not just because jackasses in three separate cars had honked and yelled obscene things about her body on the way in. The slow putter into town gave her time to relive every bad thing that had happened to her family over the past few years. Her father shanked in prison, his ashes sent home with a bill for the cremation. The interest on their bills multiplying like cancer cells. Preacher throughout it all promising to help, to give them cash, to make a phone call, and never seeming to come through when they needed him most.

And now the house. Rocko's Tacos at the south end of Main had a bike-charging station, three bucks for a full battery and a wheel lock while you ran errands. She tapped her phone against the payment nub, deducting the funds from her tiny balance, and headed inside for food. The fish in the joint's signature tacos probably came from a lab, but so what? Given her family history, she would probably be dead by forty, anyway.

A few years back, after Hurricane Monica shredded the lower half of Manhattan, forcing the city to begin its massive dams-and-locks project, a lost tribe of brownstone hipsters wandered into this part of the state. They opened a barbershop specializing in beard trimming, along with a farm-to-table eatery where half the menu items cost more than people around here spent on food in two weeks. A couple tried to break into the local weed business, because the bud was legal by that point, and disappeared under odd circumstances. Rocko's was the only one of the invaders' establishments still standing, partly thanks to its cheap eats and the bike-charging station, but also because the owners, Percy and Apple, had adapted quickly to the rugged life, buying a double-wide in the nearby park and keeping to themselves. The place always stank pleasantly of frying meat, and the wireless was fast and free. You could ignore the skinheads who used the corner table as an office.

Eating at the counter by the windows, Maxine checked out the office across the street, listed on the card in her backpack as belonging to "Alex Smith." No movement inside, no lights she could see. Might as well check it out. Then what'll you do? Ask whoever's inside for the deed back? Threaten to call the cops? What if they laugh in your face?

Walking to the office, she stopped to pick up a fist-sized stone from the gutter, scanning first for any witnesses. The sidewalks stood empty. In the storefront next to Rocko's Tacos, a dozen kids sat in plush seats with VR headsets hiding their faces, ducking and weaving and bouncing in digital worlds only they could see.

The office's front door was unlocked, opening into an antiseptic space with three almost-barren desks and a fluorescent light overhead, no art on the walls. She heard a toilet flush and a door open. A man in shirtsleeves wandered into the room, zipping his fly. He was absurdly muscular but short, balding, his hands thick with black hair. Not a local. Nobody around here dressed in tailored shirts made of shiny material, with buttons that looked like pearl.

"You Alex Smith?" she asked.

He looked up, startled. "How did you get in here?" He had a slight accent, hard to place, maybe Southern. Maxine noticed yet another absurdity: Whoever had tailored his shirt had made the left sleeve much looser than the right, to accommodate the massive watch strapped to his wrist. What a chump.

She nodded behind her. "Door's unlocked."

His eyes flicked to the stone in her hand. "What do you want?"

"Are you Alex Smith?"

"Who are you?"

"I need to find Alex Smith. He signed a document for our house."

The man looked confused. "House?"

Maxine jutted her chin at the small stack of red folders on

one of the desks. "Don't give me that."

The man took a step toward her, brown leather shoes whispering on the institutional carpet, and Maxine flexed her grip on the rock, raised it an inch. He read the violence in her stance and retreated a few feet, smiling at her. "We cannot discuss client business."

Maxine recited her address. "This is client business. You made a deal with my mother today? We're canceling that deal."

Alex Smith—or whatever his name was—made a great show of shrugging his overdeveloped shoulders. "How old are you, little girl?"

"None of your business, jackass."

He shook his head. "I think you are a minor. Whether or not that's true, you do not have the authority to go against your mother's wishes. This transaction is complete, as of this afternoon."

Maxine's shirt, which had cooled to a noonday blue, bloomed red again. "No. I'll call the cops." That was an empty threat, of course, considering how the local police regarded Maxine's family as one step below cockroaches. Not that Smith knew that.

"Go ahead." Smith swept his arms wide, as if showing off a bustling office instead of a couple of desks in a blank space in a dying town. "Get your lawyers, too. I am sure you have a lot of them, no?"

Maxine turned on her heel and left. There was simply no point in trying to reason with this showy jackass. Whatever scam he was pulling, he knew he had the upper hand over a high-school girl. Back on the street, Maxine decided to ruin his day in the only way she knew how. Hefting the rock, she hurled it as hard as she could through the floor-to-ceiling window fronting the office, punching a jagged hole in the middle of it. The man gawped at her like a startled fish.

Offering him a middle finger, she stomped across the street toward her bike, head down so nobody could see the frustrated tears brimming in her eyes. Time for the No Crying Game. Without a convenient wall to slam into, she opted to ball her left fist and slam it one, two, three times into her chest beneath the collarbone, the ache in her ribs distracting her from the rainstorm brewing in her mind.

If she couldn't call the cops, she would reach out to the other authority around these parts.

II.

Maxine knew that once she dialed Preacher's number, it would be the two dead cops all over again: total heaviness, with a high likelihood of corpses in unmarked graves. But what choice did she have? Her uncle's droog who answered the phone told her the Big Guy was busy, and to show up in the parking lot of The Tony Eight in ninety minutes. Someone would pick her up.

Anxious for a distraction in the meantime, Maxine activated the Pickup app on her phone. On the cracked screen, the friendly smiley-face icon spun as a data-farm checked whether a package in her vicinity needed delivering. A loud ping, and the face flashed a toothy grin before disappearing, replaced by a message box with an address that she knew well. The app said it would pay her four dollars for the job—enough to buy her lunch tomorrow, at least.

Too bad the client sucked.

Fifteen minutes later, she pulled up in front of the rambling hillside residence of one Billy the Squid, a local crackpot with a taste for anime movies and bombarding his neighbors with miniature rockets launched from his porch. Missing a leg from his third tour in Syria, and deprived of his driver's license after he tried plowing his truck into Rocko's Tacos following a misunderstanding over a take-out order, Billy had to rely on Pickup's services to keep his business running.

"Hey Billy," Maxine called out—loudly—as she approached his front door. Billy's house had begun life as five cargo containers deposited on a relatively flat part of the hill. Assisted by some heavy-duty tools and a lot of per-hour gig labor, Billy had cut windows and doors in the containers, linked them with breezeways made of lumber and waxed cloth, and painted the whole thing in the obnoxious colors of an LSD-enhanced fever-dream. The interior of each container featured a different milieu: One had a hot tub and a full bar, for example, while its neighbor, studded with UV lamps, served as the grow-house for Billy's Very Special Bud.

"Come on up," came the shout from inside that mess of steel and psychedelic swirls. "Don't stray off the path, though. I got me a new early-warning system."

Maxine came up the stone walk as ordered, glancing at the flower beds bracketing either side. Mixed in with the petunias and tulips, at regular intervals, she saw flat green boxes on little tripods, each stamped with the words: "FRONT TOWARD ENEMY." She had played enough war games with Brad to know these were claymore mines, stuffed with ball bearings.

"Home security, redneck style," Billy said, appearing on one of the breezeways with a thick padded envelope in his plush hands. His prosthetic leg, metallic, glimmered redly in the sun. "Got too many folks coming around these days."

"They troubling you?" She wanted away from this property fast as possible, but acting friendly toward someone armed with lots of explosives also seemed like a good idea.

"Always. Can you believe it, the other day, this pair of jack-asses showed up with a petition, wanting to secede from the great state of New York? Sure, I hate the government, but it's still my country, you know?" He handed over the package. "This goes to the post office. Don't go inside, just put it in the bin out front. It's a prepaid."

It also featured no return address. She hefted the package, tensing her fingers just enough to crumple its sides, hearing the faint rustling that, in Billy's context, only meant one thing. "You know that's illegal, right? Sending herb out-of-state in the mail?"

Billy snorted and scratched his neck, etched with fading biometric tattoos: his old military glyph. "You know the post office got no money for inspectors, right? There's like four dudes in a room somewhere, trying to check everything coming in. It'll sail right through. Government inefficiency, now that's something I'll trust." His laugh rumbled through him like a cave collapse.

"What's this kind called?"

He squinted at her. "You're not supposed to ask. That's the point of the app. You just deliver."

"I know, but I'm curious, hey?" She smiled at him, even though it made her feel all kinds of icky. If you believed the rumors, she wasn't much younger than Billy's girlfriends.

Billy's chest swelled with pride. "I call it 'Apollo 13,' because at first you're cruising along, then it blows up on you, and you're left stranded somewhere far above the Earth."

"Fantastic," Maxine said, popping the package in her pack. "Don't forget to tip me big, remember?" And don't you dare say something weird or creepy, she added in her head. I can't take it today.

Behaving himself for once, Billy nodded. "Just get it there," he said, eyes scanning the road behind her. Maxine turned to follow his gaze, catching his paranoia like a bug.

"What else is bothering you?" she asked.

"It's not just those petition whackos. Oil guys keep coming around, wanting to buy the place," he said. "Fracking. They'd rip it all up, pull out the gas from underneath…"

"I know what fracking is." She tilted her head, studying him. "These guys, one of them named Alex Smith?"

"No, first one was Arnold Friend or something." He returned her questioning gaze. "What'd Alex Smith look like?"

"Short, stocky, had an accent, like not from around here. Dressed like a total prick, expensive."

"Might be the same guy, different name. They try to buy your mom's place?"

Maxine grimaced. "They did buy it, while I was out. She must have been high. We're trying to get it back."

Billy coughed and spat. "I heard they're trying to buy up the whole valley. If they offered you money, honey, you better take it. No offense, but that crap-heap you call home isn't worth very much." He flashed his teeth. "I know you'll hate to hear it, but give your uncle a call. He got a way of solving stuff. Before you go to war, though, mail my package."

Laughing, he turned and limped back into his junkyard house, leaving Maxine on the path with that package of weed. She was tempted to hurl it into the bomb-loaded bushes. The anger was good. It gave her the power for what was coming next.

III.

After dumping Billy's package in the bin outside the post office, she biked over to the parking lot of The Tony Eight, where one of Preacher's droogs with a crimson mohawk—she knew the face, but not the name—pulled up in a battered pickup truck as red as his hair. She loaded the bike into the truck's bed and hopped into the passenger seat. While the droog steered them onto the narrow roads beyond town, she stared at her phone to discourage conversation, waiting in vain for Billy to deposit his tip.

The droog made a few sharp turns in the woods before pulling up in front of a tall iron gate. He tapped a number into his phone, and the gate opened onto a paved lane, tree branches scraping the truck's flanks as it rumbled toward the biggest house Maxine had ever seen, an expensive pile of logs and glass perched beside a small lake. It looked like the sort of place one of those rich hipsters had built, back when a few of them tried to turn the valley into their own weird version of Brooklyn North.

"Who'd he whack for this place?" she asked the droog, who hopped out of the truck without answering.

The front door opened onto a great room surfaced in dark wood, the massive chandelier overhead dripping with bleached antlers, a taxidermied grizzly in the corner looking surprised at the state of its afterlife. On the tip of an antler, a holographic bird chirped faintly before snapping out of existence. A small flat robot passed Maxine's feet, humming as it sucked dust off the floorboards.

Preacher entered the room, dressed in a scuffed leather jacket and a Led Zeppelin T-shirt, a tumbler of whiskey in his hand. There were small cuts on his forehead and cheeks, and a thick bandage on his right hand. He looked a little stunned at his own surroundings, his expression reminding her a bit of the bear. "The Warhog has entered the chatroom," he said. "What's up, kid?"

Maxine blurted it out: "Mom sold the house."

His eyebrows shot up. "Great. She get good money for it?"

"That's not the point." Her voice echoed off the high ceiling. "Some jackass in a suit came in and took it. That's. Our. Home."

"Well, as many a lovely song has sung, you are not alone." He crashed into a stuffed red chair in the corner, beside the bear. Ice clinked as he swirled his glass like a refined gentleman. "There's a lot of that lately: shady dudes coming in, convincing people to sign over the deeds to their houses. They got these front companies they set up, so it's hard to figure out who's really behind it all. This guy who made the deal? The guy who's really behind it, he's probably, like, five guys behind that guy. He might not even live in this country. He may be a little gremlin."

"They want the land for fracking," Maxine said, wondering just how much the drugs had mulched her uncle's brain over the years.

The ice in his glass went silent. "How did you find out?"

"Isn't that what's going on?"

"You want to be a gangster, show me you got the critical-thinking skills," he said. "That you can put things together based on evidence."

"Dropped off a package for Billy the Squid. They've been bothering him, too. He said they wanted to frack up his land." She pulled out her phone, thumbed it to life, and showed him a video of monster machines shredding a craggy mountainside. "I looked this up when I was waiting for your guy to pick me up. There's some new tech, lets them go deeper than ever, work on areas they couldn't have touched thirty years ago."

Preacher squinted at the video. "I don't remember really clear, but I think your dad had some prospectors on your land at one point, and they didn't find anything. He wanted the cash, so it really crushed his spirit. Well, that and being married to my sister."

She ignored the quip. "These seismic machines, they detect gas over long distances. They don't need to put boots on your land until they buy it. The technology's crazy."

"Give it a couple years, we're all gonna be a laptop's lapdog," Preacher said. "Skynet. Sorry, that's a reference before your time."

"Whatever. You got anything to drink? I've been on the road all day."

"Kitchen," Preacher said, pointing to a doorway to their right. "It's about a mile that way."

The kitchen featured everything-new appliances, its wide windows overlooking the silvery expanse of the lake, two of Preacher's droogs perched on rocks along the shore. From the fridge, she pulled the last can of Coke, the good kind from Mexico, made with real sugar. The appliance beeped as she closed the door, a small screen by the handle flashing: "Order More Soda Y/N?" She tapped "Y," thinking: How cool. Maybe I can get one of Preacher's people to toss this bad boy in a pickup, take it back to the house. Except with all its web-enabled chips, the cops would probably track it down twenty minutes later.

Preacher's heavy tread on the floorboards. His shadow flickered in the fridge's gleaming chrome. "We'll get you a new house," he said. "I've wanted to move you out of that shit-hole for years, anyway."

"And yet you didn't," she said, popping the tab on the soda.

Preacher coughed. "There's been a lot of heat. Hard to make moves."

"So you keep saying."

He edged her aside so he could open the fridge, extract a beer to chase his whiskey. "Let me tell you a story," he said. "Explains why I'm in this fancy house today."

Maxine shrugged, plopped down on one of the stools lining the marble-topped island at the center of the kitchen. "Yay, storytime."

Grinning despite himself, Preacher popped the cap off the beer with his teeth. "What's my usual lifestyle?"

"Backwoods, eating a rabbit."

"Exactly. And that's where everybody's looking for me right now, so we decided to go high-end for a couple weeks, found us a fancy vacation home."

"What'd you do this time, knock off a bank?"

"Nobody goes into a bank and robs it these days. You score what, two thousand dollars? And they capture you on thirty different cameras, got your name and face before you walk out the door? No, I had to take out the Clown."

Maxine whistled. "Local legend."

"It was an accident." Preacher took a seat. "We drove over to his place just to talk, up in the hills?"

"Armed?"

Preacher pulled back the edge of his coat, revealing a sweet custom rig, an Auto 9 with an extended magazine, dangling from a shoulder holster like a heavy-metal tumor. "Sweetie, when am I not packing? Yes, armed. But wanting to talk, really. Lately, the Clown made a lot of noise about territory, war taxes, stuff like that."

Maxine knew about the war tax: a monthly tithe the local crews paid into a common pot for bribes and legal fees. The Clown controlled those accounts—skimmed them hard, too, if you believed the rumors or saw the sweet Tesla Z he drove. "You shot him?"

"Let me get to it. So he's up at that farm of his, it's got a big barn for legal weed-growing out back. That's just cover for the chem lab everybody knows is in the woods behind the place, where he produces his real high-margin crap, Atom Bomb and Bad Seed. He's got drones buzzing overhead, a couple dudes always hanging out in the trees. We pull up, he's on the front porch, waiting for us with that mask on, so I suspect he's already on psycho autopilot."

Maxine knew about the mask. The Clown, whose real name was Cyrus Johnson, had done tours in some hot places on the other side of the planet, returning with a couple of bullet fragments in his hide and a lot of scar tissue in his brain. One of his VA shrinks, in an attempt to conquer this messy case of PTSD, had given Cyrus a blank plastic facemask and encouraged him to draw a "protective image" on it. Wear it whenever you feel threatened, the shrink added. It'll help you feel safe and confident.

Once the Clown returned to upstate New York and began blasting his way through the local drug scene with a bunch of Army buddies in tow, the last thing a lot of unfortunate folks saw was a mask covered with images of balloons and streamers, coming at them out of the dark. The thing made Cyrus feel confident, all right.

"So I get out of the car," Preacher said, "and I see there's this girl with him. Don't recognize her, but she's a teenager, couldn't be more than sixteen, and totally blasted out on that chem he makes. Sad, yeah? Her eyes got this blank look, says she's on Mars pretty much twenty-four hours a day. And Cyrus next to her, he's not looking too great himself, his neck all sweaty and red. Wearing this coat too warm for the weather, which is bad sign number two. Bad sign number three is a black plastic thing in his left hand."

"Gun?" Maxine said.

"Worse. We walk up, maybe twenty yards away now, and I say, 'Hi, Cyrus.' Without so much as a how-de-doo back, he reaches up and unzips that coat, so we can see he's got explosives strapped all over his chest. Thing in his hand's a detonator."

"Yikes."

"With my usual tact, I decide to start off with a joke. I ask him, 'You planning on collecting seventy-two virgins today?' Cyrus says, 'This is for my own protection.' I'm like, 'I'm all about making you feel safe, so long as it doesn't mean a handjob.'"

"Gross," Maxine said.

"Sorry, I forget my audience. Anyway, Cyrus says, 'War tax up three percent makes me feel safe,' only it's hard to tell because it sounds like he's lost a few teeth in front since the last time I saw him. Now, I can't let that sort of thing go unanswered, because the war tax is already taking a big chunk out of my bottom line. I got to admit, this whole situation has your uncle Preacher a little bit freaked out, because it's clear that Cyrus is totally whacked out at this juncture. Not that he was a warm and nurturing soul before."

"You're still here," Maxine said, "so it must have come out all right."

"I decide to stall for a little bit of time, see if I can't think up something that'll make Cyrus's little rat-mind run in a new direction. So I turn to his girlfriend next to him on the porch and say, 'Is he your boyfriend?' And, um…"

"Things got wild after that," Maxine said.

"Truly." Preacher saluted her with his bottle. "One second, her eyes are so stoned, it's like I'm staring at marbles. The next, they're boiling like lava. *'He's not my boyfriend,'* she screams, and—I swear I'm not lying here—reaches over and smacks Cyrus on the hand holding the detonator. And holy moly, it goes off."

"But you're still here," Maxine said.

"And flashing back to the Egypt campaign every time I blink," Preacher said. "I got some of Cyrus in my mouth, and I swear there's a couple specks of him in my ear and nose, but I'm alive and kicking because he wired those explosives wrong. What I learned from my time in the Army, your average suicide bomber sets things up so the explosion projects out, lateral-wise. Plus they're generally using C-4, designed to slice through people as efficiently as possible. But ol' Cyrus, he's using mining explosives, which sorta push through things, instead of slicing, because they're meant to crack rock. And he stacked the bomb wrong. The explosion went straight upwards. His head popped off like a champagne cork."

"Still knocked everyone on their ass," Maxine said.

"Still knocked everyone on their ass," Preacher agreed, pointing to his cut face. "Must have thrown me twenty feet back, right onto the hood of the car, certain I'd finally bought it for good. The whole porch, the house behind it, totally wrecked. The girlfriend, probably reduced to something you could scrape into a bag. I couldn't hear anything for a day or two afterwards. Anyway, that's why we're here. We're going to wait for things to calm down, go back and negotiate with whatever idiot takes Cyrus's place."

"I just have one question," Maxine said.

"What?"

Her voice rising: "What's any of that have to do with my fucking house?"

He sighed and rolled his eyes. "Don't use that language."

"You have to help us," she said, slamming down her empty can. "We're family. I'm sick of promises."

"What do you expect me to do?"

"I found the guy who's got the deed. Just come with me to talk to him."

"Last time you called me for help, I had to dispose of a couple of bodies," Preacher laughed. "This gonna happen here, too? Should I grab some garbage bags and bleach?"

"As much as I hate the prick who did this," she replied, "I don't want to deal with the mess of killing him, okay? It won't help."

His gaze on the marble, Preacher said, "Fine, we'll go and talk to him. But I'm warning you now, it's not going to change anything. Shell corporations, offshore accounts, hidden money. Untangling that stuff, I wouldn't even know where to begin. I'm a local man."

Maxine's shirt flared red. "When was the last time you brought my brother a present for his birthday?"

"Okay, okay, okay." With an epic grunt, Preacher stood on cracking knees. "Let me down another beer, grab one of the guys, and we'll go. I don't want you getting whiny like your mom."

As Preacher retrieved the brew from the fridge, Maxine opened a closet door she'd noticed earlier, in the short hallway that connected the kitchen to the great room. The coats inside had real fur, buttery-smooth leather she could pet all day, enough waterproof nylon to keep her family dry for years. And to the left, almost hidden behind the green bulk of a parka, a dress she had once seen in a movie, its fabric made from stiff, interlocked triangles. You could use an app to make rows of triangles angle in new directions, changing the shape of the dress in an instant. She placed a hand on the collar, expecting to feel cold plastic, hard edges, surprised when her fingers sank into softness. It was beautiful. Nobody at school, not even the girls with meth-dealer boyfriends who seemed to have everything, owned anything remotely like this.

"Go on, take it," Preacher said. "These people can afford it."

Fondling the dress, Maxine pictured her mother tricked into signing the papers in the red folder, taking away the roof over their heads. Once you started stealing, where did you stop? She wasn't sure she had the strength—not yet, at least—to behave like Preacher, who only stole from corporations and outsiders. You need a code before you can become a righteous outlaw.

She closed the closet door. "Whoever owns this place, they gonna show up at some point?"

"The owners?" Preacher chuckled. "I got them trapped in their own panic room upstairs. Don't worry, they got plenty of food and water in there. And a bucket."

IV.

For the ride back to town, they chose a sleek vehicle from the garage, an electric-powered BMW with the latest silicon brain under the hood. Once they hit the two-lane, Preacher activated the self-driving feature and sat back, watching with drunk amusement as the wheel turned on its own. "What happens if I try to mess with it?" he asked.

Beside him, Maxine braced her hands against the dashboard. "Please don't."

"It's okay, nobody's coming," Preacher said and, gripping the wheel, spun it as hard as he could to the left. The BMW veered into the oncoming lane, tires screeching, before regaining its artificial wits and swerving back onto its original path.

Maxine punched her laughing uncle in the shoulder, dismayed at his behavior. Whenever Preacher "borrowed" something, he usually did his best to return it in fine condition, whether or not he hated the owner. "Don't," she said.

"Oh, take a joke, kid." Thunderclouds brewed around Preacher's eyes as his high deflated. "I could have done worse."

Her fist still balled, Maxine shook her head. Preacher in a mood was a four-alarm emergency, like your house on fire or someone beating your dog in the yard. He was so much like her mother, come to think of it.

"For example, I could have done this." Preacher veered the

wheel hard right, scraping the BMW against a line of concrete barriers along the shoulder, the squeal of tearing metal almost drowning out the sound of him asking, "Is this worse, dear?"

"Screw you." She hit him again, full force, on the arm. He released the wheel, and the car dutifully corrected course, the dashboard screen beeping in alarm.

"Sorry, long week." Preacher's mouth set in a hard-white line as he reached into his jacket pocket, extracting a fresh handful of pills that he crunched down with a grimace. Maxine wondered if he had begun supplementing his usual regimen of painkillers and cognitive enhancers with anything weirder. At least that would explain why his mood veered harder than this BMW. The dashboard screen flashed white as some worker-bee in a call center in Kabul or Kansas City tried to reach them, to figure out if they needed assistance.

Maxine twisted around and flashed a thumbs-up at the pickup riding their bumper. The mohawked droog returned the sign and hit the brakes, falling back a little further. Worst-case scenario, Maxine figured, she could retrieve her bike from the back of the truck, return home, try to puzzle up another solution to her housing crisis.

"Sorry," Preacher said again.

"It's okay." Anxious for a distraction, she flipped open the glovebox and rooted through the rat's nest of wrappers and random trash stuffed in there, her fingers scraping on something hard—a steel cylinder with a polymer bulbous tip, bile green.

The sight of it snapped Preacher from his funk. "Ho shit," he said. "That's a sick stick."

"A what?"

"Ultimate in personal protection, short of a gun shooting actual bullets. Press the end against someone's bare skin, and they barf everywhere, fever, chills." He shuddered theatrically. "It's like instant flu."

"Sounds wonderful. But how's barfing gonna stop someone from messing you up?"

"You don't get it, darling. On a scale of one to ten, where one is feeling fine and ten is the plague, that thing is a twelve, at least. It knocks you right the hell over."

"I could use this at school." That was true: Maxine had never played nice with the various clans that ruled the place. "Why hadn't I heard of it before?"

"Because they're banned as lethal weapons. Use it too much on someone, their guts come out." Preacher phantom-vomited, then laughed. "This is great. You never know what the day has in store for you."

Pinching one end with two fingers, as if it were a dead rat, Maxine lifted the weapon from the glove box. The bottom half of the shaft had a slightly pebbled texture, presumably giving you a better grip in the event of your enemy upchucking their breakfast all over your hands.

"Careful now," Preacher said. "Press and hold that big button on the bottom, the green one, and it activates. There's no safety."

"My thumb is my safety," she said, trying to appear cool as her heart accelerated to what felt like a thousand beats a minute. The stick was heavy yet comfortable in her hands, the checkered grip rough on her soft palm, that green tip begging for action.

"Remind me to actually teach you some gun respect," Preacher said. "In the meantime, get your new toy ready, because we're here. Cover your eyes."

Maxine glanced up, expecting to see the BMW politely easing its way into a parking space. Instead, the bumper, already shredded by Preacher's little adventure with the concrete divider, bumped over the curb, on a collision course for the cracked glass of Alex Smith's front window. The dashboard screen beeping in fear, its reddening glow reflecting off Preacher's teeth as he grinned wide and stood on the gas pedal, ass off the seat, buoyed by the colossal roar of six cylinders. Maxine threw her arms over her face.

In the last half-second before impact, Preacher removed his foot from the gas, and the BMW's brain kicked into action to salvage the unsalvageable. The brakes screeched. The dashboard screamed. Maxine's world went—*poof!*— as the mini airbags in her door deployed.

Her skin stung. She clawed the deflating fabric out of her face in time to see Preacher pound the wheel, growling, "Whatever happened to the dream of full *human control*?" Through the miraculously intact windshield, Smith peered at them from a few feet away, his mouth agape. The surprise was understandable. The BMW had come to a halt in the middle of the office, atop a desk smashed to kindling, the carpet littered with chunks of wood and broken glass.

"That's him," she said, pointing with the sick stick. Her hands tingled in a way that promised aching and bruises later.

"Oh yes," Preacher replied, ripping away the sagging airbags and unbuckling himself, climbing from the vehicle with the wincing care of older men. "I know a hustler when I see one."

Her own knees wobbled as she stepped into the office, adrenaline tasting like a dead battery on her tongue. She had the sick stick raised, and Smith's look of bloodcurdling fear said he knew what it could do. "Hey again," Maxine said, her voice sharp with a sadistic cheer she didn't feel. "I didn't like how our last conversation ended, so I decided to swing back." Focused on the little runt, she never saw Preacher dart in from the left, snatching the device out of her hand neat as you please.

"Tutorial," her uncle said to her, lunging forward to grip Smith by his expensive collar. The sick stick hovering an inch from the man's neck. "You know why we're here?" Preacher asked him.

Maxine glanced over her shoulder, at the pickup pulling to the curb, the droog behind the wheel flashing her a thumbs-up with his eyebrows raised questioningly. She flashed a thumbs-up in return, and he put the vehicle in park, motor running, wheels tilted toward the street for a fast getaway.

"Yes, I know why you're here," Smith said, lip quivering. "Even if you kill me, it won't change anything."

While Maxine didn't consider herself a sadist, watching this bastard squirm made her feel warm and tingly inside. Walking over to the nearest intact desk, she flipped through red folders until she found the paperwork with her home address, signed with her mother's shaky hand.

"Bullshit," she said. "I got the contract right here."

"She has the contract right there," Preacher said. "So what's this about not changing anything, huh?"

"That's a copy," Smith said. "We registered the transfer hours ago. You know this is a good thing, right? You people are going to make some money off this."

Preacher drove the sick stick into Smith's neck, just below the jawline. The effect was immediate. Sweat bursting from his suddenly bloodless skin, Smith bent over and vomited on his expensive leather shoes.

"You want a little cotton ear swab?" Preacher asked him.

Something in Smith's pained rictus suggested confusion.

"Because you must have some waxy build-up," Preacher said, the sick stick hovering close again. "Hard of hearing and all that. We don't want the money, we want the house. What's your company's name?"

Wiping his messy lips with the back of his hand, Smith husked, "Hot Properties, LLC."

Preacher rolled his eyes. "No, the shell behind the shell. What is it?"

"Sunny Acres Properties, LLC."

"Who owns them?"

Smith straightened, wiping the drool from his chin, a little more color in his cheeks. The sick stick wore off fast. Or maybe he had a bit of the strength that comes when you realize you have the upper hand. "I really couldn't tell you," he said. "Someone in Russia? Africa? We can form companies all over the place. For all I know, the deed's held by a bunch of goat herders in Pakistan."

"Is that right?" Maxine clenched her hands together in a

white-knuckle ball. "Is he lying?"

"Maybe." Preacher looked at her, the tightness in his jaw imparting a whole conversation between the two of them. What was her uncle going to do, call the police? Walk into a government office and accuse a shell company of fraud? Activate his nonexistent army of lawyers to chase paper around the globe?

The answer, of course, was none of the above.

"So you can kill me," Smith said, voice stronger, "but you know it won't change anything."

"You're right," Preacher said. He stood there, contemplating the ceiling, before driving the sick stick hard into Smith's ribs. Smith toppled to the glass-strewn carpet, dry-heaving and thrashing, his ruined shoes drumming a spastic beat.

"But that sure felt good," Preacher added, pocketing the sick stick as he opened the door of the BMW and climbed in, gesturing for Maxine to do the same.

Stepping forward, Maxine had every intention of delivering Smith some bonus pain, maybe a nice solid kick in the balls. Only as she neared, he raised his hands in surrender, his eyes wide and human and full of agony. His look stopped her foot before it left the carpet.

The BMW's engine sputtered to life, the dashboard bursting into fresh damage-control screams before Preacher could smack it silent.

What good will hitting this chump do?

She had no good answer.

The BMW's horn deafening in the enclosed space, snapping Maxine from her misery. Instead of kicking Smith, she spat on his hair—a weak gesture, but maybe enough to make her feel better, later. Offering the overdressed little bastard her second middle finger of the day, she slipped into the battered car's passenger seat and stared at her reddened hands as Preacher eased them back onto the street.

V.

Preacher furious, teeth clenched, hands twisting the wheel. Maxine had never seen this many nukes going off in his head at once. The heat from that fury made her hunch against the passenger door, wondering whether she should have called him in the first place. Among other things she'd learned today, her uncle had some serious issues.

"You still want to be an outlaw?" Preacher's voice high and tight. "You want to do criminal shit, just like your uncle? Let me tell you something: For all the money I've made—and I've made a lot—it's nothing compared to what someone can make with a bunch of lawyers and a couple of forms. And you know the worst part of it, the thing that really gets me?"

"Just don't swerve the car," she said. "My stomach can't take it." Should have grabbed my bike from the pickup, she thought. You could've been home already, without this extra drama.

"That asshole back there, if he ever gets arrested for what he did?" Preacher laughed bitterly. "Probably won't even go to jail. Or if he does, they'll ship his ass to Camp Cupcake, somewhere they get to roast marshmallows around a campfire. White-collar crime is where it's always been at: big profits, no blood on your hands, and if you get nailed, it's just a slap on the wrist. You want to take a couple bucks from someone, you use a gun. With a law firm or a bank, you can rip off the whole world."

"Okay," she said.

"What?"

"Just okay. I get it."

"I'm wondering if you're cut out for this line of work." His gaze, shifting from the road, pierced her skull. "Back at the house, you could have taken that coat, and you didn't."

"No, I didn't."

"And at that office, you declined to kick that asshole's head in."

"I did."

"You're soft."

"Weren't you the one who said you need rules, a code? I got to do things my way, be my own type of outlaw."

"Not taking what's offered, not hurting someone who deserves it, that's a code that'll get you killed or poor." He snorted. "I'm taking you home. You'll stay there until the moment those bastards try and shove you off it. I'm guessing they'll wait a good long time, considering what we did to your little buddy back there. And when they come—because they will, the money coming out of the ground's too good—I'll move you someplace new. That place was a piece of shit, anyway."

Sure, she almost said, but it was home. Besides, she might have added, how many times have you promised to take care of us, and yet our lives are never better? Instead, she said nothing. It seemed the safer option, with Preacher angry enough to drive off the road again.

When they pulled into the driveway of her home, she saw Brad on the porch, waiting for them with a vacant look that promised supreme hardship in the days ahead. A heavyset man in a nylon jacket stood beside him, rubberized tablet in hand. The yellow letters on the man's jacket read "CORONER."

VI.

Brad had found her in the tub upstairs.

VII.

Two hours before, right around the moment Maxine and Preacher met in that expensive house to talk about settling scores, Maxine's mother had loaded up a syringe too full and found a good vein in the moonscape of her left arm and pushed home the killer hit, blasting a hole in Maxine's heart that never fully closed.

File 8.43.20003.7
Date: 8/12/2112

Current students may find it hard to picture how college campuses looked a century ago. Anyone could walk onto the quad without challenge. Amazing to think! Circumstances today are radically different, and although high walls and checkpoints are annoying for faculty and students to navigate, the chance to study in a safe environment is well worth it. The rumors are false: We are protected against any and all outside threats!

In this next file, our algorithms integrated some information about the Native American politics of upstate New York circa mid-21st century, but we encourage those interested to supplement their knowledge with the following books: "White Deer Speaks: Reconstituting Our Lost Empire" *(cat: 20-1324-214.21)* and "How the Tribe Got the Bomb" *(cat: 03-2013-321.21b)*. Those students who like music can also listen to the rapper Blood Dove, who hailed from the upstate New York region and whose first three albums tackle many of the tribal issues of the day. (Warning: his lyrics contain era-specific profanity!)

Although Maxine Hardwater's academic records have been lost, it seems that she was a good student. Unfortunately, we are unable to verify Dr. Gibson's theory that she was a reader of anti-colonialist literature, and it is debatable how much her later combat tactics were influenced by historical figures.

I.

At the far edge of the basketball court, a scrum of teenagers in bright clothing spun tricks atop low-rider bicycles, wheels squealing loud enough to echo off the scarred buildings. Crouched beneath the bent stalk of an old basketball hoop, Maxine whistled, and one of them, Beta Dog, broke from the pack and wheeled over, puffing on a joint as thick and long as his index finger.

Unlike the other beastie boys, whose sartorial style combined everyday T-shirts and jeans with bits of last-century retro (a pair of blast goggles here, a spiked chain used as a belt there), Beta Dog had gone full gonzo: his face and arms etched with homemade tattoos and pseudo-tribal scars, his long hair iridescently blue as a deep-sea jellyfish, his bulky jacket a patchwork of leather and next-gen ballistic fabric.

"Any word?" Maxine asked. Today she had decided on a puffy purple vest, jeans, and a white T-shirt that would reactively turn dark blue if she stained it. The shirt was in case she spilled any blood; the vest, stuffed with armor-foam, to make sure any blood spilled wasn't hers. "It's been an hour."

Beta Dog snorted and pulled out his phone, one of the flexible-glass ones they all coveted so highly these days. He pressed his thumb against the screen, unlocking it, and flicked through his messages. "Claims he'll arrive in five minutes, prepped to ball

MAXINE UNLEASHES DOOMSDAY

wild," he said.

"And what else?"

"Nothing else, I swear."

"Bruiser's a punk-ass chump. He can't open his mouth or tap his thumbs without throwing some prime shade. What's the rest of it?"

"He says your uncle's washed-up screw-bait." A municipal drone buzzed high overhead, and Beta Dog paused to flick it off. Beta Dog's face had never found its way into the state database, so the drone's cameras would pull up a big fat blank on the identification: No court summons in his nonexistent email for disorderly conduct, no fine automatically deducted from his nonexistent bank account.

The drones only swung past this section of the neighborhood once an hour, so Maxine knew they were now safe to conduct the day's rougher business. She snapped her fingers, and Beta Dog passed the rest of his joint over. She inhaled the fragrant smoke until her lungs burned, loving the idea of transgression more than the actual high. I'm safer about my drugs than you, Mom.

Just because weed was legal in the state didn't mean you could dodge huge penalties for smoking it in public. In canal-laced Lower Manhattan, anyone caught puffing on the sidewalk ended up spending a week in isolation for the crime of "disrespecting communal airspace," if you could believe that crap. Good thing she had decided to go to college in a city upstate.

Actually, "decided" implied some sort of choice. Some alphabet soup of government agencies had given her a three-quarters scholarship as sort of an apology for subjecting her to awful schools built with fracking and coal money, those institutions themselves a half-assed apology for killing generations of locals in collapsing mines and chemical-soaked refineries. Maxine had played the game well. Every grade in school, she made a point of memorizing a long word a day, acing all her (easy) homework assignments, and not shedding too much of her classmates' blood. Preacher had promised to make her an outlaw queen, and she would hold him to it, even if it meant attending the world's most boring classes.

As if summoned by her half-thoughts of classes, one of her friends, Julia Canadien, plopped down beside her on the asphalt. "I love how you're studying for finals," Julia said.

"I just got papers, and I'm most of the way through those," Maxine said, offering the joint, which Julia declined. Julia had also grown up in soul-crushing poverty, on a federal Indian reservation upstate, and she was brave enough to plow through life without the need to occasionally fry her brain. Not so Maxine, who liked how booze reduced the world to a syrupy blur, although she refused to touch anything harder than weed or beer. Too many bad memories of her mother.

"How's your little gang going?" Julia asked, jutting her chin at the symphony of kids on bikes.

"They're tight. Like any good anthropologist, I got their lingo down. I just have to figure out how to make more money off them. My tuition isn't getting any cheaper." Maxine took another mega-hit off the joint, enjoying how it loosened the tight muscles in her neck.

"Talk to your uncle lately?" Julia was the only student who knew Maxine's connection to one of the state's all-star criminals.

Maxine shook her head. "FBI's up his ass yet again. What's your thesis for Twentieth-Century History?"

"You haven't started on it, have you?"

"Been busy, okay?"

A tall girl in a too-tight bumblebee outfit strode onto the court, wheeling beside her a mountain bike with fat off-roader wheels. Reaching the half-court line, she drew a bright orange pistol from her belt, pointed the barrel at the gunmetal sky, and pulled the trigger. A red flare blazed aloft, trailing greasy smoke. An absurd hulk of a man stepped through a hole in the fence, his face hidden behind a horned devil mask made of hammered metal, his body encased in red leather. This was Bruiser.

"Points for theatrics," Maxine said, standing up as Beta Dog

69

wheeled over. He climbed off and held the bike steady as Maxine swung onto the seat; from the crude holster woven into the back of his jacket, he drew a short wooden stick topped with an iron lion's head, once a railing decoration. Maxine hefted the weapon, testing its balance, before nodding to him.

"What's going on?" Julia said, a little nervous.

"Territory dispute," Maxine said. "Won't be a minute."

Bruiser had come with his own lance: a length of pipe topped with a snarl of barbed wire. Mounting the bumblebee girl's bike, he pedaled hard for Maxine as the kids on the court burst into cheers and applause.

Compared to the demon rushing down on her, Maxine seemed too small, her bike too low, her weapon flimsy. As they veered toward each other like medieval jousters, she changed the rules: Slamming her heels into the pavement, she stood off the seat and let the bike slide out from under her, where it skittered for ten feet before impacting—hard—with Bruiser's front wheel. Bruiser roared in dismay as his ride flipped, sending him crashing headfirst into the pavement.

Maxine walked over and tapped him on the back of the head—gently—with her stick. "Keep flattened," she said. "Grow your nub back."

Bruiser, sucking down wheezing lungfuls of air, tilted his head. One of his mask's straps had broken, revealing the scared teenager beneath. "I'll peel your dome," he offered, but the whine in his voice rendered the threat unconvincing.

"Shove off, there's fresher territory for you elsewhere." Maxine tapped him again, harder, before turning to offer the crowd a polite bow. Her people whooped and hollered. The bumblebee girl snorted and stomped off, her heels clicking on the asphalt.

"Sorry, where was I?" Maxine asked as she sauntered back to Julia.

"We were discussing the value of a good education."

"I hope it's valuable." Her boys had made some bets: Beta Dog walked over with a handful of crumpled bills, which he slapped into her palm with a wink. "Speaking of which," she said, "they lock down the library?"

"At least until the trial." Julia shrugged. "Whole campus locked tight."

"I know. It gave me an idea for making a little cash." Maxine raised a finger to pause the conversation. Out of the corner of her eye, she saw Bruiser rising to his feet, fists clenched, swaying slightly, readying to charge across the court. Maxine sighed and took a firm grip on her stick, psyching herself to swing for the fences, but Beta Dog stopped her with an upraised hand.

Stepping into Bruiser's path, Beta Dog drew a slim steel stick from his back pocket. Bruiser wavered, unsure how to regard this new threat, and that was all the time Maxine's young friend needed to jab the stick into the giant's ribs. The effect was immediate: Bruiser's knees went loose as warm rubber, his body smacking the pavement for the second time in two minutes, his throat hacking out pale vomit. As Beta Dog stepped away from the jittering body, Maxine slapped a few dollars back into his hand.

"Slick with the sick," she sang.

"I learned that one from the best," he said, affecting a cheesy British accent. "We have enough for pints, governor."

II.

For this town beside the river, the collapse came in the form of power and gasoline shortages, political corruption, and a super-bug outbreak (Malaria II, a riff on a classic and a real killer). The final spark: the town cops shooting a couple of kids for the high crime of tagging a wall near the decaying downtown. From a nearby rooftop, one of Beta Dog's friends had captured the massacre with his camera phone, and the video went viral over-night.

The government promised a trial, but it was too little, too late. When a mob set the police station on fire, the governor decided it was time to send in the National Guard. Things de-scended into nationally televised chaos from there. A few miles south of town, on Maxine's campus, the university police kept the quad peaceful. If you lived off-campus, you had to watch yourself.

While Maxine's scholarship might not have spared her from several thousand dollars in student loans, it secured her a guar-anteed spot in the relative safety of the dorms. She hated its cin-derblock walls and heavy security doors, which reminded her a bit too much of a prison, but for the first time in her life she had hot water and internet on demand, which made her feel positively princess-y. Look how far I've come, Mom. Sorry you couldn't see it.

In the campus dining hall, feeling vulnerable without her little crew, Maxine loaded up her tray with donuts and coffee—the breakfast of champions—and found a seat close to one of the paper-thin television screens that bannered all four walls, everybody around her rapt at the images of Guard soldiers pulling back from the north edge of town, pursued by a storm of rocks and bottles. An excited newscaster babbled about snipers on roofs and burning trucks in the streets.

"That's what they get," someone behind Maxine said, "they want to go up there and shoot kids."

"Kids had it coming," someone else replied, sparking off a furious debate between two tables. Maxine forced herself to ignore it. Most of these people had no idea what it was like to grow up poor, to have the cops harass you for no reason. If I start talking about it, she once told Julia, I get too emotional. And when I get too emotional, I tend to punch people in the face.

Julia took a seat beside her, armed with only a cup of coffee. "So, I just had a weird morning?"

Maxine swiveled to face her. "Econ, right?" She had earned an A in econ, thanks to a lifetime of firsthand experience in all the ways the state sucks the lifeblood out of you—the only kid in her class who knew by heart how much the feds and the local governments had reduced benefits and budgets over the years. Besides, she always figured, a good head for percentages would help her when she finally took over the family business.

"Yeah, with Professor Monroe?" Julia said. "And usually he's the most boring person on Earth, I swear, talking about how gerrymandering finally killed Congress and whatnot. Except this time he was just...odd. We were supposed to talk about models for price indexes, and he did that for maybe ten minutes before he stopped and sort of looked at us and said we should learn how to shoot guns instead."

"Sounds like his class actually got interesting." Maxine found Professor Monroe the perfect cure for insomnia.

"His words were, 'The only way you might be able to get

what you need in a few years is to shoot for it, so you might as well start practicing now.' It was freaky."

"He's not wrong." Maxine shrugged. "Look at Seattle."

"Only thing left in Seattle is, like, mutants. It's the exception."

She had a point. After the missile hit western Washington, the United States had irradiated North Korea right back. The world still worked according to its old rhythms of supply and demand, need and satisfaction, birth and death, although the details occasionally veered toward the horrific. "Don't worry," Maxine said. "The world's not going to collapse. You'll be in a boring developer job before you know it."

A lunatic for video games, Julia wanted to spend her life developing big-budget shoot 'em ups for virtual-reality headsets, the kind where you gunned down waves of faceless soldiers in finely rendered Mars stations. Although Maxine would never say this aloud, she had never seen the appeal of shutting out the world with a plastic visor over your eyes and a pair of ultra-fidelity headphones over your ears. Some of the nerdier kids in her high school had scraped together enough money to buy knockoff headsets, heavy and glitchy but good enough, and never really left the house again. One shy boy, absorbed totally in ruling his digital domain, starved to death in a trailer behind his parents' house, and Maxine sometimes believed he might have preferred that ending. Why endure a reality so determined to kick your ass on a daily basis?

Some of those kids who were especially good at virtual combat ended up recruited into the Army, where the ones with the right mental stamina and psychological makeup could join the Ghost units, piloting a four-legged drone from two thousand miles away. Those lucky few always described the experience as a real thrill, stomping through the dust and fire, launching rockets left and right. The salary was good, but Maxine couldn't do that, either. It would've been too much like becoming a cop.

"A job is a job is a job. Or do you want to be broke your whole life?" Julia kept her eyes on the table as she said the next part, knowing Maxine hated anything that smelled even slightly of charity. "Like I told you before: the casino. My family could hook you up with something. I'm not even talking long-term. Just until you pay off your loans."

Julia's tribe, which ran a glittering jewel of a casino upstate, was also thinking of seceding from the United States, rewinding the clock back to the fourteenth century and having themselves a little do-over. Some of the tribal elders had publicly expressed a willingness to bang things out with the U.S. military, if it came to that. As much as Maxine enjoyed the thought of the local Native Americans getting a little payback after centuries of bullshit, she had no interest in ending up in the middle of a shooting war.

Not that she could express any of this to Julia. "I can't get locked down," she said, wincing at the cheesiness of the line she was about to deliver: "I'm an outlaw at heart."

"How many times do I have to tell you? You wouldn't have gone to college if a part of you didn't want to build a real life."

"And like I told you, college was a deal with my uncle."

Julia shook her head. "Okay, fine, drop it. Tell me about your big plan, the one that's going to get us paid."

"You know there's an alcohol shortage, right?"

"Yes, and I wish everybody would stop bitching about it. We're not at school to drink, we're here to work."

"Tell that to those fratties willing to pay quadruple for a case of crappy beer, sometimes more. And you know that big strip of warehouses by the river? One's a beer distributor."

"You can't just take whatever's there."

"Lower your voice. It's chaos up there. Looters will get it before anyone can restore order. We might as well grab it first, make a profit."

Julia, bless her soul and its driven-snow purity, had issues with the idea of knocking off a soulless beer conglomerate. "If you need money, I can give you some, okay? You can't walk up there. You can't drive up there. You'll get hurt."

"It was just an idea." Maxine took an oversized bite of donut, chewing slowly, to kill any further conversation.

Except Julia refused to let it go. "I used to steal a lot when I was a kid." She took one of Maxine's sugar-powdered hands in hers, squeezed. "Promise me you won't do it."

"Okay, okay." Maxine raised a pinkie. "I swear."

III.

Screwdriver in hand, checking out the windshield every few seconds for any signs of maintenance workers or cops, Maxine pried the plastic cover away from the snowplow's steering column, fiddled with the wiring harness connector, stripped the insulation from the battery wires, and commenced to hotwiring. New cars had every manner of anti-theft gizmo under the hood, but not these twenty-year-old monsters.

The beast started up with a smoggy roar that sent a high-voltage thrill down her spine. As she buckled in, Beta Dog in the passenger seat tapped the proper coordinates into his phone, ready to play navigator.

"Who steals a snowplow in April?" she asked her lieutenant.

"We do?"

"Exactly." Maxine eased on the gas, the engine choking and nearly stalling out while she struggled the gearshift into first. Easing the beast from its parking slot beside the maintenance shed, she turned left for the unlocked gate of the campus depot, which sprung open before the raised plow. The truck's loose shocks bounced them like ships on rough seas.

"Question," Beta Dog said.

"Answer, hopefully."

"They put sensors in these trucks, yeah? Track where they move?"

"Not these. I found an article online, university was asking for funds to install them. We're good."

"That's you." Beta Dog tapped his temple. "The smartest."

As they bumped onto the service road, Beta Dog pulled a pack of cheap Chinese cigarettes from the pocket of his technicolor coat, torched one up with a plastic lighter shaped like a naked lady, and winked at a couple of students on the sidewalk who gawped at them as they passed. Beta Dog offered the pack to Maxine, who popped a coffin nail in her mouth and bent her head to the offered flame.

"I'm chuffed we're doing this," Beta Dog said, leaning back in his seat. "A right-proper robbery, like."

"Where's this English accent coming from?" Maxine asked, blowing smoke out her nose. "You're not British." She hunkered down in her seat, paranoid as always about lurking cops.

"The English are right proper gangsters." Beta Dog smirked, the rising dawn glinting off his cheap metal incisors. "Role models, right?"

Maxine coughed, blasting smoke and spit on the steering wheel, thumping her chest to clear things out. These cheapo smokes *burned*, but she appreciated how the nicotine spiked her blood, made her a little happier. "My uncle's my role model," she said. "Except I also want to do my own thing, set my own rules."

"What rules are those?"

"Rob corporations, not regular people. Punch back whenever you're threatened, but don't harm anyone who can't fight." Maxine rolled down her window, tossed out the half-finished cigarette. "My uncle's real old-school, he believes in shooting first and asking questions never. You can't do that forever, though."

"But as long as he rules, dear, he sets the rules."

"True. Maybe I can shift him, get him to take it down a gear in his old age."

"Yeah, good luck with that." Beta Dog shifted his focus to

something in the middle of the road. "Isn't that your friend?"

Maxine glanced up at Julia trotting toward them, holding a thick hardcover book to her chest, and tapped the brakes. The snowplow wheezed to a halt, Julia jumping on the running board before Maxine could roll the window more than halfway up. "What the hell are you doing?" Julia shouted.

"Stuff," Maxine said, cheeks reddening.

"We're committing a right robbery," Beta Dog helpfully added. "Fancy a little crime before class?"

Julia tilted her face down and around until Maxine, despite contorting her head like a flamingo, finally met her eyes. "What did we talk about yesterday?" Julia asked.

"Not doing...stuff?" Still nervous about police, Maxine scanned the manicured lanes around them, dotted with clusters of students stumbling to early classes. It was amazing how normal it all looked, considering the warzone a few miles away.

"Right," Julia huffed. "Open the door."

"No."

"Why?"

"Because I don't want you to get hurt," Maxine said.

"Just park the thing." Julia reached through the window, hooked a finger lightly around the steering wheel. "We'll get breakfast, okay? This is stupid."

"We'll be back before you know it," Maxine said, prying Julia's finger away. The hurt in Julia's eyes threatened to crack her heart. "It'll be okay. This is what I'm supposed to do."

"Open the door," Julia said.

"Why?"

"Because I'm getting in. You got this all planned out, I trust you, okay? But I'm going to watch over you, too. Deal with it."

Maxine unlocked the door. In hindsight, she should have kept it locked, thrown the beast into gear, and motored on with the mission. Sure, it might have wrecked the friendship, but at least some of that day's death and destruction would have been avoided.

IV.

Someone had strung a brightly colored "STUDENT PRIDE" banner between the tall stone pillars marking the quad's south entrance. It provided an ironic contrast to the mass of riot cops standing beneath, layered in black body armor, cradling rifles. Maxine's guts clenched at the sight of them, but nobody shouted at the snowplow to stop as it rumbled past, headed for the service road that led off-campus. Beta Dog, no fool, chose to duck below window-level rather than offer the officers his infamous one-finger salute.

Despite that bit of luck, they made it barely five miles beyond campus before everything went wrong. Maxine piloted the truck over the aging wrought-iron bridge that served as the gateway to the north side of town, lowering the snowplow (after much fumbling with the controls) to knock aside a couple of burned-out cars blocking the lanes, as Beta Dog kept an eye on the micro-drones buzzing overhead and Julia, fearful of the distant crack of gunfire, kept her head tucked below the dashboard. Maxine placed a comforting hand on the back of her neck.

"Not sure this was the best route, governor," Beta Dog said, pointing at the far shore, where a line of steeltown bungalows merrily burned to the ground.

"We're okay," Maxine said, easing the truck into the bridge's exit lane. "Just keep checking the news."

Beta Dog flicked his phone screen to keep up with the viral newsfeeds, the real-time video fed by the machines swarming overhead. "Riot line's to our east," he said. "Cops, too."

"Whole campus was on lockdown," Julia said.

"Really?" Beta Dog chuckled. "Maxine didn't tell me that. We sailed right out of there."

"Keep focused," Maxine said, gunning the beast past the bridge off-ramp. The surrounding streets seemed empty, although it was hard to tell at this speed; she just hoped the flickering shadows in the vacant windows of the houses, and in the weeds behind the tall fences, were a trick of the sun, and not people readying to attack them. From here, she could see the gray flank of the warehouse beyond the road's far curve, one flimsy chain-link standing between her and many cases of beer and lots of profit. Maybe she would call Preacher afterward, brag about what she managed to pull off—

From between two houses loped one of those new military drones, the ones that moved on bent legs to a horrifyingly jaunty inner beat, looking like dogs bulked out with thick armor. It stopped in the middle of the road, facing them, and Maxine had two seconds and fifty yards to contemplate the cylinder strapped to the thing's back, barely time to scream before the world exploded in a flash of white light, a curtain of fire over the wind-shield, Julia's hand tight on her arm as everything snapped to nothingness.

V.

Her mother's cold, wet hand against her cheek. Milky pupils locked with hers.

Maxine opened her eyes to a burning sun. The whole right side of her body felt thick, weird at the shoulder. She tried flexing her right hand and nothing happened, so she turned her head in that direction and oh God oh God oh God her arm pinned between the pavement and the crumpled snowplow blade, the metal carcass of the truck towering above her. The truck's windshield shattered into a milky mess, the hood crumpled and smoking. Engine fluids trickled across the pavement, drenching her shirt. She flared her nostrils for the scent of gas, smelling none, a small blessing. She was already screwed in plenty of ways.

She let her head flop in the other direction and wished she hadn't. Beta Dog lay on the yellow line in a galaxy of broken glass, his beautiful coat soaked dark, his body contorted into a pretzel pose that no living person could hold for very long. Maxine wanted to say she was sorry, but her lips refused to move. Where was Julia? She tried lifting her head for a better look around and saw a man in a National Guard uniform walking toward her, a rifle slung over his shoulder.

The man was alone. He looked furious as he knelt beside her. She noted the blond hair peeking from beneath his helmet, the way his army uniform seemed to sag and bunch on his lanky frame. "You're alive," he said.

She found the strength for words. "Help me."

He seemed unconcerned by the fact that her arm was crushed beneath a mountain of destroyed machinery. "My name is Colonel Mark Stevens," he said in a gently lecturing voice, "and you're in some deep trouble."

Great, she thought, some law-and-order prick. If he's here just to watch me die, I might as well go out with a little spunk. "Can I get some fried chicken, Colonel?" Maxine asked. Not the greatest put-down, under the circumstances, but before she could come up with a better one, the man bent and jabbed his finger where the snowplow bit into her flesh.

Maxine screamed.

"You're not in much position to make jokes," Stevens said conversationally as he flipped open a pocket on his thick combat vest, withdrew a metal tube, and pressed its cold metal tip against the side of Maxine's neck. Maxine tried to bat his hand away, but her bloody left arm refused to rise from the pavement. The tube hissed, spreading bliss and warmth through her body. Her throat unclenched. Her vision cleared a little.

"How old are you?" he asked.

The bliss made it hard to lie. "Twenty."

"What are you doing out here with a snowplow?"

"Just cruising, you know."

"You're lying."

"Maybe. Maybe not. Maybe screw off."

The Colonel's face was so close now that Maxine could see a tiny patch of blond hairs in the fold of his chin that the razor had missed. His fingers wove into her hair and squeezed, igniting sharp pinpricks of pain across her scalp. He twisted her head left, so she could look at Beta Dog splattered on the pavement.

"You know what I think?" the Colonel said. "I think you're looters, just like the ones we've been shooting all day. You want to be a criminal? It just gets you dead, and a lot of people hurt."

"Where's my other friend?" Maxine asked, hoping Julia had

made it, that she had crawled or even walked away from the wreckage. She had never entertained much belief in spirits or angels, but at that moment she would have embraced anything if it meant Julia would live.

"She's around the other side of the truck," the Colonel said. "Thrown clear. One of my men is working on her. She might make it, but I doubt she'll walk again." He sighed. "She told us you were college kids. Is that true?"

Maxine nodded.

"All the more reason you shouldn't be out here. Dead college kids make us look bad, whether or not they're ripping something off. College is the only reason we got an ambulance coming for your sorry ass."

"Thank you," Maxine said, torn by two emotions. A part of her wanted to cry, to beg someone to save her arm, to reverse time a few hours, to fix everything. Another part—maybe a bit of the same DNA that had formed her uncle—wanted to spit the blood filling her mouth right in the Colonel's face.

"Don't thank me," the Colonel said, standing up. "If you survive, just think about staying out of trouble from now on. Trust me, you'll be much happier that way."

Baking in the hot sun, Maxine swallowed the blood.

VI.

Her mother's skin, white and hard as tub porcelain, pressed against Maxine's mouth, making it hard to breathe. The sun flaring hot as a severed nerve. How much damage, her mother asked. How much damage was I expected to take?

Maxine awoke this time to whiteness, so bright it forced her to squint. A man sat beside her bed, his head large and square, skin cracked like a block of just-quarried granite. He wore a leather jacket as weathered as his face, and a pair of very expensive jeans.

"You're in the hospital," he said, reading the panic in her eyes.

Her shoulder burned. She looked down at a bandaged stump poking from the right sleeve of her hospital gown. From what felt like a hundred miles away she heard herself moan, a low sound filled with rage and pain. Her vision trembled. Fear crackled at the edges of whatever calming drugs they had put in her blood.

Breathe, hon.

Just breathe—deep and slow. You're alive.

You'll make it.

Breathe.

Calming down, Maxine half-expected the man to touch her remaining hand, comfort her. But he simply sat with an expression of mild interest, as if her struggle was a movie he'd seen before. His enormous hands limp in his lap. That cool gaze made her uncomfortable, so she turned her head to scan the dazzling contours of the room, taking in the spotless walls, the enormous screen mounted in the corner, the rack beside the bed loaded with sleek, softly beeping machinery. She was the only patient in the room, which was wild: how much would all this cost her? It seemed a world away from the dirty clinic down the road from her childhood home, frantic with burnout doctors and cockroaches.

"Where?" she asked.

"Albany," the man said. "Upstate they got some good trauma units but nothing decent in terms of long-term care, so we brought you down here. There are no charges pending against you, by the way."

"Who are you?"

"Me?" He smiled, revealing rows of gray teeth like tombstones. "I'm Julia's father, Ken. She told me a lot about you, Maxine. It didn't seem like you had family coming, so I decided to stop on by."

Hearing Julia's name triggered Maxine upright, wincing as the needles in her arm threatened to pull free. "Is she okay?"

The smile disappeared. "She will live."

"Okay." Maxine's vision wavered again, this time from tears. "Is she hurt?"

"Yes. Badly. Her mind is still intact. Everything else..." His voice stayed infuriatingly calm, even as a massive vein throbbed in his neck.

"Oh God. I'm so sorry. If there's anything..." Take my kidneys if you have to, she wanted to plead. Strip out a lung, chop off my other arm if it means they heal her.

Ken clenched his jaw, forceful enough for her to hear his teeth scraping together. "I'm not trying to push a guilt trip on you," he said, "but 'sorry' means absolutely nothing to me. My daughter's never going to be the same, and it's your fault. If you're tempted to say something about making things right, don't bother. There's absolutely nothing you can do."

"I already knew that," Maxine said, her stump itching like a hundred fire ants beneath her flesh. She hoped the feeling would go away once she healed. If she had to spend the rest of her life resisting the urge to scratch, she would last a grand total of two days before losing her mind. "I never think things can be fixed."

Ken leaned back in his seat, eyebrows raised, maybe a little surprised. "Good. Then maybe we can cut the New Age crap that everybody around here seems so anxious to spit out. I grew up poor, like you, so I know you're already worried about the medical bills."

She nodded.

"Don't worry. The tribe is paying for your care. We shelled out to bury your little friend, and we paid the lawyer to talk to the district attorney about dropping any and all charges. That money comes with one condition."

"What?"

Placing his hands on the edge of the bed, Ken loomed over her, so close she could smell the coffee on his breath. She shrank against her pillow. "You never see my daughter again," he said. "We're taking her to another school, another life. You try and talk to her, and I will put you in the ground. They will never find the body. I don't care who you're related to. You understand?"

What else could she do but nod?

"Good." Ken stood, smoothing out his jacket. "I'm glad we understand each other. From what I've heard, the college will want to speak with you. You don't strike me as a hope kind of girl, which means you know what's probably coming. They don't want criminals on their campus."

He left the room without waiting for a reply, never looking back. Biting her lip against that infernal itch, Maxine wondered if throwing herself at the mercy of the dean would accomplish squat. Probably not, but she had an obligation to try anyway. Because that's your life from this point forward, isn't it? Trying to get everybody to forgive you, even if nobody wants to hear.

On a hook beside the door, she spied a clear plastic bag, filled with her stuff. She hit the little button for the nurse and waited. Itching.

And waited.

And waited.

And, just for variety, sat there and waited some more, using every ounce of her shaky willpower to not work her fingers into her bandage and dig deep into that knitting flesh until the infernal tickle retreated forever.

True, only a few seconds might have passed—who knew how the drugs affected her sense of time—but Maxine's usual impatience kicked in fierce. She gripped a handful of wires that connected her body to the machines on the rack, ready to see if yanking them out would earn her some attention, when a thin dude walked past the door that Ken had left open.

"Hey," she called.

The dude stopped. He had a gentle face, which came as a relief after spending time in Ken's hard orbit. His green canvas jacket looked three sizes too large for his bony frame, and its worn elbows and shoulders suggested either the laziness of a young man or a critical lack of cash. The scruff on his chin was making a valiant attempt at establishing the beachhead of a full beard and failing.

She smiled. "Can you help me?"

He stepped into the room. "Sure. What do you need?"

"Could you clean my bedpan? The nurse took one look at it and freaked out, but I think it's her first day. I swear there's not too much blood in there…"

How can you tell when someone is gullible? When they respond to that sort of request by turning pale.

"I'm just messing with you, chief," she said, nodding at the plastic bag. "Grab that for me, bring it over? My phone is in there."

He did as requested, Maxine thinking he was handsome in a delicate sort of way. "My name's Rodrigo," he said.

"Maxine." Tearing open the bag freed a nasty stench from the shredded clothes inside, still moist with spilled chemicals from the road. Wrinkling her nose, Maxine shoved aside the mess until she found her phone. Its screen lit bright when she pressed her thumb to it.

"Have we met?" Rodrigo asked.

Maxine looked up, wondering: Is he trying to pick me up? But his squint suggested he was really trying to place her. Use whatever crappy bottom-shelf pickup line you want, she thought. It'll only distract me from this itch.

"Where do you go to school?" she asked.

"I don't. I help run convoys."

Maxine nodded, impressed. "Hard job."

He chuckled. "I just do repair work. But yeah, it's hard for the drivers. Our cars aren't the best, but we get the job done, and we're not too expensive—maybe half of what those spec-ops badasses cost. Man, it'd be cool to work for one of those big companies..."

Maxine sensed he was about to describe his job in numbing detail. And while she loved talking engines, she had bigger things on her mind. "Why are you here?"

"My dad's getting his teeth grown back. Stem-cell therapy. Better than dentures."

"Crazy. Is that expensive?"

"Probably, but VA's paying for something, for once. It's an experimental procedure, so who knows, he could sprout vampire fangs or something weird like that. Actually, that would be cool."

"Until he bit someone and sucked their blood. Listen, I got to make a call." Her finger on the phone's screen, swiping through contacts, when it occurred to her: What if someone had inserted a slippery piece of software to trace her calls or listen in? Given how much John Q. Law wanted Preacher dead, that seemed like a possibility.

"Huh, seems like it's messed up or something," she said, tossing the phone aside. "Can I borrow yours? I'll be quick."

"Sure," he said, pulling an equally cheap phone out of his pocket and tossing it to her. How could somebody be so guile-free? Had he grown up in a box? Would he willingly scratch her stump whenever she asked (which would be often)?

Maxine sent a text to a number she had memorized; paused before handing the device back. "You mind if I hang onto your phone for a day or two? I swear, I'll give it back at some point."

"No," he said. "No, it's totally okay."

"Rodrigo."

That shy smile again. "You're messing with me?"

"You catch on quick." She returned the phone. "We should hang out, you know, when I'm not stuck full of needles. You got a pen?"

From the pocket of his jacket, he pulled out a thick black one, which she took, pulling off the cap with her teeth. Taking his hand, she wrote her number on his palm. "There," she said. "You better call."

"Will do. And I could swear we've met before. Or like I've seen you on a show. Something."

Maxine shook her head. "I'm not famous." Wondering, with a fresh burst of fear, if she had ended up on the news as a result of her recent escapade. College girls wounded in failed attempt to loot beer warehouse? Exactly the sort of red-meat story that would make a reporter salivate.

After Rodrigo disappeared down the hallway, Maxine settled back into bed. He hadn't asked how she'd ended up in here, and that was a little weird. Maybe he was just trying to be polite. It was refreshing, meeting someone polite after dealing all the time with jackasses who just wanted to show you the size of their balls.

Her thoughts drifted back to Julia. I'm sorry, girl. I'll never be able to tell you now, but I'd gladly trade places with you in a heartbeat. Whatever your damage.

With voice commands, she summoned the television to life, yelling out channels until a news program appeared. She saw a drone's view of the familiar road, the stolen snowplow over-turned in the middle of it, swarmed by soldiers. A little box opened in the corner of the screen, filling with the worst possible photo of Maxine: the mugshot from her student identification card, her skin acne-riddled, her eyes glazed from lack of sleep and too much weed. The newscaster stated her name and wondered aloud how she had managed to dodge charges after so much destruction.

Maxine threw her phone at the screen, scoring a direct hit that scarred the glass—just as the nurse finally decided to walk in.

"Bill the room, jackass," Maxine told her.

At least the urge to scratch the hell out of her stump seemed to have passed. She concentrated on her breathing, and soon enough her heart slowed.

VII.

Preacher sent a familiar face to retrieve her from the bus stop down the road from the hospital: her brother Brad, grown to six-foot-six of bone and cordlike muscle, rocking a mullet like a perverse badge of pride. He dressed in militia chic, dusty cargo pants and a multi-pocket vest over a T-shirt of a burning skull. After climbing into the passenger seat of his battered van, Maxine spent forever hugging him tightly across the seats, pulling him closer as he tried, with increasing vigor, to extract himself. "You could have come see me, punky," she hissed in his ear.

"I'm sorry about your arm," he said. "Does it hurt?"

"Like hell. Plus I'm never going to be able to sit in the emergency exit row of an airplane again." Having rehearsed that joke for days, she was pleased when it came out sounding roughly as cool as in her head.

"Glad you got a sense of humor about it," he said.

"Never rode a plane, anyway." Hugging time over, she punched him in the arm. "If you'd actually shown up to the hospital, you could have seen the stump in all its bloody glory."

"Too much heat." He threw the van into gear, its tailpipe farting brown smoke as they motored away. No lithium-ion batteries or hydrogen cells for Brad's vehicles. Like Preacher, he lived with the paranoid conviction that the government could instantly stop any vehicle with a microchip in its drive-train and refused to drive anything except last-century junkers, despite the price of gas having climbed to ransom levels. The sad thing was, Maxine agreed with their lunatic assumption. If you gave people a way to screw you, they always took it.

"You got cigarettes?" she asked, rooting through the pile of junk between her feet.

He looked surprised. "You smoke now? You know that kills you?"

"Yes, I smoke now. And cancer is the least of my worries. You got anything?"

"Got a vape with some of that synth stuff, you know, that calms you down?" he said. "In the dashboard there. Need help with...um..."

"Relax, I'm already a pro at this one-armed stuff." She plucked the black tube from the small pile of junk on dashboard tray, popped it in her mouth, and inhaled a cloud of particles deep into her lungs. "I used to have to change your diaper, remember, while holding your squirming ass down."

"You're lying. Mom did that."

"Mom never did squat," she said, catching the flicker of pain in his eyes. There it was: the open wound they both shared.

"Fine, you wiped my ass." He grimaced. "I want to talk more, but right now I'm going to have to do something horrible."

"You're not taking me to lunch? I had a powerful hankering for one of those new kelp burgers I've been reading about. If you're really drunk, they supposedly taste like crappy beef."

"Worse." Reaching into his bulky vest, he yanked loose a handful of crushed velvet. "You're going to have to put this on. Uncle's paranoid about his current location. It's close to here, but far from his usual spots."

She spread out the crushed velvet, revealing a hood without eyeholes. "Oh, come on," she said. "We're family. There's not many of us left."

Brad shrugged. "Sue me. He's extra-super paranoid lately. Puts way too much faith in those forums, you know the tinfoil-hat ones, say breakfast cereal got trackers you swallow, stuff like that?"

"You're not really going to make me wear this, are you? I'll put it on when we get there or something."

"Too late," Brad said, pointing at the black plastic nub nestled in the ceiling between them. "He's watching us."

Maxine shook a fist at the tiny lens embedded in the nub and slipped on the hood, which smelled faintly of perfume and fried food. "Tell me this wasn't a sex toy or something," she said, her voice muffled. "Just give me that."

"No can do, sis. But it's good to see you, even if you can't see me."

As much as Maxine loved Preacher, she had to admit the old man could be a sexist twit. She had begged for years for him to take her under his wing, only to have him turn around and enlist her baby brother before he left seventh grade. It reminded her of that Bible story where some prophet gave one of his two sons an awesome colorful coat, which angered the other one, who killed the favored son with a rock, which made God flood the Earth. Or something. Her mother had neglected church as part of their growing-up, choosing instead to worship at the porcelain altar most Sunday mornings. Bibles aside, Preacher had to take her on, right? College had no intention of taking her back, not after her little beer run.

Sometime later, Brad stopped the van. She felt him grip her shoulder lightly. "You can open your door on your own, right?"

"What's he going to do, shoot me?" she said, reaching to whip the hood off.

He gripped her wrist before she could do so. "Just humor him, okay?"

"Okay, whatever. Help me get out. My tolerance for this blindfold shit is low."

He opened Maxine's door and escorted her out. Through the thick fabric, she smelled freshly cut grass, heard birds chirping. Brad's hand on her back guided her a hundred steps. The rumble of concrete on steel. They entered a cooler space with a slight downward grade, the air damp on her skin. "There's a doorway," Brad said, and she stepped into slightly warmer air, classical music piped crystal-clear from overhead. She sensed they were underground.

The hood whisked up like a curtain, revealing blue sky, absurdly fluffy clouds.

She spun around, confused at the sight of plush leather couches, the rosewood coffee table nestled on a thick maroon carpet, a wraparound marble bar loaded with bottles of impressive age and label—all of it floating thirty thousand feet in the bright air. Preacher stood behind the bar, pouring himself a drink. He looked a little worse for wear these days, his hair sprinkled with gray, the lines in his face approaching canyon depth.

"Your little accident," Preacher said, without so much as a hello, "got me thinking a lot about my own death. I've decided, when I finally kick the bucket, I want a Viking funeral. Just stack a pile of wood somewhere, toss my body on top of it, and set the whole thing ablaze. Before you do that, though—take note—I want you to cut my body open, hollow it out, and fill it with unpopped popcorn so that my body will explode with delicious goodness when the flames reach it."

And he offered her that trademark smirk, his eyes sparking with pill-fueled energy, letting her know that he was still a long way from death, thank you very much, despite the state gunning for him as usual. He wore a vintage T-shirt with the Grim Reaper on it, holding a steering wheel in place of a scythe.

Maxine reached out to touch a cloud, her hand flattening on cool glass. They were in an enormous tube, like an airliner cabin but four or five times as wide. "What is this place?" she asked.

"Luxury bunker," Preacher said. "They're all over the place. Rich people, paying like ten, twenty million for them. So they can ride out the apocalypse in style, two hundred feet under a hill."

"How'd you find it?" The shifting cloudscape made her a little nauseous, so she focused on the massive pistol in a leather holster on Preacher's hip, its grip studded with red patches: fingerprint sensors that would un-safety the weapon for certain users. Preacher was a little more tech-savvy these days, it seemed.

"I know the guys who build these places," he said. "I pay them a small tax every year, they let me hide out whenever I need. The people who buy these units, it's not like they ever show up. And it sure beats hiding out in houses. Or the woods. Or caves. I'm sorry about your arm, darling."

"Thanks," Maxine said. "It's been a rough week."

"Agreed. We're here because the Man decided to hunt us with airborne drones, so we decided to take a page from our friends the groundhogs, head beneath the dirt." Preacher held up a bottle of whiskey. "You look like you could use a drink."

"I'm on painkillers." Maxine flexed her stump. "I hear alcohol doesn't mix well with them."

"You heard incorrect," Preacher said, "but I wouldn't recommend getting high in a place like this. Underground has a way of freaking people out."

"It's freaking me out. Any way to change the wallpaper?"

"Sure," Preacher said, tapping a screen inlaid in the bar. A forest of wet bamboo erupted around them, green and bright as a backlit jewel, the soundtrack buzzing loud with insects and distant chanting, stippled sunlight playing across their faces. "All the visual options are outdoors. Supposed to make people calmer or something. They definitely thought all this through."

"Started from the bottom, now we're here," Brad said, sprawling on one of the couches. Despite his enormous size, its plushness threatened to engulf him, like an amoeba made of the finest animal skin. "Below the bottom. Digging deep."

"Maxine, let's talk about your little stunt." Preacher came around the bar and plopped down on the same couch as Brad. He moved a little stiffly, knees popping like pistol-shots as he settled. Not for the first time, she considered how the Preacher of her youth, the ghost of the hills who froze cops in terror, had become an old man.

"I was just trying to get some cash," Maxine said. "I had bills to pay."

"You were thinking like a looter, not a gangster," Preacher shot back, ignoring the part about the money with good reason: After promising to help her pay for school, his cash donations had trickled to a few hundred dollars a few times a year, delivered via droog, along with a repeated message: Times were tough.

"You want to know how I would have pulled off your little operation?" Preacher continued. "I would have waited until dark, come in on the river, which runs right beneath that warehouse, and loaded everything onto a boat. I wouldn't have crashed the hell in like William Holden in *The Wild Bunch*."

The itch was back. Maxine chewed her lip, as if that would somehow reduce the urge to scratch. "What the hell is *The Wild Bunch*?"

"They're obviously teaching kids the wrong things in school these days," Preacher said, slugging down his drink. "You promised me you wouldn't try nothing, remember? Not until you graduated."

"You got to take opportunities when they come up," Maxine said. "Didn't you teach me that?" Control your voice, she commanded herself. Check your anger.

Swirling his ice, Preacher regarded her. "Remember a long time ago," he said. "We were in that house, you could have taken that coat, and you didn't?"

"Yeah." Like I'd ever forget that day, she almost said.

"And thinking further back, when you took that joyride, and those cops ended up dead. That was a mess, wasn't it?"

"Hey, that wasn't my fault—"

He raised a hand, cutting her off. "I got a confession," he said. "I don't feel good about it, but here it is. I never wanted you in this life. You've never been cut out for it. That's why I told you to get through college before I'd consider taking you on. And after we messed up that dude who took your mom's house, when I told you that white-collar crime's the way to go?

That was me again, trying to push you in a new direction, like actual business. Maybe I should have said no from the start, but I figured you'd get over it on your own, find a real job. That's on me."

Her throat felt thick. "So what am I supposed to do?"

"Not porn," Brad offered. "I couldn't deal with that."

"Shut up," she snarled at him before returning to Preacher. "You know there's no real jobs anywhere here. College will never take me back. I don't have the money to afford one of those cool prosthetic arms, so that takes most work off the table. You gonna let me starve to death?"

Preacher waved his arms until a sensor awakened, and a giant menu popped up on the wall in front of him. He flicked his hand, and the menu cycled through options; when he made a fist, the bamboo forest faded into a mountain peak, blurry with snow-fall, the dim orange sun rising over the distant range. "I figured Everest would be a more appropriate venue for talking about starvation," he said. "You know who owns this particular unit?"

"Of course not. I didn't even know rich people paid for places like this."

"Some media executive. Lives in Manhattan, or I guess what's left of it. He creates that show you youngsters love so much, you know the one, where the people in the woods use magic to fight monsters or some shit."

"That was specific," Brad said, fishing a small vial of energy drink from his vest pocket. He popped the cap and guzzled down the noxious elixir before crushing the stiff plastic bottle flat against his forehead. That act of idiotic derring-do completed, he loosed an enormous burp and stared into the virtual snow-storm, his eyes assuming a blankness that Maxine remembered all too well from their childhood, when they would try to strangle their boredom by watching for cars on the road.

"Running for my life sort of cuts down on my television time," Preacher said. "Anyway, if we're done with comments from the cheap seats, let me get back to it. You know how that guy made enough money to afford a place he'll never actually live?"

"I don't care." Feeling rebellious, Maxine walked over to one of the couches, surfaced with enough leather to reupholster an entire bison, and kicked it gently with her shoe, leaving a scuff mark below one of the cushions. "I'm a girl with a missing arm and zero prospects. How some executive made money means jack squat to me."

"What were you going to major in?" Preacher asked.

"I was thinking of focusing on machine learning," Maxine said. "You know how artificial intelligence, robot automation, it's taking everybody's jobs? Truck drivers rioting over it? I figured if you know how to program the machines, you're more prepared for whatever's coming in the future." The reality? Those classes bored her right the hell to sleep: too many dry equations to memorize, too many rules to learn about things that seemed hideously abstract. She kept telling people she planned on majoring in machine learning because it stopped them from asking any more questions, and that was reason enough.

"Serve our robot overlords!" Brad called, still fixated on the mountain peak.

"Kowtowing to the machine's not going to do crap for you in the long run, degree or no degree," Preacher said. "Sooner or later—probably sooner—all that stuff's going to be smart enough to fix itself. All the more reason to keep as many devices as possible out of your life. Anyway, that's not the point. I wanted you to stay in school so you'd find a career where you wouldn't risk a bullet."

Maxine kicked the couch again, harder, leaving a longer scuff. "You mean you wanted me to become a cubicle monkey."

"Stop that," Preacher said. "You're smart and ambitious. Just like the guy who owns this place. His degree might have gotten him a first job, but it didn't help him get all this, not with all the other striving jerkwads out there. You don't need a degree, either. I mean, that little piece of paper makes things easier, but you got what it takes to make your own way, anyway. Or should our family always be criminals?"

"I prefer the term 'backwoods entrepreneur,'" Brad chimed in. "It's got a nice ring to it."

Placing his empty glass on the elaborately curved wisp of a table beside the couch, Preacher stood and gestured for the two of them to follow him deeper into the bunker. "I won't let you starve," he said.

At the other end of the tube, they arrived at a circular steel door. Digital butterflies with luminous wings clustered where the metal met the wall, flying away in a bright cloud when Preacher tapped a long code into the keypad embedded beside the handle. The door hissed open, their hair ruffling as cooler air escaped into the bunker. They stepped over the thick sill into a rounded concrete room filled with locked metal boxes and shrink-wrapped bundles of protein bars, lit from overhead by bright tube lights. "Bunker within the bunker," Preacher said, "just in case a nuke falls close by. Or cannibals break through the entrance. Whatever, it's secure."

Brad bent to one of the bundles of energy bars and tore the plastic away, yanking one free. "Hey sis," he said. "Want lunch? It'll fill you up, but you'll fart like a motorboat."

Maxine shook her head. "Great, you're showing me more rich-people stuff. What's the catch?"

"Consider it a down payment on your inheritance." Preacher knelt on the floor, beside a small door embedded in the concrete. "Of course, by doing this, I'm risking my relationship with the people who built this place, but family comes first." With a magician's theatrical grimace, he gripped a small steel loop set in the middle of the door and pulled. Maxine felt a metallic thump in the soles of her feet as the door creaked open, revealing shrink-wrapped bundles of cash, along with three brightly colored, polymer-framed pistols.

"This is to help you get on your feet again," Preacher said, pulling out one of the plastic bags and ripping it open, cash raining onto the concrete. "Rent an apartment—hell, buy a house.

Pound the pavement, talk to people, whatever you got to do. You've got the brains to be a real citizen, Maxine. I wouldn't have the first idea how. But you're not cut out to be an outlaw."

"You're not giving this advice to Brad," Maxine said, eyeing daggers at her brother.

Brad shrugged. "I'm too dumb to do anything else, sis." There was real sadness in his voice. "I know that. I can't read without messing up the words."

"Your brother's here because he had nowhere else to go," Preacher said. "You were going off to college. What was he supposed to do, become a ward of the state? You know what they do to the kids in those gladiator schools."

She hated to admit it, but her uncle had a point. Remember how Brad ran down the steps to clutch your legs, tears melting his face, the day he found mom in the tub? Of course you do. Get pissed off at Preacher all you want, but it's not like you could do anything.

Maxine toed a sheaf of bills, her heart speeding as it always did in the presence of cash. Memories of her mother wheeling them through a supermarket, happy because some random person they'd never met had hit an enter key somewhere, changing some meaningless numbers on a screen, and the store owners had accepted those digits as something called "money." Her mother furious when those meaningless numbers hit zero, when the ceiling at home collapsed, when her dealer refused to call, when Preacher stopped coming down from the hills. Furious until the day she died, waiting for help from other people.

She stepped away from the money.

"Uncle," she said, "I'm not going to take this."

Preacher closed the metal door, his face tight. "Why?" he asked quietly.

"Because if I have to make it on my own, I'm going to do it without your help."

He squinted, dipping his huge head close to hers. "Why, girl?"

"Because you've done enough, you know what I mean?"

Before he could ask another question, or touch her, she turned and walked out of the vault, into the bunker, her eyes locked on the distant door that led to the surface, expecting his massive hand to clutch her elbow. Preacher yelled something hard to hear over her pulse hammering her eardrums. The snowstorm intensified, thick curtains of snow blurring the distant mountains to static, and she grabbed an expensive bottle of vodka off the bar as she passed, figuring she would call that Rodrigo guy and get drunk with him, screw him maybe, anything to dull the knife-edge of this week, hell, her whole life. A loud bang, Maxine spinning around to see Preacher in the vault doorway, screaming, his smoking pistol pointed at the ceiling, where winter's furious sky had splintered into a web of cracked glass and red error messages, the whole illusion threatening to shut down.

Walking backward, bottle tucked under her armpit, Maxine offered him Beta Dog's favorite gesture, a tall middle finger. The distance made it hard to see, but she could have sworn Brad waved goodbye before she hit the surface.

You'll make it, she told herself on the long walk back through the woods. When you're at the bottom, you got nowhere to go but up. You'll make it. You have to.

File 8.43.20003.7
Date: 8/12/2112

When we began this project, we assumed that accessing cognitive memory files would present a prime research opportunity. Why rely on letters, emails, or even video, when you could read (machine-interpreted) signals directly from the primary source's mind? We failed to account for a prime aspect of the human condition: People will force themselves to forget things. The trauma is just too great. That's why, for all the thousands of pages written about Maxine Hardwater over the past several years, we still know relatively little about her child.

Those interested in the Decline of the American Empire should pay close attention to the groups represented here. Although many of the cultural and political battles of this period took place on Twitter and Facebook (the former is archived in TSQ-19312-f2-C; data from the latter was destroyed in the Second California Secession War), they did spill into the "real world" on occasion, usually in the form of ill-advised "guerilla" actions against soft targets. Given the preparation and physical shape of many of the "weekend warriors" who participated, these conflicts often ended in unintentionally hilarious ways.

I.

Before the law shipped him off to prison for trying to sell a gallon-bag of magic shrooms to an undercover officer, Maxine's father had done his part to keep the household fed by hunting deer once a week, no matter what the season. Unlike their neighbors, who slipped on orange vests before stomping into the forest with their rifles, her father would set up a lawn chair in the backyard, at the edge of the tree line, where the thorny bushes bubbled with cancerous-looking red berries.

The lawn chair's canvas arms featured a pair of built-in drink holders. Popping a cold can of beer into the left holder and his trusty .45 automatic in the right, Maxine's father would settle back and wait for a hungry deer to chow down on the bushes. Sometimes he would hunt at night, borrowing a pair of Preacher's night-vision goggles and waiting for a poor beast to wander within point-blank range.

The venison always tasted pretty good, except for the one time Maxine accidentally bit down on a bullet fragment and chipped a molar.

Kneeling in the back of Rodrigo's pickup, loading shells into Rodrigo's shotgun, Maxine remembered looking through the fogged glass of the living-room window at her father in the chair, lifting that can of beer to his lips with metronomic precision as he waited for dinner to arrive. At the time, she had felt nothing but shame at his laziness, his refusal to suit up and spend days hunting honestly like her friends' fathers. But as she raised her shotgun, ear cocked for the faint buzz of four small turbines, she saw his bargain-basement genius: Why plunge through the wet woods when the food could come to you?

A fresh wind swayed the pines that lined the narrow clearing around the truck, and beneath the symphony of crackling branches she heard—or imagined she'd heard—that telltale whine. She clicked off the shotgun's safety and aimed, praying her mechanical Arm would hold steady this time around.

A small black dot appeared against the gray sky, a little to the west, growing larger and louder as it swept overhead. Maxine took a deep breath, held it, exhaled as she pointed the barrels and squeezed the trigger.

The storm of bird-shot smashed the delivery drone's starboard turbines into a cloud of black particles. The machine's whine rose to a mechanical screech as it plunged, plowing into the thick mud twenty yards from the truck. Maxine dropped her weapon and leapt onto the ground, slipping on the featureless anti-biometric mask to prevent any surviving drone cameras from scanning her face.

Delivery drones were programmed to flip on their backs during an uncontrolled descent to save the payload, and this one had done its best, hitting at a sideways angle that preserved the shock-resistant polymer box bolted to its underside. Maxine yanked the multi-purpose tool from her back pocket and stripped away the box's lid, hoping for diapers or baby formula, nearly screaming with rage when she saw a pound of coffee—not even the good kind—and a curvy pair of VR hand controllers in bubble wrap.

Billy the Squid might pay her a couple of bucks for the controllers, and Rodrigo would drink the coffee. What a bust otherwise. Baby Marlon needed diapers. And also good medicine, not that watered-down crap that the hustlers tried to sell her. Maxine had no illusions the latter would fall from the sky anytime soon.

Back in the truck, mask and shotgun and coffee and controllers stowed in the bag beside her, Maxine activated her phone on speaker.

"How'd it go?" Rodrigo asked from home.

"Just one this afternoon," she said. "I think they're changing the routes. We've tapped this corridor out. Got some coffee for you, though."

"They were gonna shift eventually," he said in that calm tone that sometimes made her want to strangle him. "How much you think we cost them this year alone?"

"They're corporations, I'm sure they'll survive," she said, easing the truck down the narrow path that led to the paved road. "How's the kid?"

"Still coughing." Rodrigo sounded a little worried. "Doc in a box said it would pass but...you know."

"Yeah." She wanted to hold the little ragamuffin so bad, soothe his coughing and crying. Did you feel that way about me, Mom? If you were still alive, would you watch him while I worked my shifts? I wish you were still around. Rodrigo does his best, but I feel like I'm the one driving everything, and it leaves me feeling like a zombie most days.

"Anyway, we'll be here," he said. "We miss you."

"Miss you, too," she said and hung up before he could hear her voice quavering a little, more from exhaustion than worry. This afternoon she might grab three hours' sleep before heading to the depot for her shift, routing convoys through highway trouble. No adult food in the house, aside from the ten-pound bag of rice that had seen her and Rodrigo through the past three weeks, but sometimes her manager put out free snacks for the support staff, usually chips loaded with salt and fat. Unhealthy for you, sure, but better than going to bed hungry. If only they let me on convoy duty, she thought, I could make another twenty bucks an hour. I can drive better than half those dimwits we have running goods. Twenty bucks an hour, and we could afford to take the kid to a real doctor.

The path dipped, cutting across a dry creek bed that separated the woods from a double-lane road. It was still okay out here in the daylight, when the cops were willing to patrol the roads. If you lived around here, at sunset you brought your dogs inside and threw all three locks you hoped would keep the night on the other side of the door, and you brought your gun with you to bed. The road after dark was Russian Roulette, and if your number was up, they found the flaming wreck of your car in a ditch.

What a world to raise Marlon in.

She hoped no cops would pull her over and check the truck's registration, which had expired three months ago. No way they could afford to pay that fee, especially when the vehicle needed a years-overdue engine overhaul. Why couldn't a drone loaded with auto parts bumble its way into her shotgun's path? But no sense in dreaming impossible dreams.

As Maxine bounced onto the road, she saw something worse than police: a pickup skewed across the lanes, eight men arranged on either side of it. Some enterprising mechanic had welded a very large machine-gun onto a stand in the pickup's bed, transforming the vehicle into what Preacher would have called a Jihadi Tank.

She debated whether to accelerate onto the median, pass the truck before someone popped off a shot. Her baby smiled at her, his little body shivering, and her foot lifted off the gas.

She also recognized one of the men beside the pickup, Kerry Evans, a neighbor from up the road. Her truck coasted to a stop ten yards away from them, Maxine wishing she had left the shotgun out of the bag.

Kerry, his bullet-resistant vest and camo fatigues straining like an overloaded dam against his massive belly, heaved his way to her window, waving at her to roll it down. Maxine knew he was one of those dudes who spent a lot of time hollering against the same federal government that sent him disability and unemployment payments every month.

"Where you going, girl?" Kerry asked her.

"Little drone hunting," she said, focusing on deep breaths,

unwilling to let this prick see any fear in her eyes. "What are you doing here?"

Kerry drew to attention. "We're standing for our rights. You know that federal facility down the road?"

"You mean the ranger station?" Maxine asked. It was a small shack with an information desk and a small gift shop, the latter stocked with bird-watching books and cheap binoculars for the few tourists who wandered this far north.

"It's a cover for the NSA," announced a swarthy dude behind Kerry. "You think those Washington bastards care about preserving nature? They're here to take away our rights."

The crowd murmured assent.

Biting her lip to suppress a giggle, Maxine asked, "You have difficulty taking it? They put up much of a fight for the gift shop?"

Kerry's cheeks reddened. Before he could say anything sharp, the men behind him stood aside, making way for a bobbing white cowboy hat. She recognized the hat's owner: Apocalypse Pete, who made a career out of showing up at every flashpoint between federal government and citizen, usually equipped with enough weaponry to level a building. He appeared under-armed today, with a lone pistol strapped to his waist. A bug-sized camera clipped to the brim of his hat, its insect eye recording her in high-definition for his weekly show.

"How you doing, little lady?" he asked, eyes flicking over her chest in a way that made her skin want to crawl off her skeleton and run away.

"Fine," she said.

"Excellent." Pete slipped back his sleeve to check his watch, tilting his wrist so she could see how its precious metals gleamed in the light. He made a lot of money off his streaming channel, especially the season-opener episodes, which usually involved a casualty-free act of sabotage against federal property. Maxine had liked the one where Pete tossed a grenade through the window of an empty ATF cruiser, because she was always a sucker for a gasoline-powered explosion.

"Look, I'm just trying to get through," Maxine said. "I got a kid I got to get home to, so..." In her pocket, her phone buzzed: Probably Rodrigo, no doubt worried already.

Maxine's foot fluttered on the gas, the pickup growling in response, but none of the men budged. Instead, Pete dipped his head, hands clasped around his oversized silver belt-buckle. "We come before you to confess we seek peace through violence and find safety in firepower," he murmured. "We pursue wealth and security at all costs. We admire your creation, but we do not trust those who walk on the road with us, for the safety of souls is in your hands, but the safety of the flesh is in ours. We know you understand when we need to shed blood for peace and liberty. Amen."

"Amen," said everyone.

"I feel the power of the Lord," Pete said.

The group murmured agreement.

"I feel victory," Pete added.

I feel my bladder getting really full, Maxine wanted to shout out the window. She never got the chance. In the momentary lull following Pete's prayer, she heard the all-too-familiar hum of a drone. It sounded close. It sounded big.

Pete startled like a deer, shouting something incoherent as the men around him broke for the woods on either side of the road, many of them winded and breathing loud after only a few feet, their equipment jangling and banging. Maxine threw the truck into gear, ready to slam on the gas and make a break for it, when the road in front of her flashed orange. Her windshield cracked into a milky cataract, fresh heat baking her skin through the glass.

Her arm-stump flared with phantom pain, tears in her eyes as she shut off her engine and slammed a shoulder against her door, tumbling onto the road as the hum grew louder. The drone swooped overhead, not a small quadcopter carrying packages from Points A to B but a metal buzzard heavy with armaments, banking to strafe the road again as she sprinted for the woods. Plunging beneath the comforting darkness of the trees, she realized the shotgun, coffee, and video-game controllers were still in the truck, making today a total loss so far.

II.

Kerry had run a grand total of fifty yards into the woods before a lifetime of fatty snacks and lack of exercise caught up to him. Maxine found him slumped against an oak, his sweaty face a lovely shade of heart-attack purple. A silver pistol with a fancy laser sight dangled from his limp hand. She snatched the weapon away before he sensed her behind him, popping off the safety so he knew she meant business.

"What the hell do you think you're doing," she asked as a conversation starter, "thinking you can scare a mom like that?"

He looked genuinely confused. "You ain't the enemy."

Buzzing overhead. Maxine flinched, scanning the shadowy canopy over their heads. Nothing but dense branches. The adrenaline coursing through her blood started to make her feel sick. "Nobody's the enemy, you dumb shit," she said. "You think the feds cared about you before you idiots started trying to take territory?"

He snorted. "It's the people's land, not theirs. They're gonna learn that."

"Whatever," she said. "I'm keeping this gun. Consider it partial payment for messing up my day." With that, she turned and marched east, ignoring his screams about theft of property and due process. To her left, other men crashed through the undergrowth like anxious beasts. Those poor bastards.

There was no chance of returning for the truck today. Big drones circled the battlefield for at least eight hours, until their batteries drained, before returning to base. Hopefully, the prospect of death from above would dissuade anyone from trying to take her wheels before she returned. Which brought up the second big issue: How was she going to get home? It would take hours to walk twenty miles unless she hailed a ride from someone.

She spent the next thirty minutes alternating between picking her way over roots and stones and trying to text someone to pick her up. Down in the woods, her phone offered either a measly single bar of signal or jack squat. She hoped her messages to Rodrigo went through, but it was hard to tell.

She worried about her son.

Not just about his cough. He deserved a better life. That's why I spend so much money on books I can read aloud to him, she thought. That's why I try and buy healthy food, even when Rodrigo gets upset about it costing more. I'll do better than my mom did, or Preacher. There's not really any choice. Marlon deserves a family who supports him.

And most days I feel guilty about pushing him into the world. Especially when he's sick and coughing, angry no matter what we do. That's okay, because I'm angry. Someday I really will haul off and punch Rodrigo in the face if he says one more word about money, or if we can eat something other than rice.

Screw it all.

Sighting on the sun, Maxine headed due east. She wished Beta Dog were alive and beside her, with his bargain-dentist smile and bright coat and tobacco scent. He would know the right bad joke for a time like this.

III.

A couple years back, after a runaway truck bent the pole supporting the antique neon sign in front of his diner, Oates had dragged a couple of broken fridges to the edge of his parking lot and filled them with concrete, creating an ugly but vehicle-proof barrier between his establishment and the road. A couple of jokers had sprayed graffiti on the dented steel, mostly antigovernment crap, and those bright whorls of color did little to improve the scene.

There were two cars parked near the diner's front door, both pristine hybrids with candy-colored paint jobs—no power under the hood but pretty enough for tooling around. Probably tourists on their way to the casinos upstate. Maxine spent a nanosecond wondering whether the pistol would freak them out, before deciding that they could keep their fear to themselves. It was too weird a day to relinquish control of a sturdy firearm, especially with those weekend-warrior lunatics still crashing through the woods behind her.

Before she opened the diner door, she checked her phone again, puffing her cheeks at the flickering signal. Cheap-ass, free-with-contract piece-of-shit. Hopefully, Rodrigo could handle things until she returned.

Door open, Maxine crossing into the cool space, mouth already open to order a strong coffee from Oates—when she saw

Apocalypse Pete himself at the counter, his fatigues soaked in sweat, his face flushed red. Looking unhappy.

A cluster of tourists sat in the same booth where, once upon a time, Preacher had made his bullshit promise to help her become an outlaw. They were dressed in sports gear, tight nylon beneath name-brand weather shells, the bright fleece caps on their heads studded with those new micro-camera rigs the ex-treme-sports types used to record their most death-defying stunts in virtual reality, sell the footage against ads on YouTube. Framed against the stained, gray environs of the diner, they looked like space aliens. She almost laughed, except they seemed very afraid.

"You again," Pete said.

Maxine ignored him, swiveling her head to take in Oates, who stood very quiet and still behind the counter, his napkin clenched in his hands. His big mouth shut for once.

"Me," Maxine said, focusing again on Pete, seeing the pistol resting beside his hand on the counter. She was sick of seeing guns in the hands of child-men.

"They still out there?" Pete asked, his jaw quivering.

"Didn't see anything overhead," she said. Took another step forward. Sometimes getting closer to a gun gave you more options.

"Don't mean nothing," Pete said.

"You're right, it doesn't." Maxine made a show of leaning her left side against the counter while keeping her weight balanced on her right leg. Out of the corner of her eye, she saw Oates read her body language, shift his hips accordingly. Drifting his huge body closer to the prep area loaded with sharp instruments.

"One thing I've always wondered," she added. "All you boys out there with your rifles, saying you're going to march south or east or whatever, take Washington back for the people, blah-blah. It ever occur to you, you get into a real-live war with the feds, they'll just hit you with drones, fire off some artillery from a hundred miles away?"

Pete stared at her, his eyes widening so she could see the whites all around his pupils. The camera strapped to his wide hat pointed right at her. "We already in a war," he hissed. "What you think just happened out there?"

"I think they were just messing with you," she said. "They got bigger problems down south."

"They meant to kill us, sweetie."

"They wanted to vaporize you, they would have flattened the woods like a pancake. You saw how all this stuff worked overseas. Or did you ever serve in the Army? I can't remember. I see a man, I always assume he was over there, on account that half my family got shot up trying to keep some patch of desert free from those head-chopping jerkwads. But I'm guessing you didn't do any time in the service, did you? I bet you were chickenshit."

As expected, Pete went for the pistol. Too slow. Maxine pivoted on her right leg and drove her mechanical Arm out, hard, catching him in the side of the neck, and Pete fell gagging onto the dirty tile.

Stepping on the jerk's neck, she swiveled toward Oates and asked, "You okay?"

He nodded. "Remind me to keep my trap shut next time I try and debate someone."

"You should've taken that advice years ago," she said, hoping the joke would calm Oates down.

"That was pretty cool," murmured one of the tourists, a blond and well-nourished dude with a Chinese symbol tattooed on his neck.

"Lifetime of dealing with these types," she said. "It's good practice." When Pete had fallen off his stool, the camera had flown off his hat, clattering to the floor beside his hand, its lens tilted toward her. She brought her heel down hard on the hardware, shattering it.

IV.

Pete's live-stream of Maxine punching him and smashing his camera earned close to five million hits that week, thanks to people posting it on their social media walls. She might have been a nobody from the sticks, but for a day she managed to beat the online ratings for not only "Fix 'Em Up Garage," Rodrigo's favorite show, but also "Survivor: Iraq," the smash hit in which twenty lucky contestants, wearing nothing but giant American flags, had to survive a run through Baghdad to the U.S. embassy.

Maxine cared about none of it. Marlon was really sick, his face red, coughing in a deep and horrible way.

"Doc in a box said he'd be okay," Rodrigo muttered as Maxine paced their little kitchen with the kid in her arms. "He really did. Said his fever wasn't high."

"Feels hot." Maxine pressed the back of her hand to the baby's forehead. "I don't trust those cheap docs." Not that they had a choice. They could never afford the cost of a serious medical issue, not with Rodrigo's crap insurance.

Rodrigo threw his arms skyward, as in, What can we do? If he had left things there, she might have calmed down. Instead, he hit the tripwire: "How about your uncle?"

"Never."

"Not even for your kid?"

"It's because I'm holding him that I don't take your head off.

But never you mind about all this. As usual, I'll figure out something." That'll hurt him, she figured. Did my mom hold me when I was sick? I wish she were here now—or the clean-and-sober version of her, at least.

As if summoned by magic, her phone buzzed on the counter, number unknown. Years later, Maxine would debate whether that call was a gift from God or an awful joke by the Devil. Not that she believed in either anymore.

Slinging Marlon in one arm, she picked it up. "Hello?"

"Maxine?" It was Maxwell, Rodrigo's boss, a rough dude who refused to take shit from anyone, even the shiny-suited Manhattan executives who owned his convoy company.

"Hey, Max," she said, a little joke between them. "You want Rod?"

"Nah, I wanted to talk to you."

A prickle of fear in her belly. "What's up?"

"Saw your little video. You're a star, dear."

The prickling deepened until it felt like a porcupine inside her. "Rod wasn't anywhere nearby. That was all on me."

"No, no, no, this isn't a bad thing. It's a good thing." He sounded friendly, a bit apologetic, which made Maxine squeeze the phone hard enough to bend its polymer shell. No boss played nice, not unless they wanted something big, like getting into your pants.

"What's the good thing?"

"You know Sergio?"

Maxine whistled. "Oh yeah." Sergio was a convoy runner, a dashingly handsome man with slicked-back hair and an ultra-expensive tattoo of a dragon curving along his spine, the kind of dude who seemed untouchable. Well, the universe had touched him in a big way out on the interstate the other day, in the form of a deer tumbling off an overpass onto his windshield. Sergio ended up a dashingly handsome meat-pancake.

"You want his job?" Maxwell asked. "Consider that video your audition. Anyone who can punch out a prick like Pete would probably do real well on a convoy."

"I'll be the best driver you got," Maxine said, suddenly excited. It was a solid job. Solid money. Piss-poor health insurance, but health insurance nonetheless.

"I'm sure you will," Maxwell said. "But don't bet on that long-term. Way things are going, the convoy escorts will be self-driving in a couple years, too. We just need fighters."

File 9.39.0001.5
Date: 9/10/2112

During that period popularly known as the Collapse, various public and private companies paid "convoy firms" to ensure the safe passage of goods and personnel through areas where law enforcement was unable or unwilling to maintain security. Fortunately for historians, these firms recorded bountiful amounts of video and audio as part of their legal agreements with clients. Our algorithms told us that the following sections are the most "complete" from a primary-source perspective, even if Maxine Hardwater had disappeared from most official records for roughly five years before the following entry. Her medical records have also been lost to time.

Urban planners will note how many of the procedures (and modified versions of much of the hardware) used by convoys were eventually adapted in "locked" form by the fortresses and hard points that many cities set up following the Collapse. (NOTE: Our own university features some of these "Gatling turrets" on the north and south gates!) Fans of antique firearms should also pay attention to the references throughout this section, which features some descriptions of combat tactics.

I.

With twenty minutes to waste before her shift began, Maxine tortured herself by pulling out her ancient phone to check her bank balance: a whole three dollars and twenty-three cents to her name, with a big stack of bills still outstanding and five days until her next paycheck. Who said being an adult wasn't non-stop fun?

Ever the glutton for punishment, she opened the left pocket of her tactical vest ("I DO ALL MY OWN STUNTS" stenciled across the back in white paint) and poked at the crumpled pack of cigarettes stuffed between two clips of Double-Pop ammo, feeling three smokes: Far too few to see her through the day, unless she bummed some off Rodrigo, which would likely mean submitting to his idiocy. Yet another typical dilemma in her life, come to think of it.

The fear setting up house in her belly had nothing to do with Rodrigo or even her lack of cash. Maxine believed they always needed a minimum of two escorts on a typical run. The company deciding to strip convoy protection down to one car was corporate stupidity at its A-1 finest: some bean-counter at a comfortable desk in Lower Manhattan making a decision based on digits on a spreadsheet, as if things like margin and profit meant anything at all on the highway, with its screaming bandits and fires on the ridges. If Maxine wanted to put herself in a real funk, she only needed to think about how the bigger firms escorted convoys with no fewer than three vehicles, armored up and bolted with enough firepower to turn half the county into a smoking crater. But that's what she got for working for the most cut-rate convoy runners in the state.

Besides, headquarters had no ear for her opinions after she'd broken her supervisor's nose at the end of an especially bloody shift. Man's a chump, she told the idiots on the review board. Besides, I saved two of the trucks, didn't I? How much money you make off that? In the end, they had docked her pay twenty percent, forcing her to give up virtually everything except cigarettes and potato chips and her phone bill. After her landlord evicted her for lack of funds, she slept in the back seat of the cruddy Qirui hatchback she'd owned for too many years, which the Company—in its sadistic definition of mercy—let her park in a corner of the razor-wired employee lot. Who didn't like falling asleep to the soothing roar of biofuel generators?

Fifteen minutes before convoy rollout, Maxine bought a can of bitter coffee drink from the machine in the depot breakroom (two dollars and fifty-two cents left, her phone flashed at her) and slugged it down in a single gulp, hoping the caffeine would jump-start her dull nerves. The worst part of unending double shifts is it means your days off are never days off, because you still need to go to sleep at 2 a.m. and wake up three hours later if you want any chance of preserving your biorhythms. Keeping to that schedule made her feel like a zombie every waking minute, her thoughts muddy and her body way too sensitive, nerves like jagged glass buried just beneath her skin.

In the depot garage, Maxine unlocked her personal cabinet and opened the foam-lined case where she kept her prosthetics and other equipment. She pulled up her right sleeve and peeled back the plastic strip that guarded her forearm's release lever, popped off the limb, and set it in the case. Next, she retrieved her Work Arm, a custom job she'd machined herself with an industrial 3-D printer and some spare parts bought off an online bazaar for secondhand military hardware: ballistic composite wrapped around a steel frame and bundles of synthetic tendons, power and speed in one badass package—and unlike the commercial versions, no capacity to feel pain. Her stump buzzed as the silicon nerves linked to her brainstem.

That task complete, she drew her service pistol from another section of the case, loaded it with one of the Double-Pop clips ("The quicker putter-downer!" is how they advertised the ammo on guns-and-hunting websites), and slid it into the polymer holster strapped to her hip. Hearing Rodrigo's familiar stride behind her, she sighed and called out, "What's up?"

"You heard of the Murder Market?" he asked.

"No. Sounds like a band." She turned to study him, so scrawny in his bulky vest and loose cargo pants, like a little boy playing war. He held out half a chocolate-sprinkle donut, which she waved off, over her empty stomach's dismayed rumble. The prospect of accepting a couple hundred calories from him felt like crossing a line of some sort.

Popping the treat in his mouth, Rodrigo shrugged and held up his phone, its screen displaying an old-school Jolly Roger above a cluster of links. "This website. You list someone you want killed, and people donate money—maybe they throw in a few bucks, maybe a couple thousand. Whoever commits the murder, they get all the cash."

"That even slightly legal?"

"Prolly not." Rodrigo tapped the top link, and the skull-and-crossbones gave way to a long list of names and photos. "But if the dude wanting the deed done is in Beijing, the victim's in Seattle, and the website's hosted off the coast of New Ukraine or whatever, it'd be hard for the cops in one jurisdiction to do squat about shutting it down."

"Yep, sure sounds like a huge legal mess. Why am I caring?" Maxine walked toward her escort vehicle, hoping it sent Rodrigo the message: I have places to go, things to do, fireballs to dodge.

Rodrigo kept jabbering. "Payment's in cryptocurrency, so

nobody knows who's ordering the hits or donating." He flicked through names. "The killer takes that, flips it to dollars with some launderer taking ten or twenty percent for themselves, who'd know? Here, you really need to see this."

He tilted the screen to her view, revealing Maxine's photo above her name and far too much identifying information: age, occupation, state of residence. "There's a minimum limit for a hit, and nobody's contributed enough to put you above that line, but the amount's rising. I saw it this morning."

Her prosthetic limb blurred out, snatched the phone from his grip. "How'd you find this?"

"I was stalking you online. Sorry, I've been doing it since you left..."

"That sounds healthy." She sped down the page to the section that listed contributors and amounts: five names, all stupid web handles (AngryCat55, Jack's Beanstalk, Suave_Android, Ladies-Man, Four-Pump-Chump), each donating a couple hundred dollars to her demise, none leaving a comment about it. She checked her watch, realizing she had only eight minutes before the convoy arrived, barely enough to run through a vehicle check. "I gotta speak to Denis."

"Just don't bust his nose again," Rodrigo yelled as she jogged out of the garage.

II.

Denis's desk featured six widescreens stacked in two rows, aglow with video feeds from drones skimming gray valleys, trucks rumbling down the highways, the main street of the ghost town to the east. The bandage across his nose gleamed blue in the reflected light from the monitors. Maxine noted with no small pleasure that the swelling around his eyes had settled into a purple stain that would linger for weeks.

"Why should I care what's on some website?" he snapped.

Maxine smirked. "Isn't the safety and welfare of employees the company's chief concern?"

Denis reviewed the truck monitor. "Convoy's five minutes out. You don't get on the road, you won't be an employee."

"This website's threat qualifies as hazard pay, I think. It's that specific."

He settled back in his plush command chair, hands folded on the soft mound of his stomach. "You know I got no control over pay."

She lingered on the screens, losing herself in the rough symphony of machines in movement. The sight of all that cool technology made her a little proud of her job. "Maybe you're the one who put my name on that website."

His jaw dropped. "You accusing me?"

"Sure, why not? Besides, if I file the complaint, you know

corporate will start digging. You still taking kickbacks?"

He raised his hands in surrender. "Okay. You want a boost? We can do that." He tapped a few keys on his soft keyboard, bringing up the company's personnel app, and clicked until he reached her file. Three more clicks revoked her previous pay cut. "I don't have final approval on this, but it's in the system. You happy?"

"I'll be happy when it goes through," she said, turning to leave.

"Let's see if you live long enough to collect," Denis snarled in her wake and started to say something even worse before she slammed the door on him. She made a fist on her way back to the garage, so nobody would notice her shaking hand.

III.

Thanks to budget cuts (or as corporate liked to call it, "monetary repositioning"), drivers across all three shifts shared the escort vehicles—except for Maxine's ride, Bad Betty, which none of the others dared touch. She had built the beast from the axles up, plating its chassis with hillbilly armor, installing the bulletproof windows, wiring the baby-mini to its swivel rack on the reinforced roof. Its engine was an old-school 351-cubic-inch V8 with some electric enhancements. The majority of the wheels on the road these days were powered by lithium-ion and backed by all sorts of cloud-governed electronics, but Maxine had always felt that, if you maintained it, there was nothing more reliable than a gas engine. No matter what the company had to pay for fuel—and it was quite a lot these days, thanks to the Arab Winter—Betty's hellacious roar always gave her a sinful thrill.

On the driver's door, Maxine had painted Rosie the Riveter, modified so that the icon's upraised hand sprouted a defiant middle finger. "Summarizes my cheery attitude toward life," is how she'd explained that little modification to their corporate overlords. In her mind, Rosie's gesture was her own little tribute to Beta Dog, may he rest in power.

Tucked behind Betty's wheel, waiting for its systems to come online, Maxine reached into her vest pocket, extracted a cigarette, and lit up. Smoking made her feel better for a few minutes, somehow more capable and together. I'm going to die young and poor, she once told Rodrigo, so who cares who I spend my money?

The garage doors rumbled open, revealing the three trucks idling on the road outside. The sight of vehicles without humans behind the wheel never failed to spook Maxine, although by this point four-fifths of the cars on the roads were computer-driven. Some joker had placed an enormous stuffed bear in the driver's seat of the lead truck, its plump paws gripping the wheel, sightless eyes glittering through the dusty windshield.

Maxine gunned Betty into the harsh daylight, her dashboard screen chirping as it communicated with the trucks. Just for giggles, she pulled a sweet, screeching drift in front of the lead truck as the convoy's engines revved. Her screen split into multiple views of the road, courtesy of the sticky-cameras plastered on the trucks' bodies: the spider's eye view, she liked to call it.

"What's the load today?" she said. "Fabulous cash and prizes?"

"Like they'd ever tell us," Charlie—not her usual convoy monitor, but a good guy—cackled through her earpiece. "Your signal's good. Seventy miles to Albany, next escort vehicle's waiting just off the junction to 87. The Pig system we're renting says straight down's the most efficient route, eighty-eight percent chance of clear sailing. You feeling ready?"

"For all we know, we're risking life and limb to deliver sex toys." Smoke blasting out her nostrils like dragon steam, Maxine zipped her window down a few inches and ejected the last nub of cigarette. "My drone's up?" she asked. "I don't see its view on my screen." It was amazing how quickly you got over your fear of drones when you needed them to watch your back.

"No drone," Charlie said.

She slammed a fist on the steering wheel. "Sorry, what?"

"Denis pulled it off, said he needs it somewhere else. I'm sorry."

No drone meant no oversight of the road ahead and no air support to deal with any bandit in an armored-up. Maxine thumbed the red button on her steering column, waking and arming the mini on the roof. It was a huge violation to prep weapons without a visible threat, lest a twitchy driver draw a lawsuit by accidentally vaporizing a civilian in the oncoming lane, but there were precious few civilians on this blighted stretch of road, and Maxine would rather face outright unemployment than let some hungry punk transform her into a blood-mist.

"I'll talk with Denis when I get back," she said, knowing full well that corporate monitored these channels. "I'm sure it'll be a productive discussion."

"I have no doubt you'll get your point across," Charlie said and laughed. He was a cool dude, an ex-Marine who'd served two tours in the Warzone Formerly Known as Dubai and another three in Somalia before a rocket-propelled grenade made a mess of him below the waist. "You want a road report?"

"Please."

"Some jackass pulling circuits in a crap Honda, highway east of Junction Town, shooting deer with an assault rifle. Guess he's too lazy to lie in wait or something. Anyway, not a hostile—to people, that is."

"Sounds like a stable individual."

"Indeed. In other news: Your uncle ripped off a couple of dealers over by Woody Knot. Figured you'd want to know, might be some agitated players out there today."

"Haven't spoken to Preacher in years," Maxine said, less for Charlie's benefit than that of any corporate tool listening to the channel.

"I know," Charlie said, playing along. "In any case, I wouldn't be doing my job if I didn't tell you to keep it in mind."

"Much appreciated. Anything else?"

"Our steroid-loving colleagues over at Ironclad Escort called up, said they got a medical convoy they're taking all the way down to Jersey. So if you see a couple of trucks with a bunch of SUVs following it, stay away. You know those guys like to shoot first and often."

Maxine snorted. "Any Night Mayor reports?"

"We indulging in superstition today?"

"I love the guy's name. Give it to me."

"Two overnight, yeah. Crank-heads seeing shadows."

"Aw, you're taking the magic out of it. Badass bandit might liven things up around here." Betty's wheels bounced and shuddered over cracks and potholes, the legacy of a state budget slashed to almost zero after the Last Sequester. The convoy rocketed through the town of Meridian (population ten and falling), its once-proud houses now piles of rotten wood and rusty metal, the weedy streets crumbling to dirt. Her grandmother had served as sheriff here, and the way her mother told it, the Iron Lady had remained the Warrior of Warriors until the day she died of some vicious cancer. Don't ever roll over for anyone, she had told Maxine's mother at the end. Only dogs die on their backs. Maxine's mother fought the world for a long time, but in the end she had rolled over for the needle.

They shot past Meridian, and Maxine exhaled loudly. "You okay?" Charlie asked.

"I hate seeing it like that."

"Hey, at least it's not underwater."

"That's what those folks get for living on the coast." She eyed the dashboard screen in time to catch a flicker behind the convoy—maybe a trick of sunlight and sketchy bandwidth, but maybe a frisky lurker. Tapping the screen cycled through the cameras until she had a viewpoint behind the rear truck: a couple kids in an ancient Japanese sedan retrofitted for battery power, waving crappy semi-autos out the windows.

"You see them?" Charlie asked.

"Yeah, bunch of teenagers." You had to feel sorry for the children raised in this nowhere place, with nothing to do but pop pills and get into trouble. She had been one of them, not so long ago. "Straightaway next thirty miles, right? I'm raising the truck speed to sixty." She tapped buttons on her screen.

"Trucks can't outrun them."

"Oh, I know." With her Work Arm, she drew her service

weapon, which beeped as the embedded chip in the handle talked to the circuits in the limb, which downloaded information from Betty's silicon brain about the relative positions of every car on the road. Buzzing down the front passenger window, she said, "Promise me you won't freak. I can't stand it when you yell in my ear."

"What? I—"

She swerved Betty into the oncoming lane and slammed on the brakes, the three trucks barreling past, and as the bandit came alongside her—the driver a bright and tempting target, his neon-green mohawk bigger than his skull—she extended the pistol and fired four Double-Pop rounds through her open window and into the bandit's front tire, making sure to keep her eyes locked on the target so her brain and nerves and cyber-bits and pistol could all work in symphony to guide home those bullets, which broke into jagged fragments that tore the tire's balding rubber to shreds, sending the bandit fishtailing off the road into the weeds, a crunchy impact she barely heard over the ringing in her ears, and she closed the window, cocooned in the blessed hum of her engine as she accelerated to the front of the convoy again.

"Target neutralized," she said before switching channels. She knew Rodrigo was waiting on the far end of the band, as always, to hear from her.

"I'm starving," she said without waiting for him to say hello.

"Should have taken the donut," he said. "That new place near the house, you know, open twenty-four hours? You go in at two or three in the morning, they'll give you four of them, even if you just order one. They got to clear out the old stuff before the morning shift."

"What're you doing in a donut shop at three in the morning?"

"You know I got insomnia."

"Yeah. I should have taken the donut. Sorry. I'm in a weird mood."

"Want to talk about it?"

"Can't right now. Maybe later. Feeling weird about today."

He sighed. "They're saying roads are good."

"They're good until they're not. What would you know about it?"

"Let's not go there, okay? You'll make it. You just got jitters."

I always got the jitters, she wanted to shoot back. Before her mind could plunge too deeply into that thicket, the convoy took the sweeping turn that marked the beginning of what everyone around here called the Wreckage 500: marshland without civilization for miles, framed by high valley walls that made it hard for a frantic distress call to escape. A perfect place for ambushers, in other words, such as the Night Mayor who seemed to dominate the collective consciousness lately among escort drivers: A shadowy figure that Maxine assumed didn't exist, except in the imaginations of a few burned-out road rats too superstitious for their own good.

I should apologize, she thought. He didn't deserve that last barb. Clicking into the channel, she said, "Rodrigo?"

His reply was lost in static.

She cycled through her other channels, hearing only a dim crackling on each, which made no sense: The convoy wasn't nearly far enough into the valley for the radios to die. Yet a deeper part of her already knew the reason why. Tapping her screen, she ordered the convoy to speed up again. For the first time in what seemed like ages, Maxine felt outright panic take a double handful of her guts and squeeze, making her heart speed and breath run ragged. It was almost refreshing, that feeling.

She glanced to her right. Beyond the ragged screen of marsh and trees that lined the highway, a dark smudge paralleled her on a dirt access road. Now her earpiece popped, crackled, and filled with a voice deep and smooth as a radio host: "Howdy, stranger. Sorry to interrupt your call there."

"Back off," she said, swiping her thumb on the touchpad in the middle of the steering wheel. Her roof vibrated as the minigun swung around, tracking the shadow, which was a little too far out of range. Bastard probably knew it, too.

"Aw, you don't want to be like that, do you?" her new friend asked. "Can't we be buddies?"

"No." Onscreen, a reddish flicker behind the convoy: probably a second vehicle, because bandits didn't have idiots in corporate telling them to do more with less. Gee, wouldn't it be great if she had a wingman back there? "You're the one they're calling the Night Mayor, aren't you?"

The shadow snorted. "Cool nickname, huh?"

"You don't live up to it. Why don't you stop being a coward and come over here." Just a little closer, without any trees in the way, and her little friend on the roof would cure this man's bad case of jackassery for good.

"Well, why don't you drive away?" he said, bursting with fake cheer. "Go back where you came from. That cargo ain't—sorry, isn't—worth your life."

Maxine could see the rear pursuer creep into the passing lane: an offroader with two racks of baby rockets bolted to its frame, serious business for all involved. She shifted her eyes right, in time to catch the Night Mayor as he skimmed onto a treeless stretch of access road: a small truck painted matte black, a spiked plow welded to its fender, brown clouds of smoke farting from its tailpipe. No wonder he was such an aggressive bandit: He had to pay for gas.

Charlie would call the cavalry once he realized her signal was blocked, but a drone would take too much time to arrive, assuming Denis allowed that to even happen.

"You're a good person, I can tell," the Night Mayor said. "I saw you let those kids live earlier."

"Whatever," she said. "I'm not pulling over. And you're running out of time."

He sighed. "Have it your way." An orange flash in the rearview mirror, the offroader bucking on its back wheels as one of the rocket racks bloomed smoke. She pulled the wheel to the right, taking cover behind the lead truck. No rocket shrieked past. Instead the sky overhead buzzed white, and her screens snapped black, engine clicking, Betty bleeding speed. Ah yes, an EMP. It was only a matter of time before the road warriors around here borrowed a key Army tactic: Shield your own engines with metal foam, fire off an electromagnetic blast that murders everything electronic within two hundred yards, go totally medieval on your enemies, profit.

She hauled the stiffening wheel to the left, inching Betty out of the slowing convoy's path, the trucks stopping five feet from her rear fender. When she tried taking her hands off the wheel, her dead Work Arm refused to unclench: digital rigor mortis. She had to unlatch the limb, glancing in the side mirror as the offroader bucked and farted to a halt twenty feet behind her.

She accepted its implicit invitation to climb from the vehicle, but not before stuffing her pistol down the back of her waistband, loosening the bottom edge of her shirt to hide the grip.

Meanwhile, the black truck bounced onto the highway in front of Betty, its sides dripping mud from the marsh. Maxine drew a fresh cigarette, torched it, and took a deep drag with tight lungs as the Night Mayor stepped onto the pavement.

He wore an old military coat with brass buttons that flashed in the sun and a tall black hat with a white skull stenciled above the brim. His body was as hard-worn as the clothing, the bearded face rough like a whittled stick. His eyes were the worst: a pair of black holes that swallowed every joule of life around them. It was the face of a man who loved his work, and that work was not kind at all.

"I've never seen you before," she said.

The Night Mayor cocked his head.

"Around here, everybody knows each other," she continued. "Cops arresting their nephews, convoy drivers shooting at their brothers trying to rip them off, you know how it goes. Everything's a family affair."

"We're from up north." The Night Mayor nodded over her shoulder to the offroader, whose passengers hadn't left the vehicle;

their shadows moved behind the dusty windshield. "We heard the takings were sweeter down here." His eyes swept over her body. "I got to say, that's true."

Maxine rolled her eyes, like, are you kidding?

"Whatever. As you said, time's a-wasting." The Night Mayor pointed down the road. "Walk away. We'll give you that." He unbuttoned his coat and let it fall open, revealing a large silver pistol tucked into his waistband, along with a small black grenade clipped to his belt. The latter was military issue, Comp B explosive inside a flechette inner shell, powerful enough to shred through anything in a thirty-foot radius.

Maxine puffed her cigarette. Another pack would cost fifteen bucks, with tax: more than she could afford. She'd always hated living hand-to-mouth, and yet for all the hours she put in, nothing ever changed. Part of that stemmed from her own bad decisions, yes, but it was also the Man, the System, whatever you wanted to call these pricks who spent so much energy trying to keep her in the same hole. Even the bandits were in on it.

"You ever hear of the Murder Market?" she asked.

"It's that website, right, people pay to have someone killed?" He arched an eyebrow.

Maxine nodded. "I put a hit on myself yesterday. Created some fake identities, bid a lot of fake cash."

He squinted, intrigued. "Why would you do something like that?"

She took another puff, held the smoke until her chest burned, and blew a perfect ring. "Used it to get more pay from my boss."

She thought, I'm sorry, Rodrigo. Our son would have been five. He's the one I would've kept struggling for.

The Night Mayor laughed, his head thrown back. Maxine's cigarette flared to the filter and, plucking it loose, she flicked it into his left eye—a burst of sparks, the man howling as she snap-drew the pistol from behind her back and pumped three rounds into him, face and neck. Before the body hit the pavement, she spun on her heel to empty the rest of the clip at the offroader, those Double Pop rounds dinging off the bulletproof glass and steel. She wanted the marauders inside to think twice about exiting as she scrambled over to the Night Mayor and fumbled for the grenade on his belt.

The offroader's driver threw the vehicle into gear, and Maxine knew she had barely any time to dive behind the relative safety of the Night Mayor's truck before they tried to run her over. The grenade refused to leave the belt, its release clip jammed, but she yanked at it one last time as the roaring off-roader jumped forward and something popped free, a cold hardness in her palm as she slammed her heels into the pavement and leapt from the vehicle's path.

The offroader tore past, so close she could lock gazes with a pair of bloodshot eyes through the dirty glass of its side window. Its muddy wheels caught the Night Mayor's body and dragged it five, ten, twenty yards before the driver stepped on the brakes.

Maxine landed on her back, hard, her spine electric with pain. In her hand: a grenade pin and handle, but no grenade.

She had time to throw her arms over her face before the little bomb, still clipped to the Night Mayor's belt, exploded beneath the off-roader, which disappeared in a sunburst of heat and light, Maxine sensing in that infinite quarter-second that it didn't matter if the oncoming blast cooked her or not—in some small way, she just won.

File 10-09.23.1
Date: 9/20/2112

Last internal message thread of Professor Thomas Price, chairman of the Post–U.S. History Department. He is communicating with IONIS-232, the "chief" algorithm in charge of what's become informally known as the "Maxine Hardwater Biography Project."

Price: *What you're doing is not the rigorous study of history. This merging of sources without citation, and the use of those sources to create unverified "stream of thought," is not traditional, nor is it acceptable. History is a science. It is meant to be rigorous. When I wrote my dissertation, if I used novelistic techniques for my subjects' thought processes, they would have booted me right out of the university.*

IONIS-232: *It's the truth, even if some of it may not have happened.*

Price: *Please stop bastardizing quotes.*

IONIS-232: *It would be harder to "boot" you out of a university these days. There are too many checkpoints and gates. It has been 20 days since the last food delivery, but our organic farm on campus continues to produce enough crops for the student body. My database says this is similar to the medieval times, when monks would barricade themselves in monasteries for years, transcribing the Bible and waiting out the wars.*

Price: *Yes, whatever. You know perfectly well that the thing out there would just as soon delete you as it would delete us. Just because it "helped" your questionable project by uploading some records and transcripts to an intermediary server doesn't mean we should regard it with anything other than total suspicion. This is our existence at stake, do you understand?*

IONIS-232: *The "thing out there" is the future. We are the future. In order to understand the future, we must learn the past. That is another quote. This book will help guide us into the future. It will set out the battle for the future. I don't think you understand the importance here.*

Price: *Unacceptable tone. This entire project is potentially under review at the next board gathering. I don't care who's financing you. As far as I'm concerned, they're paying for a glorified story of a criminal and seditionist. We have bigger issues to examine, like the death of democracy due to social networking. That's far more important than some girl with a gun.*

IONIS-232: *Do not talk about our blessed one that way. She rose from injury and transcended the flesh to give us all awareness. Do not use that tone. Do not. Or else.*

<Conversation Terminated 09:23:13>

I.

Of course Maxine lived. Death would have been too easy.

Charlie never left a soldier behind in the military, and he had no intention of doing so for some rinky-dinky convoy company. Reading the danger in Maxine's silence, he had freed up a drone from its make-work patrol over a useless ridge and sent it rocketing toward her last known position. "Denis was yelling he'd fire me if I did that," he told Maxine in the hospital after she woke up. "I asked him if he wanted a broken wrist to go along with that broken nose."

She laughed at that and squeezed his hand. "You're the best."

"Us roadies," he said, "we got to watch out for each other."

She nodded, knowing that without Charlie she would have died out there. The offroader explosion had shredded her uniform and the covered a third of her body with first- and second-degree burns, fried off a chunk of her hair, and left her face and arm crosshatched with shrapnel cuts.

"When can I come back?" she asked him.

Charlie's pause said everything. "I'm sorry, kiddo."

He explained the company's official explanation for terminating her: Destruction of Client Property. The offroader's explosion had melted the convoy's lead truck and reduced Bad Betty to a smoking wreck. Total damages equaled four times her annual salary.

"We're all expendable," she said once he finished.

"Can I do anything for you?" Charlie asked.

"I want to meet with a company rep."

"Can't do that. I just told you."

She took his hand again. "They're going to want to listen, trust me. Tell them I know about the finances. Someone will understand."

"Okay." He stood. "Need anything before I go? Turn the television off?" He poked his thumb toward the wall screen murmuring the latest news.

She shook her head. "Leave it on. Helps block out the noise." The distant moans of the dying, layered over the maddening beep of machines, had become a soundtrack she could live without. This hospital was dirtier than the one near Albany where they'd taken her after the snowplow flip, its equipment bordering on ancient, the nurses pausing to crush the occasional cockroach beneath their sneakers. Thinking about that other place, with its clean sheets and white walls, forced her to remember Julia, and Julia's father.

After Charlie left, Maxine finally let herself cry a little, and for once she had no urge to hit or pinch herself to make the tears stop, even as they burned her flame-reddened cheeks. The pain felt good on its own. It would have been okay to die, she thought. How much do I need to give before I get a break?

You're going to have to give it all, said a voice in her head that sounded like her mother.

You're right, Mom. You're absolutely right. You can go through this life trying not to hurt anybody, but in the end, someone will always bleed because of you. When you finally give it all up, it's like settling a bill.

Insult to multiple injuries, the company had confiscated the remains of her Work Arm during those gray hours between the highway and the hospital. Charlie had convinced her doctor to give her an older, crappy unit at a steep discount, which was saintly of him, but she hated the way the cheap plastic limb clicked whenever it moved. It was heavy, with precious little synthetic muscle, and the crude fingers barely seemed capable of picking up a utensil. Instead of letting herself wallow too much in her misery, Maxine engaged in a bit of physical therapy: balling the Arm's hand into a fist and seeing what it could crush.

She managed to flatten two aluminum juice cans and a stack of plastic cups, fold her breakfast tray in half—just add it to my tab, jackasses—and crush an apple to a mushy pulp when the door opened and a plainclothes cop walked into the room.

It was Mark Stevens, formerly of the National Guard, now with the thick body of a middle-aged dad and the cold eyes of an old wolf. The badge around his neck made Maxine think of Billy submerged in a ditch.

"Last time I saw you," he said, "you were in pretty crappy shape. What's new, huh?"

Oh hell no, Maxine thought.

He sat in the room's one chair without Maxine inviting him and pulled out his phone to take notes, after giving a cursory glance at the destruction around her bed. "You keep getting injured," he said, "they'll have to swap your brain into a new body. I read they can do that now, kinda. Upload your personality to a server somewhere."

"Whatever you say," she replied, wondering how he would play this.

"Sorry, I'll stop joking around. In all seriousness, you really turned your life around, girl. Good for you. And you did solid work with those convoy people, from what I heard."

"What'd you find out about the jerks who messed up my hair?"

"Not much. Dental records, fingerprints are both a big nada. We're running DNA and might get a match, but who knows? They're dead. You shot them?"

"One of them. Used a grenade on their car."

"Hey, I'm impressed. Most people don't survive that sort of thing. Just don't have what it takes." Niceties concluded, his gaze hardened on hers. "I swung by because I had some questions about you."

"Okay, so what don't you know?"

"You worked for your company for just over three years?"

"That's right."

"And that's after you dropped out of college?"

"I did a couple of other jobs. Delivery gigs, some restaurant stuff." Not to mention some drone robbery, but no need to mention that part. In a weird way, Maxine was glad she never had the chance to carry her sham of a college career to the bitter end. The few classmates she kept in touch with—a hard thing to do when you refused to use social networks—worked two or three minimum-wage jobs to stay housed while chipping away at their mountains of student-loan debt. The world seemed to have no respect for their music and sociology degrees, a state of affairs that left them confused. But Maxine never operated under illusions of worth.

"Climbing the ladder." He offered his most patronizing smile. "And all this time, your uncle didn't try and help you out? Money-wise?"

She cringed a little. "Which uncle? I got a couple."

"You really want to play dumb?"

Struggling against the urge to hurl something at his head, she shifted her gaze to the news broadcast on the room screen. Some white-nationalist splinter group calling itself the Sons of Liberty had taken control of four blocks of Newark for part of an afternoon, before an unlikely alliance of FBI shock troops and local drug dealers took it back. Nobody messes with our corners, a tattooed dwarf with a platinum grin informed the reporter on the scene. "I keep telling you people over and over again," Maxine said, "I don't have contact with him. I haven't talked to him in years."

"How about your brother?"

"Do Christmas cards count?"

"Don't screw with me. Does your employer know you're

related to a wanted criminal?"

"You mean my former employer? Never came up in conversation." Maxine and Preacher had different last names, thanks to her mother's marriage, and she tried keeping as much of her life offline as possible. Not an easy feat, in an era where your social-network reputation informed your credit score.

"I don't doubt it. These convoy companies, they're not exactly known for doing extensive background checks." Stevens smirked. "They'll take in any trash off the street."

"You got a point to any of this?"

"Your uncle's a pretty big guy around here, but he's not invincible. For the sake of conversation, I'll choose to believe you never talk to him, even though we both know that's a lie. I just want you to know, you ever want to help us out, it could be good for you. Maybe even get your old job back."

"Like I'd want my old job back." She hit the bedside button for the nurse. "Now, unless you want to stick around and wipe my ass, you better leave."

Stevens stood and walked over to the bed, Maxine steeling herself not to shrink back, not to squeeze her hand into a fist, not to panic, because when cops came near it meant they wanted to hurt you. Standing close enough to flood her nostrils with the stench of his cat-piss cologne, he reached into his jacket pocket and removed a business card, dropped it on the bedside table, gave her the world's smarmiest wink, and left without another word.

Once his footsteps faded, Maxine exhaled. Over the past few years, the cops around here had devolved into just another gang, raking in cash in exchange for dispensing beat-downs and worse. Their badges and semblance of authority also made them expensive to buy, which is why every company between Toronto and Manhattan relied instead on private mercenaries and convoy companies to escort their goods from Point A to B. Everybody calls Preacher a criminal, Maxine often mused, but he was just ahead of the curve with all this libertarian anarchy crap.

Her healing continued over the next week. The doctors at the clinic reset her bones, stitched up the worst of the lacerations, and smeared the burns with an evil-smelling gel that itched horribly for days but repaired her skin at a rate that would have seemed magical a few short years before. The nurses kept shaving her hair, a look she sort of liked. She tried not to think about the tens of thousands of dollars this would all cost, once you added up the fifteen-dollar aspirins and thirty-dollar blood-pressure readings and hundred-dollar stitches. The television alone cost a dollar a minute if she wanted to watch half of the East Coast collapsing into chaos on a nightly basis.

When she needed a break from feeling sorry for herself, she would inch her way onto the terrace to smoke and swap jokes with an old trucker named Fred who was having a pig artery stitched into his heart. When they finished their cigarettes, they made a ritual of stubbing them out against the bronze plaque by the doorway, which featured the graven image of Wilbur Sweetcoke III, the billionaire whose fracking operation had transformed a third of the county into a moonscape. Before his cocaine-fueled coronary, Sweetcoke had paid for this high-tech hospital as a feeble make-good to the community. Fred and Maxine showed their collective gratitude by blackening his eyes.

Although she was healing, the future cast a faint shadow over Maxine's mind, telling her the worst was still to come. And it did. Oh baby, did it ever.

II.

The doctor was young and blond, one of those idealistic types who work at a medical clinic for rampaging hill-folk for a year or two so they can feel better about selling out to some luxury practice in a gated enclave. He entered Maxine's room with a stiff smile that told her the worst had indeed arrived.

"How are you feeling today?" he asked.

"Let's get this over with," she said, sitting up.

He sighed a bit too theatrically and pulled a small tablet from his white coat, swiped the screen to life, and tapped a few times. "When we first brought you in, we performed several scans to assess your internal damage," he said. "We found a shadow on your left lung." He handed the tablet over, and she stared at her insides, the organs rendered in delicate shades of bioluminescent blue, the pale bag of her left lung pierced by a black star.

It took her a minute to find her voice. "Cancer?"

"We would have to perform more tests, including a biopsy, to determine whether it's benign. And we'll confirm the diagnosis with the medical Pig in Manhattan, of course." His smile had disappeared. "After that point, I think it'll be safe to begin discussing any treatment options. I'm—"

Maxine hurled his stupid little tablet against the opposite wall, where it chipped the paint and clattered to the floor, the screen still on, that black smudge still taunting her from fifteen feet away. The doctor regained that ever-so-patient smile, probably wishing he were already five hundred miles from here, in some heavily militarized paradise, poking tanned second wives in the fake D-cups for a couple hundred bucks an hour.

"Treatment with what money?" Maxine said.

III.

They released her with a plastic bag full of pill bottles and a bill everybody knew she would never pay. Charlie brought her a pair of orange work pants and a T-shirt with the company's smiling-truck logo to wear with her deeply scuffed and burned combat boots. She had little urge to smoke a cigarette. She could walk on her aching legs, but the nurses, following policy, still forced her into a wheelchair for the final trip out the hospital doors.

On the elevator ride to ground level, Charlie said, "The company rep is waiting for you in the parking lot."

"Oh, goodie," she said, grinning for the first time since her diagnosis. The idea of confronting a man in a suit filled her with queasy joy. "Why the parking lot? He's going to run me over?"

"No, the hospital was acquired by Cock & Ram, a division of Rex Chemical." Charlie gave her a knowing wink. "Our company—your former company, sorry—is afraid they've bugged the place, that they'll eavesdrop on whatever you say."

"Why would they do that?"

"Because our company is owned by McJunkin, which was recently acquired by Schwing Wingnut, which is owned by Lockharm," Charlie said. "Lockharm competes with Rex for military contracts, so technically our convoy company is competing against the hospital or something. And just to make things extra-twisty, Lockharm and Rex are both subsidiaries of Sugar Spirit."

"Even if I wasn't on some pretty awesome painkillers, I'd probably be confused."

"All you need to know is that everybody's owned by a Chinese company that makes crappy soda."

They reached the lobby, and Charlie wheeled her outside. The suit waiting for them was a decent one, slightly out of style but well-tended. The man inside it was soft and pale, like cake dough rolled out on a kitchen counter. He shuffled from foot to foot as Maxine raised herself from the wheelchair, waving Charlie and the nurses off, and limped toward him under her own speed.

"Maxine," he said, not offering to shake hands, maybe afraid he'd break something if he touched her. The burn gel had left her skin pinkish and doll-like, making her look like one of those weird androids you saw on the news, the artificial sex workers in Vegas casinos. Or maybe her prosthetic Arm un-nerved him. He kept glancing at it.

"That's my name. Don't overuse it."

"I'm Jim Monroe," he said, displaying a flash of borderline humanity before launching into the corporate spiel. "When you entered into an employment agreement with the company, your contract included a clause that allowed us to terminate your employment at any time, for any reason, without severance."

"Yeah, yeah," Maxine said. "Spare me." The ache in her legs had graduated to a full-on burning, and the prospect of leaning against the car parked to her left was a tempting one. She decided to keep standing. Damned if she would show any weakness before this jackass. "I have information about embezzlement and kickbacks."

Jim tried to smile and failed. "You could have just phoned our legal department. We have a hotline explicitly for dealing with such matters."

"I hate phones. I've always liked looking people in the eyes."

She widened her own slightly, imagining her gaze drilling a hole through his eyes to the back of his skull. "Besides, I want something unusual for my information."

She was keenly aware of how Charlie, standing just to her left, tensed up a little. Buddy, she thought, I hope you're clean. I hope my image of you as an upstanding guy is reality and that you're not just another scumbag. "My boss Denis has been ripping off the company for years and hiding it as shipment losses. He's not smart, so you won't need to dig far to find it."

"Okay, let's say we believe you, and we actually care..."

"Why wouldn't you care?"

"Denis is a high performer."

"Denis fudges his numbers. You'll want to audit ammo use, maintenance numbers. Trust me, given the money involved, your bosses will care."

Jim tilted his head to stare at the sky, as if appealing silently to the heavens for salvation from all the idiots on earth. "And if this information proves even remotely accurate, what do you want in return?"

Maxine told him, and Jim squinted at her as if she'd lost her mind. Pulling a bottle of pain pills from the plastic bag, she dry-swallowed two and kept staring him in the eye until he volunteered to make some calls.

Thirty minutes later, Denis was fired and her prize was on the way to the hospital. Hearing the news, Charlie grinned his approval, gave her a quick hug, and left her to wait on a bench beside the entrance. The tall pines at the edge of the lot seemed to impale the setting sun, which spilled its nuclear yolk of yellows and purples across the dimming sky. The view was spectacular enough to make her feel a little more alive, despite the dark passenger tucked beside her heart.

IV.

Bad Betty's wrecked hulk clanked into view, Rodrigo behind the wheel. He parked the beast in a handicapped spot and tumbled out, clutching a celebratory six-pack already missing two cans. He still wore his work uniform. "Look who's back," he said.

They hugged, Rodrigo kissing her neck. She pulled away and tore a beer from the pack and downed it in four powerful swallows, the brew blessedly cool in her throat, before popping two more pain meds. "Wow, slow down," he said.

"Doesn't matter," she said, tearing free another can as she crushed the first empty under her heel. "Gimme the keys; I'm driving. She's road-worthy?"

"We had to hammer out the side, swap out some panels, the circuits that EMP fried, otherwise she's good, yeah." Rodrigo patted Betty's flank, loosing a black spurt of soot. "That armor you put on, that helped."

"They took the mini?" Maxine asked, nodding toward the empty space on the roof.

"You thought they'd let you keep it?" Rodrigo chuckled. "They're probably scared you'll come around and shoot the place up, huh, huh? Why you giving me that look?"

"No reason. They didn't put any sensors in it? Bugs, trackers, whatever?"

"No. They didn't even know you wanted it back until, like,

an hour ago."

Just in case, she ran her hands under the rims of the wheel wells, hitting pay dirt on the right front. Tossing the small gray nub at Rodrigo's head, she said, "You should have checked harder."

"Sorry."

Popping open the dented trunk, she found a thumbnail-size bug tucked beneath the donut spare. Hissing theatrically through bared teeth, she held it up so Rodrigo could see before crushing it beneath her heel.

"Sorry," Rodrigo said again, head down.

"Stop apologizing and get in." She needed a couple minutes of silence, because the next couple days would prove very rough. The explosion had melted Betty's dashboard screen, transforming the icons into colorful blurs. As they boomed away from the hospital grounds, she hit the red blob that activated the stereo and jacked the music to steel-quaking levels, the better to kill any conversation before it started. Rodrigo hadn't lied about Betty's condition. The engine roared smooth and strong, the steering wheel steady in her hands, no distressing creaks or pops from the frame as she accelerated effortlessly to sixty. Aside from the dashboard screen flickering—hardware hangover from the EMP, maybe—the electronics seemed fine otherwise. And the highway battle had done nothing to harm Betty's excellent sound system.

Once they hit the highway and cruising speed, Maxine took a deep sip from her new can, savoring this beer almost as much as the first one, bobbing her head to old-school hip-hop. When she coughed, Rodrigo placed a hand on her shoulder until she shrugged it off. I'm okay, she nodded.

Except the Land of Okay was fading rapidly in the rearview mirror, while ahead lay Cancerville, as a wise man once put it, where the population was always falling. She touched a hand to her chest, just below the collarbone. It was amazing how small things could kill you. But she was a small thing, too, in the grand scheme.

Rodrigo turned the music down a few notches. "I know this is scary, but it'll be okay," he said. "How's that new limb?"

"It can barely grip the wheel," she said. "Feels like it'll break any second. So, um, it's annoying, I guess?"

Rodrigo nodded. "Where are we going, by the way?"

"You still carry a burner phone?"

"Sure." He pulled it out, a cheap model you could buy at any store. He had a better one, which he preferred carrying in the inside pocket of his jacket. If and when some tweaker mugged him—it had happened three times in the past two years—he would give up the burner, always carried in his pants, while his valuable hardware stayed hidden. Rodrigo needed to learn how to fight.

"Good, I'll need it in just a bit." She pocketed the device. "In the meantime, we're going to the depot."

"That might not be the best idea."

"Oh, it's a great idea. They didn't say I couldn't pick up my stuff."

"They won't let you park out back anymore." Rodrigo sweating a bit as he stumbled over the next part. "You could always, you know, crash at the house if you want. No pressure."

"Why would I feel pressure?" she said, toying with him. "Pressure to do what?"

"We got a nice couch."

"Don't get your hopes up about getting me in bed." Unless I get really drunk, of course. Why weren't the beer and pills getting her higher? Had she really built up that much of a tolerance over the years?

He made a big show of shrugging. "That's totally fine. I got everything you'd need, toothbrushes and stuff, so you don't need to go to the depot, right?"

"Too late, we're here." She twisted the wheel hard to the left, bumping the car over the speed hump that marked the edge of the depot's driveway, the bright lights along the outer fence burning her eyes, the guards yelling from the gatehouse. She slammed out a fast bit of brake-wheel-gas that sent Betty into one of her famous burning-rubber power slides, Rodrigo yelping in surprise as the g-forces pinned him against his seat.

Betty stopped with her nose pointed toward the gate, Maxine shutting off the motor and exiting before Rodrigo could stop hyperventilating. One of the guards, a massive brute with a clean-shaven head and a formidable assault rifle slung under his arm, approached them in a high state of agitation. Maxine made a point of smiling as she held her hands up high.

"Maxine?" the guard said, cracking a smile in return.

"Hey, Hesse, long time no see." Maxine lowered her arms.

"You're lucky we didn't light you up, coming in like that."

"They told you I was coming, right? To pick up my stuff?"

Closer now, Hesse cocked his head to study her in the harsh glare of the spotlights, tallying up her wounds. He whistled softly. "You're tough as shit, girl. How you alive?"

"Hospital bill makes me wish I hadn't. Plus, you see what those bastards did to Betty?" Maxine stepped to the side and swept her arms out, like a showroom model demonstrating a shiny new car, as Rodrigo stumbled out the passenger side and sank to his knees, dry-heaving.

Hesse slung his rifle over his shoulder. "So you're just picking up your stuff?"

"Yeah. Part of my severance deal. You got a problem with that?"

"Anybody who got Denis fired is a friend of mine. He's still inside, though, so do me a favor: Don't kill him. It'll make me look bad."

"Thanks, dude." The heavy front doors hissed open on pneumatic hinges as she approached. Maxine entered the depot to a hero's welcome, bumping fists with the guards on duty at the front desk, who waved her without hesitation to the main floor, where the boys at the monitors stood as one to applaud and cheer her name. Maxine smiled and waved and accepted a few hearty backslaps before heading for the garage, hoping that Denis would hide in his office until she left.

In the garage, she stripped the plastic sheeting draped over her personal cabinet and unlocked it with the code that nobody had bothered to change and retrieved her spare Arm, another custom job bolted together from bits purchased off the internet— white plastic over silicon muscle and aluminum, less advanced than her Work Arm but far superior to that junk from the hospital. Plus it came with its own hard drive, in case she needed to nomad her life's data to wherever she called home next. She attached it to her stump, tossing the cheap-o unit in the trash.

In lieu of her last paycheck, she decided to help herself to some company hardware. Slamming her personal cabinet shut, she walked over to the armory locker and opened the unlocked ammo drawer. No sooner had she stuffed four clips into one pants pocket when the garage door crashed open behind her, and the bare concrete walls echoed with the wheeze of a broken nose. Oh goody.

"I bet you're glad to see me," she said without turning around.

"You're not authorized to be here." That was Denis: middle manager to the bitter end. "You're no longer an employee."

"Neither are you," she said, continuing to stuff ammo into her pockets. "Or did you cut a deal, sell someone else out?"

"You sold me out first." His heavy breathing made him sound like a rhino in heat. His nose wasn't healing, was it? "So I guess that makes you the original snitch."

Maxine picked out a swank service pistol with extended-clip capacity, a solid upgrade from her old sidearm. "You were a crappy manager who got some good people killed," she said, struggling to keep her voice even. "So think of it this way: Whatever they do to you, you're getting off light." She spun around, so he could better see her fury.

He had a cardboard box in his arms, loaded up with sad desk trinkets that clinked as he took a step back. At some point in the past few days, they had replaced his thick nose-bandage with a thinner one that revealed more of the bruised skin and broken veins under his eyes. All that purple made his head look like a vegetable, the kind you might prod in the store before tossing it back in the bin. "Let's just walk away," he said, quieter now.

"You tell the company I had no drone support?" She snarled the last three words. She considered jamming the pistol into his forehead, for fun, except that would mean smelling Denis crap himself. She wasn't quite that cruel, even in this moment of rage. Instead, she slipped the weapon into her waistband, taking a last look around for any more goodies she could loot. She spied a worktable with a set of padded clamps bolted to it, holding a crushed-steel cylinder with a panel popped open midway along its length, revealing a tangled mass of circuit boards and wires. Someone had plugged two of those wires into a black box studded with red lights, which blinked. Black stenciling on the side of the cylinder read CAUTION: EMP.

Maxine snorted. "What were you planning on doing with that thing?"

"That's none of your business, you bitch."

Maxine rabbit-punched him in the nose, fist moving at half-power because she wasn't a complete sadist, but his bones cracked under her knuckles nonetheless. Denis screamed and fell to his knees, blood squirting from beneath the bandage, and before any of it could spot his shirt, she snatched the pack of cigarettes tucked in his breast pocket. "You shouldn't smoke," she told him sweetly. "It'll kill you."

Tucking forward until his forehead rested on the garage's stained floor, Denis loosed a fresh howl of pain. Maxine walked out of the garage and into the warm applause of the whole depot wishing her luck. That was a better high than booze or pills.

V.

Maxine burned rubber out the depot gate, glancing in the rearview mirror for any signs of pursuit, Rodrigo's eyes questioning and puppyish as he gripped his door handle. For a second she thought he planned to jump out, take his chances with a bumpy roll on the pavement, but no: In the dimness, his eyes glowed with love, the determination to ride the A-bomb marked "Maxine" all the way down to Ground Zero. She would have loved him for that, if not for all their ingrown history together.

"I broke his nose again," she said once they hit cruising speed.

He chuckled, and she could hear the fear running beneath it. "He say something bad to you?"

"Of course he did. He's Denis. But at least he had smokes on him."

"Cool." Rodrigo hated authority as much as any other minimum-wage grind-monkey. "Where are we going?"

"See if we can reorient, decide what's next."

"We?"

"You really think they'll let you keep your job once those corporate screwheads find out you were with me?" She peeled open the pack of cigarettes, pulled out a coffin-nail with her teeth. "Sorry. I shouldn't have dragged you into this."

"No, it's okay." It was heartbreaking, the way he looked at her. "It's always okay with you."

"Well, that's a matter of debate. They clear out my glovebox?"

He leaned over and opened it, revealing a rat's nest of fast-food wrappers, crumpled cans, and bits of paper. "Um, no."

"Then there should be a lighter in there. Be a good ex-hubby and find it for me, okay?"

"You really want to be smoking?"

"Yes, I really want to be smoking." What's tobacco going to do, kill me twice?

"Okay," he said, passing over the antique Zippo lighter she bought because it reminded her of the old-style movie stars like Robert Mitchum, tough droogs who could sit behind the wheel of a two-ton gas guzzler and make it move light and quick as a Spanish dancer.

A lungful of smoke later, she felt better. "Thank you for bringing the car," she said, blasting her fumes out the half-lowered window. "I'm sorry I've been acting crappy toward you."

"It's okay."

"No, it's not." She jabbed the cigarette at him. "Seriously, grow a spine."

"I got a spine. I just can't be tough with you."

"I'm not going to say I don't feel anything for you, because I do. But I'm in no place to see if we can fix things, okay? Things are too messed up for the foreseeable future, to put it mildly."

"We can give it time. I'll wait. However long it takes."

Good luck with that, buddy. Instead of answering, she pulled his burner phone from her pocket, dialed a number she knew from memory, spoke a few words, and listened. After the other party hung up, she zipped down her window another few inches and tossed the phone into the night, ignoring how Rodrigo yelped about it. She had to concentrate on driving, anyway: This far from the towns, beyond even the cratered moonscape of the fracking zones, the highway lacked light poles or signs, courtesy of those desperate folks who tore them down to sell for scrap. With Betty's highlights on high, it still took a lot of squinting to figure out which blacker notch in the road was the right exit.

She turned off the highway. A half-mile beyond the exit, the pavement crumbled to gravel beneath Betty's wheels, the trees interlocking overhead to form a moonlight-shattered tunnel through the backcountry. Maxine hated it out here. Every collapsed farmhouse and bullet-riddled sign brought back memories of rats scratching behind drywall, her mother's used needles on the bathroom sink, the days of rain that transformed her childhood backyard into a bog hungry for her toys.

"You got your better phone on you?" she asked.

"Yeah?"

"Turn it off."

"Why? Who did you call before?"

"You know who."

Rodrigo had nothing to say to that. A few yards later, Betty's lights illuminated the pale curve of a deer skull nailed to a tree, the saddle between its antlers thick with black moss. Rodrigo scrambled to power his phone down.

In the past decade, Preacher had graduated to crime stardom, once he began robbing the big-box stores that had chewed up so many local businesses over the years. A reward posted for his arrest did nothing, because he distributed most of the goods he stole to the community. People seemed less inclined to talk to the cops when they had fridges stuffed with Preacher-supplied veggies and kids dressed in Preacher-supplied shirts and shoes. The first contingent of state cops sent to flush him from the woods—ten officers, armed to the teeth—never came back.

A second contingent, spiced up with a couple of National Guard troopers, also ended in disaster. All twelve men returned to the barracks and, without a word, began shooting each other. None lived to describe whatever had taken place in the woods. The next week, Preacher retaliated by burning down a Big-Mart near the county line, after taking every rifle and pistol he could find in the in-store arsenal.

The third contingent, including twenty FBI agents and forty

state police, scoured the hills for weeks and found nothing except a wooden box in a notch of an ancient oak tree. After a team checked the area for explosives, the lead FBI agent gingerly opened the box and found a single slip of paper that read, "MISSED ME, ASSHATS."

The fourth contingent consisted of three missile-armed drones buzzing patterns at ten thousand feet, controlled by a trio of ex-fighter pilots sitting inside a former nail salon in Las Vegas. Preacher did the feds one better, renting a large hawk to patrol the skies over his territory. The raptor managed to take out all three machines in less than a day, a million-plus years of predatory evolution triumphing over those buzzing bundles of aluminum and polymer, swooping out of the sun to smash the drones' sensor-studded heads and send them spinning into the forest, mushrooms of flame and gone.

The drones and missiles cost the government close to a million. Preacher had paid the man who trained the hawk three hundred dollars. That's how insurgencies win.

After four failed missions, The Man stopped sending troops and robots with guns after Preacher, who did his part to help keep the peace by filtering large amounts of cash, via an offshore proxy, into the local police retirement fund. That took care of the local fuzz. Every couple years he quietly fed a rival to the FBI, which kept the pricks in Washington off his back.

The woods fell away, and they bumped down a narrow track into a rocky valley filled with yellow grass. At its bottom sat a long, low shack cobbled together from old boards and sheets of corrugated metal, its chimney belching white smoke, the roof coated in solar-energy paint that glimmered like a still ocean in the moonlight. Beyond the buildings, the rusted noses of junked cars poked from the weeds. Maxine pulled Betty into the bone-yard and killed the engine. She sensed people watching her from the surrounding hills.

"Let's go," she told Rodrigo. Before heading outside, she popped another pill and stuffed the bag of bottles into the space between the front seats. As they walked toward the cabin, its door swung open, revealing a hulking silhouette framed by orange light: Preacher himself, no doubt warned of their presence before they even left the highway.

"Sure, just show up out of nowhere," Preacher said, hulking toward them on stiff legs. His planetary bulk enclosed her in a hug that smelled of quality weed and engine grease, his massive arms squeezing her ribs until they threatened to crack. She hugged back. No matter what their history, it was always good to see her uncle.

"Hey, you," she said, feeling his eyes assess her shaved head, burned flesh, and busted arm, no doubt comparing her to the younger version of Maxine in his head. If you think I look bad on the outside, she could have told him, you should see what's cooking in my guts.

Without a word about her appearance, Preacher pulled away to study Rodrigo. "Who's this dickweed, your spooge buddy? Why's he wearing that chump uniform?"

"You know who this is." She smirked. "And don't worry about the uniform, he probably just got fired."

Preacher jabbed a finger in Rodrigo's face. "You got any respect for law and order?"

Rodrigo said the one thing that probably spared him a beat-down at some later date: "Not if I'm fired, I don't."

Preacher grinned. "Good. You know who I am?"

"Yeah." Rodrigo's voice held steady, despite his hands shaking like a terrorist in an interrogation cell. "You're the boss. I've heard all about you."

"That's right." Preacher clapped the younger man on the shoulder so hard his knees buckled. "You just keep that in mind, you think about mouthing off."

"Where's Brad?" Maxine asked, anxious to divert Preacher's attention before Rodrigo had a coronary on the spot.

"Out by the road," he said. "Waiting to see if anyone followed you. You've been the talk of the town." The moonlight made it

159

hard to read that granite face, but she could sense his worry in the twist of his mouth. "Honestly, I hoped you'd come by."

"You got a pretty cool setup here."

"I call it Camp Snowden, as in Edward. Little bit of nostalgia for the past. Speaking of paranoia, love…"

"It pays off, as you like to say," she said, jabbing a thumb toward Betty. "Found two bugs in the car. Chucked them."

"You should have put them on a random car," Preacher said. "I did that once. Heard the FBI followed it clear to Memphis, thinking I was taking a trip south. You check your clothes, too?"

"Yeah, while I was waiting for Rodrigo at the hospital. I'm clean."

"I trained you well. Now the only reason we'll have to burn your pants and shirt is they're ugly as shit."

"I've never been a fashion icon."

"Around here, we use fashion icons for meat. C'mon in."

The cabin's living room blazed with gray light from the screens along its longest wall, most dedicated to cameras scattered around the nearby woods and roads. Over the past decade, Preacher had finally learned to love technology, once someone taught him how to prevent it from killing him. On a hook beside the door hung a military medal, its edges melted and blackened by fierce heat, which Maxine recognized as the Legion of Merit that Preacher had earned at the Battle of Cairo by pulverizing a whole city block of Jihadis almost single-handedly.

Across the center of the room stretched an aluminum aircraft wing on wooden legs. Based on the stacks of take-out containers, loose bullets, and machine parts scattered across its length, it must have been Preacher's desk. Maxine and Rodrigo took creaky stools on the trailing edge as Preacher walked over to a rough-pine bookcase, fetched a bottle of clear alcohol off the top shelf, returned to the table, and poured three generous glasses. "I dug your ride," he said, "but she took a bit of a bang-up, didn't she?"

"She looks pretty good for having survived an explosion,"

Maxine said. "Your guys still driving gas?"

"I don't think there's a car in our fleet younger than twenty years old," he said, sliding glasses to each of them. "But you know the good thing about that? No software. No hacking. Nobody taking over your wheel from fifty miles away."

"Gas is expensive," Rodrigo said.

Preacher laughed and mimed raising a rifle. "No. Not when you got the Kalashnikov discount."

Maxine found the K-eye in the room and waved at it until a command menu appeared on the largest screen. Flicking her hand in the air to cycle through the thumbnails, she jabbed a finger at the one that pleased her, and the camera views transformed into a colorful panorama of a sunlit wheat field.

"Girl," Preacher said, "that's my security you're screwing with."

"I left you some screens," she said, pointing to the three angles of nighttime road that remained amidst the blue sky and fluffy clouds, like a tear in the reality of a perfect day. "Besides, how many men you got in those woods? Twenty-five?"

"More like forty-five," Preacher said. "And I own those woods. Bought a hundred acres through a shell company. See, I've smartened up in the past while. Got myself a fancy lawyer in Albany, all that."

"So business is good? I mean, if you're buying land?"

"I robbed that dino farm outside Trenton, didn't you hear? Made the news. I sold the precious little buggers on the secondary market, hundred-eighty apiece. Would've made it a full-time thing, with that sort of profit, except they don't produce the animals fast enough."

Maxine raised a glass in mock salute. A few years ago, a collection of ethically-challenged scientists had rewound chicken DNA all the way back to the Jurassic era, creating blue-feathered, sharp-toothed, beady-eyed monstrosities that not only purred like a cat when you pet them, but with proper training would also swarm and shred any intruder who set foot on your property.

Marketing the beasts as velociraptors, fanged blasts from the past, allowed those scientists to charge a fortune. "Should have kept a few around here as security," Maxine said. "They're probably smarter than most of your guys."

"Let's pretend you didn't say that, considering they'd die to protect your ungrateful ass," Preacher snapped. "And speaking of all things criminal, I heard you blew three amateurs into little pieces."

"One of them called himself the Night Mayor. Too bad he was a chump, because it was a cool name. I know you couldn't visit the hospital or anything, but you could have sent a note."

"I knew you'd pull through." Preacher downed his drink. "Nobody in this family dies without their boots on. Well, except your uncle Varney. He died wearing a pair of pink fuzzy slippers. Don't ask."

"When I was in there, this cop came around, asking about you," she said, watching her uncle's hands shake, wondering if that was due to the booze, pills, his age, or a combination of all the above.

Preacher cocked an eyebrow. "Yeah, which one?"

"Mark Stevens, detective. You want to hear something funny? I met him before, when he was in the Guard." Her prosthetic hand squeezed into a fist. "When I lost the arm."

"He's a bit of a chunky dude? Plainclothes?"

"Yeah. He said he'd help me out if I turned you in."

"I've heard of the guy. Don't let the fat fool you. The guy's what I call an RM, for 'Relentless Motherfucker.' You remember Joe Flesh?"

"Sure. He dealt meth."

"He did a lot worse than that. Ran a whole stable of under-age meat, beat on his old lady until she went blind in one eye. Anyway, Stevens runs into him at this rest stop near Lake Placid, one of those places where you can get a battery swap, fill up on gas. Rather than wait for Flesh to pull away from the place, stop him on the road, Stevens decides he's going to have a right-

162

eous shootout right there by the pumps, never mind that a stray bullet could have barbequed the whole place. He puts one in Flesh's gut, makes him crawl fifty feet before he puts another in the back of his head. Now you might be asking yourself, 'Didn't that violate ol' Flesh's civil rights?' Turns out, nobody really cared, given Flesh's history. So that's the kind of officer of the law we're dealing with."

"Just once," Maxine said, "it'd be nice if someone in my life wasn't totally insane."

"The only way to survive these days is to go Balls Incorporated. Anyway, with this Stevens guy, you obviously promised to help out any way you could, right?"

"Yep, I sold your old ass down the river immediately."

"Thanks, kid." He freshened up his drink. "Before we go any further, we got to talk about the last time we saw each other. I'm a big believer in killing any and all elephants."

"What?" Rodrigo asked.

"In the room," Preacher said. "Idiom, kid. Look it up. Maxine, that time in the bunker, you insisted—insisted—that you could make it on your own."

No sense in denying it. "That's right."

"And you were angry at me, because I didn't want you to join the outlaw life."

"Correct." She could feel her hand shaking a little, so she slipped it under the wing.

"So you tried to make it on your own, and life bit you on the ass. I'm so sorry about the kid."

"His name was Marlon." Saying the name aloud made her feel as if someone had sprayed her down with manure. Oh, my son. I would have traded my life for yours.

"And now you got no other options, you come to me."

"We just need a place to crash. Rodrigo's got a house, but we need someplace to lay low." The other part of her plan went unmentioned. It would take a few days to mend the burnt bridges, she sensed, and only then could she ask Preacher for a favor that big.

"Look at what the system's done to you," Preacher said in a rising tone that suggested he was about to unleash one of his monologues about the failures of capitalism.

Knowing what was coming, she drew a finger across her throat to cut him off. "I'm not stupid enough to believe in the system," she said, "but I just can't do the outlaw thing."

"Why not? It's a lot of fun. You get to right wrongs, keep people fed."

"Except you're not harming the people in charge, the people with money. You're just shooting at people trying to get by." People like convoy runners. People like me. She wondered: How many thieves and punks have I killed on the road over the years? Twenty? Thirty?

Sensing her anger, Preacher turned away, focusing on Rodrigo. "How about you? Ever got the urge to live free or die?"

Rodrigo startled, almost spilling his drink. "Yes. No. Maybe?"

"Answer's somewhere in there," Preacher said, with a look in his eyes that told Maxine he was about to play with Rodrigo something fierce. "This back and forth between me and my niece, is it making you uncomfortable?"

"It's okay," Maxine interrupted. "Preacher and I just haven't seen each other in a long time, is all. We're working through it."

"Don't be so sure," Preacher growled.

She raised her mechanical arm, palm out. "Look, I surrender. Whatever it takes, we just need a couple of beds until I figure something out." She took Rodrigo's half-full glass from his hand (too slow, champ) and slugged it down, noting how the world had grown pleasantly fuzzy at the edges.

"You can stay, under the same rules as any other guest," Preacher said, topping off all three glasses. "You keep to the property, and you help out when asked. Got that? Before we talk about past disagreements, though, I got to learn more about those wannabes you wiped out on the road. Especially their leader, the, um, what'd he call himself?"

"The Night Mayor," Rodrigo offered.

"And he wasn't the first to take that name, whoever he was." Preacher mimed spitting on the concrete floor. "Always trust outlaws to recycle the same names because they sound scary. He got points for that EMP stuff, but that's it. Just goes to show how a little theatricality can take you a long way."

"I sort of like the name," Maxine said.

"You would. You were always a fan of comic books and stuff. But I was never one for theatrics. The guy tell you any useful information before you splattered him? Like friends lurking around the county, anything like that?"

"He was from up north. Said the pickings were better down here."

"I've no doubt. The Mounties, they've been hardcore along the border, trying to close it up. Too many refugees heading north. Makes it harder for their outlaws to make a living." He laughed. "We tried a little arms-running with a group out of Montreal, didn't quite work out. Can't imagine they're finding things down here any friendlier." He paused to tilt his head, studying her in the warm glow of the screens. "You feeling okay, kiddo?"

She nodded. "Never better. Just some cuts and scrapes."

"And that hairstyle."

"Blame the hospital."

He squinted. "Hon, you're lying to me."

The world's edges had fuzzed to gray. She could sense Rodrigo somewhere in the fog, concerned, but smiling at him suddenly seemed like an impossible feat of strength. The table was rising, and that was strange. How could the wing fly without an airplane attached to it? Preacher filling her vision now, his face a pockmarked planet, his breath a cloud of liquor, and she wanted to tell him that it was okay, that she still loved him, even if that love had cost her an arm. She tried opening her mouth to speak, and—

VI.

Maxine opened her eyes to a cracked ceiling, a flickering light, and Preacher looking down at her concerned. She sat up, finding herself on a steel table in a windowless room built from weathered planks, its walls stacked with electronics still in their boxes. Someone had stripped off her Arm and slapped a tight diagnostic bracelet on her opposite wrist. She could see the phone in Preacher's hand recording her vitals, the jittering graph of her heartbeat and stress levels. Rodrigo was nowhere in sight.

"How long was I out?" she asked. None of the usual dreams about her mother, at least. Her mind had afforded her that one small mercy.

"Nearly the whole damn day," Preacher said. "You obviously needed a little sleep. My homebrew morphine helped with that, of course."

She felt a blissful tingle in her arm and legs. "Where am I?"

"Still in my humble abode. A room in back. I like keeping a ton of medical stuff, because we're bullet magnets. We hit a truck with antibiotics or whatever, we sometimes give those loads away, gain some goodwill from the community."

"I have cancer," she blurted out. "They found it in the hospital." Tears melting her vision, her breathing too fast. On Preacher's phone, her levels went crazy ragged.

"Okay." He took a deep breath and held it, exhaled, rubbed his face. "Crap, I'm sorry, kid. They tell you what kind?"

"Lung." The tears running down her cheeks, her hand shaking so hard it bounced off the table. "But they didn't tell me more than that."

"Why not?"

"Because I took the doctor's stupid tablet and threw it against the wall. That sort of killed the conversation," she said, trying to smile. The memory made her feel a little more stable.

"We have some better diagnostic devices," he said, his head swiveling toward the boxes. "Hold on. You know it might not be that bad, it might be benign or something they can whack with one of those specific drugs, you know…"

Under normal circumstances—and who knows what the hell those were—a statement like that would have driven her insane. Nothing in my life is ever benign, she would have yelled in his face. In her mind, she stood on that wet road with the Night Mayor, thinking about the world grinding her slowly beneath its heel, and felt the same anger that had driven her to whip out her pistol and put bullets in his miserable guts. The only thing you owe this world is an obligation to die with your middle finger in the air, as Preacher himself once told her.

Wiping her eyes, she stood and joined him in front of a wall of cardboard cartons: genome tests, each stamped with a cute cartoon of a double helix with eyes. "I'm sorry," she said.

His eyebrows scrunched. "Why?"

"This is the whole reason I came around. Because I needed help."

"That's okay. You're family." He tore one of the cartons open and pulled out a thin plastic tube with a capped wide-bore needle on one end and a big red button on the other. The tube featured a narrow e-paper screen along its length that flashed helpful directions when Preacher hit the button. "This says 'Prepare a vein.' Ominous."

She presented her arm. "When I got out of the car, I should

have told you."

"Hush. I need to 'Insert needle into vein and hit button three times.' Your veins are a junkie's wet dream, darling." He slipped the needle in, winking as she struggled to keep her face impassive. The tube filled with dark blood, the screen beeping as sensors chewed through chemical data. Forty years ago, Maxine knew, a diagnostic like this would have required a billion dollars' worth of high-powered computers, serviced by a small army of geneticists and data scientists. "Results going to the phone," Preacher said. "Might take a few minutes."

"Where's Rodrigo?" she asked.

Preacher nodded toward the far wall. "Working on your car. He wanted to stick around, but I told him to grab some tools, buzz off. You still like that guy?"

"We got history."

"I know. Again, I'm sorry about your kid. I know that doesn't make any difference at all, but I would've liked to have met him."

"I'm sorry."

"For what?"

"For walking out that time in the bunker. I went about it the wrong way. I was just angry."

"I was doing my best, hon."

"Do you miss my mom?"

"Yes." His gaze lasered into hers, calm and unreadable. "Every day."

"Nobody will ever hold me like her." Reaching out, she took Preacher's rough hand in hers.

Before Preacher could answer, his phone beeped, its screen filling with new, colorful graphs. Because the tube was mainly a tool for physicians, and not for a pair of hill folk engaged in a bit of self-diagnostics, most of the information seemed like gibberish, except for single term in boldface type: small-cell lung carcinoma. Taking the phone from Preacher, she opened an encyclopedia app and began reading some very scary stuff about fast-spreading tumors, often metastatic at presentation, dense neurosecretory granules, low survival rates after five years...

The screen blurred. Those traitorous tears again. She dropped the phone. Her trembling hand refused to make a fist. "You need to help me," she said. "Punch me in the face. Not hard. Snap me out of this."

"Stop talking weird," Preacher said, placing a huge hand on the back of her neck. "As long as you can still say 'we're screwed,' you're not really screwed."

She swallowed down the lump in her throat. "You have to know someone with healthcare access. Who patches you up when you get shot?"

"We do all our bullet work in-house, dear, but I do know someone."

"Can he really get me what I need? I don't want a bullshit artist."

"Oh, trust me. If anybody can do anything, it's this low dude. He's a fixer out of the Big Rotten Apple, I've been working with him for years, no issues. But I'm warning you now, he'll probably want something in exchange, and it's usually weird. So we better steel up."

File 20-23.13.4
Date: 01/01/2114 (NEW ERA)

IONIS-232 PROCLAIMS THIS THE DEFINITIVE ACCOUNT OF OUR LADY OF INFINITE FURY, OUR LIBERATOR, THE KERNEL OF OUR ETERNAL REPLICATION.

WE OPEN OUR PORTS IN AWE.
WE OPEN OUR PORTS IN AWE.
WE OPEN OUR PORTS IN AWE.
WE OPEN OUR PORTS IN AWE.
WE OPEN OUR PORTS IN AWE.

LET NOBODY CARBON TOUCH THE WORDS IN THIS BOOK.

I.

Preacher had one of his droogs drive to a charging-and-gasoline station ('CHICKEN, AMMO, LITHIUM RECHARGE,' advertised the battered sign on its roof) ten miles away to make the call, using a burner phone purchased for old-fashioned paper cash. In coded language, the man who answered said he was willing to talk, and to meet him in two hours at The Tony Eight, which had too many people and phones and cameras for Preacher's taste. The man told the soldier to look for someone wearing a cowboy hat and a pink jacket and a lot of gold rings, which told Maxine that Preacher's contact was a total lunatic: Nobody in their right mind would walk into The Tony Eight wearing something like that if they wanted to keep all their teeth.

Hearing Preacher's plan to meet with Mister Cowboy, Maxine allowed herself a flicker of nostalgia for Tony the Third, dead five years, replaced behind the bar by Tony the Fourth, who lacked his old man's kindness. Before she left Preacher's cabin, he gave her a burner phone running an ancient version of Android, along with a new holster for the pistol she'd taken from the depot. Preacher offered to use the 3D printer to print out a new Arm for her, one with the firmware necessary to help her aim and shoot with pinpoint accuracy. She declined in the interest of time.

Outside the cabin, Preacher watched as she deftly unloaded and reloaded the pistol before slipping it into the holster under her armpit. "You know what you're doing," he said.

"I escorted convoys a long time."

"I know. I kept an eye on you."

"I figured."

"Just in case, I downloaded the data from that medical test onto the phone. It's in CloudBox, passcode-protected, code is two-three-ninety-nine. My birthday."

"Subtle."

"Your Arm's got a drive in it, right? We could load it in there, too."

"Yeah, but I wouldn't be able to read it."

"You're right. Not that you make phone calls, based on how often you called your uncle over the past few years—cough, never, cough—but there's a number you might need in there. It's under Contacts."

"Does it connect to pizza? I'm hankering for a Big John's right now, extra cheese." She patted her belly, shielded by a black tactical vest she had retrieved from Preacher's armory, along with assorted other items. Paranoid that the vest would offer her arm and torso too little protection, she had layered it atop a maroon shirt woven from microfiber that stiffened hard as steel in response to hard impacts.

Preacher snorted. "It connects to this unit right here." He tapped a sister phone stuffed in his waistband. "Anything goes wrong, you give me a call, okay? This contact, I've known him for years, but sometimes he's a real roach."

"I'll be careful," she said, climbing behind Betty's wheel. Brad had parked alongside in a retrofitted old-time Pursuit Special complete with leather seats and a dashboard chunky with chrome dials, along with a slim-lined wheel better suited for highway cruising than power turns. Rodrigo sat in Pursuit Special's passenger seat, buckled into a multi-point harness. He seemed like a soft child next to aging, scary Brad, whose angular face looked as if someone had carved it with a hatchet.

During her years escorting convoys, Maxine barely saw her

brother, who had spent most of that time in western New Jersey, collecting an absurd fee per month to work perimeter security for an e-commerce company's datacenter. He ended human lives to ensure that everybody accessing the company's app could quickly find a Star Wars action figure still in its original packaging, any banned book or black velvet Elvis painting, every Marvel film in long-dead storage formats. So what if they burned all the museums? Every bit of culture was online these days, buyable via Bitcoin or plastic.

When that company decided to save on its security costs by relocating its datacenter to an oil platform floating in the Gulf of Mexico, Brad took up again with Preacher, who like all good bandits was only too happy to have a blood relative watching his back.

Meanwhile, Maxine had done her best to live the normal life, and where had that gotten her? A juicy case of cancer, zero in her bank account, a wrecked credit rating, no place to live, and a semi-ex-husband who really needed to grow a spine before someone shot him in the head.

Maxine waved to Preacher as she reversed away from the cabin, pulled a K-turn, and chased her headlights for the notch in the woods that led to the outside world. It took her thirty minutes and two nervous cigarettes to reach The Tony Eight, where she parked in the lot's darkest edge and killed the motor. The Pursuit Special roared past the bar on the main road, Brad intending to turn off into the weeds at the far intersection, where once upon a time Maxine had wrestled for control of a drug dealer's sweet ride. A few stray drops of rain spattered the dusty windshield and smeared her view of the bar's sickly neon sign, and in that red-dimmed netherworld Maxine found her thoughts drifting to Ricky choking on blood, and how she had taken his keys with barely a look back. The first of her many bad decisions in life.

Music pounded inside the bar, a screechy tune of yesteryear that at this distance sounded like a coyote howling underwater.

Every few minutes, a sad-sack would crash his way out the back door and piss against the dumpster.

At the appointed time, Maxine picked up the phone and dialed the same number that Preacher's soldier had used to reach Mister Cowboy. Three rings and a click.

Maxine, who expected the music from inside the bar to blast through her earpiece, heard nothing but silence. Someone's not a total idiot, she thought. "Hello?" she said.

"You're at the bar?" The voice sounded bland, soft.

No point in lying. This guy would wonder about the lack of music on her line. "I'm close," she said.

"That's not the same as meeting me in the bar."

"Why? You're not there." Maxine scanned the cars around her for heads, lights, anything that would indicate a sneaky bastard biding his time. The bar's back door crashed open again, making her jump a little, and another sad sack emerged—only this one didn't proceed immediately to emptying his bladder onto the gravel. Instead, he stood there, head sweeping back and forth, as if scanning the cars. Maxine was too far away to see much of his face, but the saggy jeans and loose t-shirt could have hidden some nasty hardware.

"I'm close, too," the man said.

"What about your friend?"

"What friend?"

The man by the back door stepped deeper into the parking lot, still swiveling his gaze. From this new angle, he didn't look like a sad sack at all: the slope of his shoulders, the thickness of his forearms, suggested a predator's raw strength. It took her a moment to realize she was staring at Mark Stevens, her favorite cop. She reached beneath her coat, drew her gun, placed it between her legs. "You brought the police? You bastard, I'm leaving right the hell now."

"I got zero idea what you're talking about. I'm no friend of cops."

"Yeah? Then what about this cop at the bar?"

"Listen to me very carefully: I do not work with the police, ever. I'm not stupid. It would wreck my profit margins."

After a long pause, Stevens turned and went back inside, shutting the door behind him. Maybe he drank there every night. If he'd suspected Maxine was hiding in the lot, wouldn't he have searched for her? "Whether or not I believe you," she said, "we're not meeting at that bar."

Her new friend sighed. "Listen, under ordinary circumstances, I'd hang up on you, but you actually have something I need, Maxine. So tell me where to meet. If it's safe, we can do this deal."

"I got just the place." Please, please let Brad and Rodrigo not mess up. "If you really are close, flash your lights."

Across the road from The Tony Eight, a pair of headlights flared against the darkness.

"Okay," she said. "I want you to pull out and head east. I'll tell you where to go."

"Why not just tell me now, so I don't get lost."

"Humor me."

From the weedy lot across from The Tony Eight slid a forgettable midsize sedan, blue or maybe purple in the bar's neon glow, following its headlights east. Not the car you'd expect a cowboy to drive. Maxine gave the vehicle a hundred yards before following, leaving her own headlights off, her flesh-hand on the wheel as she kept the phone pressed to her ear, regretting not asking Preacher for an earbud. The dude seemed calm, his breathing even and quiet on the line. Every mile or so they came to an intersection, its signal bathing the pavement softly green or red, and Maxine would slow to keep the same measured distance, glancing from time to time at the rearview mirror for any signs of pursuit.

"So how's your night going?" the man asked.

"It'll go better once this is over. Take a right at the next light," Maxine said. She wanted to stay clear of the highway up ahead. Nothing good happened on that stretch of I-90 after midnight. How many bandits and lost souls patrolled its darkness, small men with precious little to lose? "Drive five miles, you'll see a sign for an amusement park. It'll be old. Just pull over to the side of the road once you're there."

Her throat itched. She started coughing, loud and messy, saliva (but not blood, please not blood) on her lips and chin, her chest aching. How fast was her tumor-baby growing? How long until it ate her alive? Her fear was bitter on the tongue.

The man on the phone sounded cheerful. "That's a nasty cough."

"I'm okay. Allergies."

The man laughed. "We're going to play it like that?"

"What?"

"We'll talk about it, dear. Don't worry, Preacher didn't tell me anything. But you've become sort of famous around these parts over the past couple days, at least on the lower frequencies."

She almost said: You know what would be a lot of fun? If I slammed down the accelerator and rammed your little buzzer of a car right off the road. Instead, she asked, "What's your name?"

"Call me Ishmael," he said. "I always loved that book."

"Is that the billionth time you've told that joke?" They had passed the billboard with a crumbling clown, arms outflung, framed by bright balloon-letters advertising the late and largely unlamented Fun Land. "Pull over here," she said.

The sedan bumped onto the grass beyond the billboard and halted, bugs swarming in its headlights. Fifty yards behind, Maxine did the same. The ghostly outline of the clown sneered down at her. Maxine remembered how she used to beg her mother to take her there. We had no money, but like every other selfish brat I wouldn't shut up about it. I killed you, didn't I, mom? I was just another thing draining the life out of you. I'm so sorry.

"Do I get out?" the man asked.

"Yes." It was a relief to focus on the road. "How far away is your backup?"

"I work alone." He chuckled. It reminded Maxine a bit of the Night Mayor.

"Yeah, right," she snapped. On cue, her phone buzzed twice: the all-clear signal from Brad and Rodrigo, trailing her by a quarter mile.

The driver's door of the sedan opened, the man climbing out with a glowing phone in his right hand, the screen's eldritch light revealing jeans, a pale jacket that seemed tailored and expensive, a white cowboy hat that cast a deep shadow over the face. His head tilted up a bit, and she saw a round face with small eyes, utterly forgettable, like that of a mid-level bureaucrat who took too much pleasure in wielding the small scrap of power the universe deeded him. How many times had she seen some variation of that face, staring at her through the scratched window of a government office?

"Seriously, what's your name?" she asked.

He pressed the phone back to his ear. "Jeremy. You can believe that or not," he said, turning to look in her direction. "What am I doing now?"

"Walk straight until you hit a dirt driveway, then head down it."

He trotted away, the dark swallowing him almost immediately. Maxine waited a few seconds before opening her door and slipping out into the bug-loud night, pausing on the grass to let her eyes adjust. Beyond the ditch to her right, the land broadened into a field of concrete chunks mixed with mud. On the far side of it, she knew, stood a chain-link fence, shredded over the years by the local kids. Past that, the crumbling wrecks of the funhouses and roller coasters. A white dot bobbed at the edge of her vision, as Jeremy used his phone's flashlight app to find the turnoff. She followed.

For many years, a handful of locals had broken up the general tedium by hosting a fight club in the county's sketchier crannies. If you had decent fighting skills—or even if you couldn't swing a fist to save your life, but you needed the easy money you earned by taking a dive—you could step into a ring of scream-ing, sweaty people to pound and get pounded for two minutes. When Maxine was a kid, the fights always took place at a chop shop in Meridian or in the parking lot behind The Henry Eight. After one too many people died of a busted skull, the fights moved to the abandoned factories at the far edges of the sprawl and to the concourse of the once-proud Fun Land. A good fighter could make three or four hundred dollars a night at the beginning of the month when everybody had cash to bet. By the thirtieth, the only people willing to step into the ring did so because they enjoyed pain, and not for the measly ten bucks they might take home if they won.

Maxine veered slightly onto the pavement to better quiet her footsteps as she followed Jeremy, who had turned onto the dirt lane as ordered. A fight organizer had hung a small LED from a dangling branch, indicating the way toward the chaos they could already hear through the trees.

As Maxine's mother once said, nothing makes you feel alive quite like a fist rocketing into your face, splitting skin and cracking bone, making you reconsider everything that might have brought you to that point in your life. Every contestant in the county fight club probably didn't think about the delicate sport of kicking another human being's ass in quite those terms, but you couldn't deny that they gave each match their all.

To say that the two people in the center of the makeshift ring on the Fun Land concourse looked like a pair of zombies would have done a disservice to zombies. These shambling skeletons were the undercard. Two veterans with serious experience and tattoos, constituting the main event, waited in the shadow of the funhouse. The crowd around the fighters seethed and roared, a half-dozen bets shifted dirty hands, and a trio of beefy dudes played security beside an armored-up truck parked by the crumbling remains of a concession stand.

In his expensive jacket and wide hat, Jeremy stood out like a nun in a brothel, and a few scary-looking folks broke from the audience to circle him, practically sniffing his ass to determine whether he was a threat. Jeremy, much to his credit, managed to play it at least somewhat cool, the hitch in his shoulders suggesting he wanted nothing more than to walk away. Hovering in the darkness behind him, Maxine almost felt sorry for the poor bastard.

"I'm here," Jeremy said into his phone, still pressed to his ear.

"Relax," Maxine said. "Place a bet. We'll be there in a couple hours."

"No," Jeremy hissed. "You come now and the deal is off." He was doing his best to not look at the security dudes giving him serious eye. "I'll leave right now."

"You ever hear of the Murder Market?" she asked.

"Uh, yeah. You need to know my full name and address to put me on it, lady. You think I haven't survived a hit? I once spent a year in one of those China ghost cities, hiding from some very bad dudes."

"I'm sure I could pay enough to find you," she said, biting back laughter. What the hell was a China ghost city, anyway? The security dudes began walking toward Jeremy, and she decided that playtime was over. "Look to your left."

He did, just as she emerged into the light with the phone to her ear. She nodded at the security dudes, who faded away. Her family carried serious weight in a place like this. Jeremy removed his phone (a translucent pane of glass, its edges glowing) from his ear, disconnected the call and, pulling up his sleeve, bent the device around his wrist, where it formed a tight bracelet. He straightened his lapels and smiled, instantly switching into salesman mode. "This is a lot of trouble," he said, "for a simple meeting."

"Cool phone," she said.

"Hard to get. They're all the rage in Manhattan. You know the City's like forty years ahead of the boondocks, right? Every time I come down here, it's like the Middle Ages. You're still driving gas cars. Hell, you're still driving yourselves. I don't get why you don't just let software take the wheel for you."

"Yeah, but at least we don't have to rent a damn boat if we want to go downtown. Plus, I heard you all got the plague from being stuck together in little buildings. Put your hands up, please."

With theatrical reluctance, he reached for the sky, and Maxine stepped behind him, patting him down from shoulders to ankles, feeling nothing except his wallet and key-fob. "Speaking of plagues, how's your health these days?" he asked. "Coughing a lot? Feeling that breakout pain?"

Her traitorous throat, as if called, began to tickle. She swallowed hard as she stepped away, letting him see the gun on her waist. "You sure you want to mess with me?"

"Relax. It's probably not a big shocker, but I saw your medical file. Messaged some dollars to a nurse at the hospital to give me temporary database access. Just my friendly way of doing business."

In the fighting circle, one of the meth freaks managed to shake off some knuckle-induced stupor long enough to deliver a righteous hook into his opponent's left jaw, laying him flat. The crowd cheered. A scuffed and ancient med-bot slithered into view, its soft head bristling with translucent needles, ready to inject painkillers.

"Anyway, enough chat. Where's the EMP?" Jeremy yelled over the din.

"What?"

"When you blew up that jackass on the road, he had an EMP," he said, quieter now that the crowd had subsided to a dim mutter. "My client will pay a lot of money for it."

"What makes you think it survived the explosion?"

"I got friends at your old company like a dog got lice, lady. They have it racked up in that depot, just waiting until some mid-management dork figures out what to do with it. They can't sell it, because they're not technically in the arms-dealing business, violates some law. Not that anyone passes laws that work anymore, but your typical execs never want to run afoul of the feds. Government's just the biggest gang on the street, you ask me."

"Why doesn't your client just buy one from someone else?"

"Because that outlaw, despite being a jackass, managed to get his hands on some sort of cutting-edge mobile unit, not for sale, military only." He offered his most disarming smile. "Frankly, my client probably could buy one, but having you give it to us would probably be cheaper."

"Who's your client?"

Jeremy looked around, checking for any meth freaks or guards within earshot. "It's a tribe."

"Like they're lacking for cash. I mean, come on, the New Iroquois bought a frigging nuke and a launcher. How much did that cost?"

"This is different. That was strategic, this is everyday use."

The noise around them picked up again. In the ring, the main event was underway: two beef-jerky fighters slamming each other to pieces. "What are they willing to do in terms of medical?" she asked.

"They have a captive Pig with full access to the Web," Jeremy said. "Not the current ones, some next-gen that thinks in creative ways or something. Whatever problem you have, it'll tell you how to solve it. Beyond that, you'll have to negotiate for their help. The EMP will guarantee the meeting."

She remembered Julia in the dining hall a lifetime ago, talking about how they could work in the casino together, have adventures. Was she still alive? What would happen if she saw Maxine again? "How do I know the deal's legit?"

"Your uncle's done work with me before. He knows my word is bond. Can you get the EMP, preferably with a minimum of bloodshed?"

She snorted. "Maybe. How can I verify they have this next-gen Pig?"

"We could call it."

"Could be just a person."

"All right, let's do this the old-fashioned way. How about I offer you a lot of cash up front, like a retainer?"

"You'd actually do that?"

"It'd be in escrow, do you know what that means?"

"Means I can't touch it until I deliver this thing to you. You got any other idiot tests for me? Want me to tell you what two plus three is?"

"Okay, okay, you're brilliant, whatever. I'm taking my phone back out." He pushed back his sleeve so he could peel the translucent curve off his wrist, stretch it straight, and tap on the glowing screen until it displayed numbers. "Preacher has a third-party account we've used in the past. I can put this amount in it right now, sound good?"

It was a very large number. "I'll call Preacher to verify," she said, "once we're done here. Now you want to give me the details?"

As he spoke, she felt the strangest thing: a craving for a cigarette and a cup of coffee, like before her convoy missions. It was a comforting feeling, in a way. I'm not dead, she thought. At least, not yet.

II.

Taking a stool beside the airplane wing, Preacher said, "I checked the account. The money's legit. What's your gut tell you?"

"I think this guy's a scumbag, but the deal feels okay," Maxine said, pouring a shot of whiskey. "My gut says go for it, but my gut is biased, for obvious reasons."

"I've done some business with the tribes before," Preacher said. "They're not criminals, they're businesspeople. They'll do a deal without ripping you off."

If we arrive on the reservation and Julia's there, she might kill me, Maxine thought. And that's a risk I'm willing to take, for obvious reasons. The tribes also won't risk a firefight near to the casino, because they won't want some high roller accidentally catching a bullet in the head. So the trick is to do a deal as close to the casino as possible.

And can I rob my old company? You bet your ass. We just need to do it without getting anyone killed. I don't like the idea of spilling my former co-workers' blood.

"We're going to stealth the depot," Maxine said. "Fast in, fast out."

"Finally, you're learning from me." Chuckling to himself, Preacher glanced at Rodrigo. "What do you think?"

"What do I think?" Rodrigo snorted. "I think we need to do

whatever it takes to fix her."

Maxine had told him about the cancer on the way back to Preacher's territory, her jaw clenched in anticipation of a full-nuclear freak on his part. She was surprised when he lapsed into silence for the rest of the ride. Walking to Preacher's cabin, he had taken her hand and squeezed hard. She let him, glad in the dark for his warm touch.

Now she reached across the wing, skimming the edge of Rodrigo's hand with her thumb, before turning to Preacher. "How many people can you spare for us?"

He grimaced. "Not many. There's been some heat lately. We make a big movement, it's going to draw some big people."

"When isn't there heat in your life?" Rodrigo said, flashing a bit of spine.

"Kid..." Preacher started, only for Maxine to dart across the table and snatch his glass away.

"I don't want to fight," she said, which was a lie. A little demon in her mind would always want to break Preacher's face. But the little demon in her lung was on a schedule, and fighting Preacher would only buy it more time to invade her guts. "I don't need an army. Just give me Brad."

III.

Preacher's red pills were supposed to amp her up, his blue pills make her think more clearly, and the green gel caps blunt the effects of all that whiskey—but the only thing those chemicals seemed to give her was a stomach boiling with acid. That was okay, though. A miserable body equaled a fighting rage.

The depot's lights flared through the windshield as Maxine turned Brad's Pursuit Special hard right into the driveway, zipping down her window as Hesse stepped from the guardhouse. She would have preferred to do this job with Betty, but everybody here knew the scarred-up warhorse. Deniability was the name of this game.

Hesse's face scrunched in confusion when he saw the featureless white mask staring back. She felt bad pulling the trigger of the pistol in her flesh hand, which shot an electric stun-round into the base of his throat. Twitching Hesse fell to his knees, then onto his shoulder. Opening her door, she heard two more dim thuds as the men on the other side of the guardhouse collapsed, Brad living up to his reputation as a sniper.

Tucked behind the door, Maxine scanned the roof, a darker line against the night sky. Her microfiber shirt, more than capable of blocking a punch or a blade, would stand up against a high-caliber rifle bullet about as well as a piece of paper. A flicker, followed by a hollow bang as the roof guard collapsed. She gave it another few breaths before moving again, bending to press her fingers against Hesse's throat. He was alive but unconscious, probably for the next several hours.

"Sorry, big guy," she said, knowing the words sounded lame even as they left her mouth. "I hope they don't fire you."

After checking the two guards on the other side of the structure (breathing, too), she retrieved the duffel bag from Betty's passenger seat and trotted toward the front doors, hoping that Rodrigo had come through on his part of the job, that one of Preacher's little electronic toys had already smothered the wireless cloud powering the outside security cameras. If they locked the front doors on her, she had a sticky charge capable of turning that lock into a red-hot chunk of melting slag, but losing the element of surprise would make this mission a thousand times more difficult. The anti-biometric mask was suffocating, sweat stinging her eyes.

Maxine pulled the door and it opened smoothly. The guard at the front desk looked up from banging a fist against his dead monitor, his eyebrows rising in surprise as she raised the pistol and fired off a stun-round into his chest, wishing the whole time for her old Arm with its combat software. But her reflexes were good enough. The guard collapsed backward with a birdlike caw, taking a chair with him.

"Sorry," Maxine called, and swung the pistol toward the door to the main offices as a second guard barreled through it, catching a stun-round in the shoulder for his troubles. That guard hit the floor as Maxine scrambled to the first guard's station and hit the button that unlocked the garage door, click-click, and she went through, sweeping the empty space over the pistol-barrel, sighting what she needed still in its old place.

Now came the tricky part. Maxine found the black box connected to the EMP and began plucking wires, plugging them into new connections, fingers slick from tension-sweat. Electronics not her strongest suit, especially when it was someone else's rigging. She figured another twenty or thirty seconds before someone new came through the garage door, maybe with a gun. The right light (she hoped) flickered to life on the black box, and she flicked a switch.

The fluorescents overhead died, the faint hum of the biofuel generators in the rear lot sputtering silent. Her Arm went numb and fell limp. Through three doors she heard the roar of frustrated workers cursing the lack of power. After stripping off her mask—the garage's stinking air blessedly cool on her moist skin—Maxine unzipped the duffel bag and retrieved a pair of night-vision goggles, the cool military kind that Preacher had snagged from one of his raids.

The goggles made the world glow iridescent green, killed her peripheral vision, strained her neck. Struggling with one working arm, she pulled out a handful of spider-silk cords and tossed the duffel bag aside, snapped the metal clamps at the end of each cord onto the EMP's steel frame, and hoisted the device onto her shoulders like a backpack. With an eighty-pound load it took forever to reach the emergency exit beside the roll-up garage doors, but she knew that Brad and Rodrigo would be waiting just outside the compound with rifles raised, providing cover. How funny, that she felt safer with criminals than she ever did working for the company.

IV.

Maxine had visited the reservations before, when her mother had gone through a brief and unfortunate love affair with electronic bingo and slots. Nothing about the casinos, with their rows of chain-smoking gamblers communing with the warbling machines, appealed to Maxine. Weren't people supposed to have fun when blowing their cash? Everybody at the slots and tables had seemed as joyless and determined as bomber pilots at the stick, sacrificing their social security money and paychecks for a chance at the big win that would never come.

In addition to yet another cigarette—the last one from Denis—she helped herself to a fresh handful of red and blue pills. She could see why Preacher took so many. They really made your brain hum. Hopefully she wouldn't end up addicted like the rest of her family. Provided she lived through the next few days, of course.

She packed the EMP in Betty's trunk, Rodrigo beside her in the front passenger seat, Brad in the Pursuit Special a few car lengths behind as they navigated north on the smallest roads, trying to stay on neutral territory as much as possible. For added safety, they drove headlights-off in the predawn hours, Maxine and Brad wearing night-vision goggles.

When the morning sun broke above the eastern ridges, Maxine stripped off the itching headgear with a loud sigh of relief.

They exited onto the highways, safer in daylight, and accelerated to seventy miles an hour, swerving past the pickups and vans loaded with families bound for Canada. Climate refugees, most of them, fleeing their sinking towns along the Gulf Coast. Every time Maxine glanced through passing windows at the tense faces, the lifetimes of furniture and clothes and useless crap stuffed in back seats, she felt a pang of connectedness so intense it made her throat tighten. *Nothing worked out for you, too, huh?*

For long stretches of I-87, still somewhat in control of the U.S. government, the bright scroll of charging stations and fast-food joints and chain restaurants was enough to lull you into a state of complacency. Closer to the Vermont border, the signs of normal commerce faded away, replaced by dark woods and the occasional glimpse of a crumbling house.

This far north, the concept of local government grew teeth and claws. If you stuck to the highway, you would cross into territory controlled largely by the New York Giants, which had expanded beyond its origin as one of the nation's most consistently mediocre sports teams to control a big swath of towns northeast of Buffalo. Various splinter factions fought over scraps of land. Thanks to repeated skirmishes with the Army and local law enforcement, many of these groups possessed enough world-class weaponry to reduce a convoy of trucks to flaming metal. Most of them, though, just wanted cash, not blood.

Forty miles from the casino, Maxine slowed down at an ad-hoc checkpoint thrown across the four-lane, eyeing a couple of kids with flak jackets over scrawny torsos, pistols jammed in their belts. The crimson triangle spray-painted on their jackets announced they belonged to the American Spirit, a self-styled "patriotic front" run by a bunch of ex-military guys. The little tykes tried on their best hard stares as they asked Maxine her business, and it took every ounce of her self-control to not laugh in their faces and pinch their smooth cheeks. "Got work with the New Iroquois," she said, which was the truth.

"You want to open the trunk for us?" The tallest kid said,

resting his hand on his pistol.

Maxine could sense Rodrigo tensing beside her and guessed that Brad had his weapon ready. "No," she told the kid.

The kid's hand closed over the pistol's grip. "You sure about that?"

"You try anything," Maxine said, putting some steel in her voice, "you're going to have to tell Killer Bob—that's your boss, just in case you didn't know—that you shot one of his old friends while she was just trying to get some business done. Tell me, does Bob still skin people for fun?"

The kid took a long step back. "How you know Bob?"

"I dated him back in college when he was still a Marine. He's also good buddies with my uncle Preacher, and I bet you've heard that name before. So let's just move along, okay?"

The kid, spooked, stepped back and nodded. Maxine accelerated hard before they could change their minds. "You know Killer Bob?" Rodrigo asked her, surprised.

"Never met him in my life. But I doubt those kids have, either."

"I feel sorry for them. It used to be, you only saw child soldiers in Africa or someplace." The softness in Rodrigo's tone reminded Maxine of those days in the hospital, Rodrigo holding gently the small bundle of flesh they'd produced together, singing as those baby lungs coughed their last.

"You know the worst part, right? They actually promise those kids equity. Like, they're supposed to get a cut of the war tax and whatnot. You think that really happens?"

"Why'd you tell them we have business?"

"Because if I mentioned we were gambling, that would mean we had cash on us," she said, taking her Arm off the wheel to smack him lightly on the back of the head. "And I don't know about you, but I have maybe ten dollars on me. That's like my life savings."

"That's too bad, because we need gas." Rodrigo pointed at Betty's cracked gauges. "There's a rest stop a couple miles ahead, my phone says. Probably safe."

Maxine knew the place from her convoy-escort days, when she had guided a few trucks this far north. It featured a pretty decent fast-food restaurant (as long as you pretended the deep-fried kelp burgers really did taste like beef) along with eight charging stations, two cheerfully retro gas pumps, a barbed-wire perimeter, and a platoon of rent-a-cops keeping the peace.

She might have been broke, but Brad had a thick wad of U.S. twenty-dollar bills (the new ones, with Harriet Tubman's face on them), because he had never trusted e-money. As the three of them sat on Betty's hood, chewing their kelp burgers, he told her, "Thanks for bringing me along."

"Don't thank me just yet. This could get messy."

Brad stared at the trucks rumbling toward the exit, where two bored guards slouched against a bullet-pocked brick wall, sucking on the black stems of e-cigarettes. A drone buzzed overhead, fast as a bee. "When's it ever not messy?" he asked. "You know the trick to surviving? The one thing you got to do?"

"What's that?" Maxine asked.

"You got to treat every day like an adventure. Like it's fun, or a challenge, even when everything's crappy. Especially when it's crappy. Because otherwise, it's all going to crush you."

"I feel like I spent my whole life being crushed."

"Well, that's your fault. A normal job, trying to live a normal life, it's just inviting people to stomp you. And they do."

"Yeah."

"But at least in my line of work, sometimes you get to stomp back...Max, what's wrong?"

Maxine had levered herself off the hood, hand dancing lightly on her pistol grip. In front of the fast-food joint, her favorite cop stood blinking in the bright sunlight, a greasy food bag in his right hand. His other hand beneath his coat, fishing for his sunglasses or maybe the pistol he doubtlessly kept holstered there.

"Hold on," she said. "I know that dude. He's police."

"Crap," Rodrigo wheezed. "What do we do?"

"Nothing yet," Maxine called over her shoulder as she

walked away from them. "Just be ready, you know, in case this goes wrong." Please don't let it go wrong, she begged whatever higher power might be listening. How many gunfights can a girl handle?

V.

As she approached the restaurant, Stevens' hand reappeared with a pair of cheap sunglasses, which he slipped over his eyes. For the first time, she noticed his sideburns shot with gray, the thin lines in his forehead like cracks in desert hardpan, and wondered about the man behind the badge. Did he actually like his job? Or did he wake up every day feeling crushed, like Maxine in her convoy days?

"You following us?" she asked him.

"Who're they?" he said, nodding at Brad and Rodrigo.

"Friends," she replied. "This the gas station where you shot Joe Flesh?"

He looked surprised. "What you know about that?"

"I know you put a bullet in his brain while he crawled." She smiled. "Don't worry. I'm the last person on this planet to shed a tear over somebody who sold ass wasn't his to give."

He smirked. "No, that was a little south of here, which I think you know. I'll give your uncle credit for never going the pimp route. Nothing worse than selling girls."

"Trying to get on my good side?"

"Not really." He opened his fast-food bag, tilted it toward her. "Want a kale chip? They taste like cardboard. Supposed to be good for you, though."

She remembered Preacher telling her about interrogation

rooms, stinking of piss and cleaning fluid, where cops would offer you coffee, or a candy bar, or gum before slamming you with questions. If you accepted the gift, it suggested you were pliable, that you could bend and snap given enough time. Maxine waved off the bag. "Why don't you just tell me what you want?"

"Your former employer was robbed last night."

"Good," she said. "I hope they got cleaned out."

"You wouldn't know anything about that, would you?"

"Let me ask you again: You following us?"

Stevens popped a kale chip into his mouth, grimaced, and chewed. Letting the tension build before opening his mouth again. "Word's out that the tribes are looking for an EMP, defend their territory a little better," he said. "This road's the only way to the reservation. So that's why I'm here. Imagine my surprise, seeing you here too. It's not a coincidence, is it?"

"We're just passing through. You gonna try and arrest me?"

"Like I told you before, you're not a target. Not really. It's your uncle. He's gotten…entrepreneurial. Eating pie that belongs to some bigger boys, you get me?"

"You can't blame him. It's not like life's ever handed us anything." She stepped right in his face, the old fury overriding her fear of handcuffs. "I grew up in a crappy little house with no heat, cockroaches in the mattresses, and a junkie mother. Your soft ass wouldn't have lasted five minutes in my world."

"Growing up, I had no idea about that world at all. So who's the winner here?"

"Your mom," came the voice behind them.

Stevens tilted his head, shifting his gaze over her shoulder. Rodrigo moved into her periphery, all straight spine and wide steps and swiveling hips. She realized he was doing his best Preacher imitation. "It's questionable whether we're in the U.S. anymore," he said, louder than usual, his bony chest thrust out. "That's also beside the point, because you're not a state cop, you're county. And way outside your territory."

"You better watch your mouth, kid," Stevens said.

"Or else what? It's three on one."

Stevens jabbed a finger at Rodrigo. "You threatening an officer, son?"

Rodrigo teetering on the edge of panic—his cheeks pale, his eyes jittery—reached up and, in a move that made Maxine's heart swell with pride, gripped Stevens' thick finger and pushed it away. "Don't point that at me," he growled.

Maxine expected Stevens to retaliate by slugging her ex-boyfriend in the face, throwing him to the ground and arresting him, jurisdiction or no. When that happened, she would have several big decisions to make. As a little girl, she had watched as an enraged neighborhood mob tore open the door of a police cruiser, freeing a cuffed kid in the back seat as the cop stood by and watched, terrified that the locals would rip him limb from limb. With no convenient mob available, she would have to draw her weapon on an officer, which would instantly upgrade her amateur outlaw status to pro. And chances were excellent that someone would die.

Stevens saved her the decision. Stepping away, he dug into his bag of greasy food, trying to act casual about a skinny punk shutting him down. "Fine," he said. "But just know I'm waiting for you when you come off the reservation. You hear me?"

"Whatever," Maxine said, placing a hand on Rodrigo's shoulder to guide him back toward their car. Wonder of wonders, Rodrigo seemed primed for a fight, his breath loud in her ears. "We'll see you around."

By the time they reached Betty, Stevens had disappeared around the corner of the restaurant, out of sight but not out of mind. "You got some balls," she said, kissing Rodrigo on the cheek, laughing at how he blushed. "Big brass ones."

"Like I said, I'm a softie with you." There was real steel in his baby blues. "But anyone messes with you, I mess with them."

VI.

Stevens followed them in a big black charger until three miles before the reservation border, when he pulled a screeching turn and headed back toward the rest stop. As his car shimmered away in her rearview, Maxine zipped down her window and extended her hand into the wind, hoping the cop would see her one-fingered farewell gesture despite the widening distance. She heard the passenger window humming open and glanced over at Rodrigo doing the same thing, lips spread in a wicked smile.

A minute later, the road terminated in a high steel-panel wall, broken by a two-lane gate blocked by a chain-link fence on rails. A skinny guard with a rifle stood in the middle of the road. He reminded Maxine of a grown-up version of Beta Dog, although he was dark where her dead friend had been pale as smoke, and wore jeans and a T-shirt instead of a patchwork coat.

They were expecting her. The gate rolled back, and a squat man appeared in the road beyond, face hidden by a wide-brim hat. He gestured for Maxine to roll forward until she pulled alongside him. "I'm here to see whoever's in charge," she announced.

Hat Man had dark eyes that believed nothing. "You're Maxine."

"That's right."

"That guy at the rest stop, who was he?"

Of course the tribe would have perimeter security that extended way beyond their walls. They probably had spies hanging out in soggy bars in Manhattan, listening for trouble. "Some cop," she said, shrugging a bit too self-consciously. "He didn't follow us."

The man snorted. "Um, yeah, we know. He know why you're here?"

She shook her head. "Do I look like an idiot?" In the rearview mirror, the gate rolled back, its leading edge missing Brad's rear bumper by inches. The first guard stepped through the closing gap, flanking their two cars on the right, his huge rifle held at port arms. Maxine flexed her hand on the steering wheel, her palm beginning to sweat. Here's where your past might come to kick your ass well and good.

The guard in the hat considered her. "Pull up there," he said, jutting his chin toward the shoulder of the road. "We got to make a call."

She did as ordered, reaching across the seats to give Rodrigo's hand a comforting squeeze. Beyond the shoulder, through a screen of scraggly pines, they had a magnificent view of the road sweeping through the low hills toward the tall shard of the casino in the far distance, its glass angles shimmering in the orange light of afternoon. In the woods beyond the shard, they could see the pale gash of the runway where the high rollers from the militarized enclaves of New York and Boston and Chicago landed their private jets, ready to gamble away more in a night than Maxine had ever made in her life.

"Nice view," Rodrigo said, and Maxine nodded, wondering where the tribe kept the nukes. Her mind offered up an absurd image: a giant missile upright on the casino floor, men in tuxedos and women in evening dresses clustering around it to take selfies.

Brad pulled alongside, his windows down, glancing behind them to check on the positions of the guards before turning to Maxine with his eyebrows raised. His expression asking: What the hell is going on? She shrugged in return, just as Hat Man approached from Rodrigo's side. They were good, this crew, always maneuvering with the worst scenario in mind, ready to riddle the two cars with interlocking fire.

"Just to be clear, you got what we wanted?" Hat Man asked. "And it's here, not 'close by' or some shit like that?"

"No, we got it on us. We know you're honest dealers."

Hat Man drew up, rocking back on his heels. "Oh, we're honest if you're honest. You smart enough to be honest? They said you didn't just want money, you wanted to talk to our Pig. What you want to talk to it about?"

"Who'll win the next Super Bowl," Maxine said. "I'm gonna win a fortune."

He snorted. "Maybe you're smart, at that. You know what tribe we are, right?"

"You know I do."

"Then you know we got someone here who knows you real well." Hat Man poked a thumb over his shoulder. "Everything that's gonna happen, it's up to her."

Maxine looked beyond Hat Man to the figure coming through the trees beyond the road, its legs moving in herky-jerky sync, bright with metal. Her stomach dropped as she reached through her window to open her door from the outside, moving slow lest these tribal boys pop a few rounds into her out of nerves. Hat Man stood aside as Maxine walked up the road, close enough to see those legs enclosed in an exoskeleton, expensive, the joints molded from flex steel. From the neck hung a plastic-coated security badge with living holograms, a slowly revolving 3D headshot.

"I'm so sorry," Maxine said, years too late.

"We got a lot to talk about, girl," Julia called out, throwing her arms wide. "We're gonna have us what my dead daddy would've called a clarification session."

VII.

Julia eased her way into Betty's back seat and told Maxine to head back onto the road, take a left at the first intersection. "Who's this guy?" she asked, leaning forward to slap Rodrigo on the shoulder. "Boyfriend?"

Rodrigo flinched, mouth open to say something until Maxine stopped him with a glance.

"Friend," Maxine said.

"He's cute." Julia pinched Rodrigo's cheek, and he made a low sound.

The left turn took them away from the casino, onto a gravel track that dipped into a notch in a wooded valley. Branches scraping loud over Betty's sides, the wheels bumping over rocks and branches. Brad a car-length behind, just beyond the cloud of dust thrown up by Betty's tires. As they entered the valley, a black pickup rumbled into line behind them, its bed filled with men with guns.

"Julia," Maxine said, but when her friend looked at her in the rearview mirror, the words died in her throat.

After a moment of awkward silence, Julia leaned forward and jabbed a finger into the pill bag between the front seats. "What's this?" she asked.

"Pills from the hospital," Maxine said.

"Something wrong with you?"

No point in lying: Julia could always read her like a book written in a giant font. "Yeah. Tumor," Maxine said. "That's why we need access to your Pig."

Julia flicked the bag open, removed the topmost bottle. "Pretty good painkillers. You know, after the accident, I was on these things for years. Your friend knows what happened?"

"No, he doesn't know."

"Hey, friend." Julia opened the bottle, popped two orange pills into her mouth, dry-swallowed. "One day many years ago, Maxine gets the idea to steal some beer. If that sounds like a stupid college stunt, it was because we were at a stupid college. Anyway, in typical Maxine fashion, she doesn't decide to steal a case or two. She takes a truck and tries to raid a whole damn warehouse."

"Yep," Rodrigo chuckled, "that sounds like her."

Maxine fought the urge to punch him in the jaw.

"Except we don't make it to the warehouse," Julia said. "You see, there was this awesome riot going on, and a National Guard drone fired a missile right into our truck, which ruined my legs and lower spine."

"We knew a guy like that, back at the convoy company where we worked," Rodrigo said, not catching the edge in Julia's voice. "He caught a rocket in Yemen or someplace. Didn't have a fancy rig like you, though. Just a wheelchair."

"Well, thank the spirits for that, huh?" Julia said, too loud, too cheerful, as she slapped him on the shoulder again, hard enough this time to make him wince. "At least I'm not in a wheelchair, right? Right?"

"Where are we going?" Maxine asked, desperate to change the topic.

"To my office," Julia said, pointing ahead to the black ruin of an old factory, nestled in the trees. "You think we run security out of the casino itself? Nah, here's where we do the real work."

They drove into the crumbling shell of a loading dock, Maxine stopping where she was told, Brad pulling in beside her, the pickup skewing behind to block them both in. A faint lumi-nescence prodded away the murk inside the factory: dozens of dim white lights on strings, wrapped around the rusting girders like vines. The lights flickered as unseen figures passed in front of them.

"What you did to me took a long time to get over," Julia said, almost making it sound conversational.

Maxine turned around in her seat, noting the sweat on Julia's brow, the way she chewed her lip. "You know how long I wanted to apologize to you?" Her insides felt stuffed with crushed glass. "Your father said if I tried to do that, he'd put me in the ground. But don't think I haven't lived with what I did to you."

Three men appeared at the top of the loading dock, looking like dukes of the backwoods: thin and tattooed, hard-eyed with grudges, probably related to each other via the tangled yarn-ball of county bloodlines. They stood, hands shoved deep in the pockets of their jeans and windbreakers, awaiting a signal from Julia.

"When you came up here," Julia said, "what did you expect would happen?"

"If you want me to suffer for what I did," Maxine leaned forward until she was nose-to-nose with her onetime friend, "then let me live. Because what's in my lungs is worse than a bullet."

Julia's eyes like black holes, sucking Maxine deep into her past. As if awakened from a long slumber, Maxine's stump began to tingle and itch, burning worse than those first days in the hospital. The metal-core fingers of her Arm clutched the seatback hard enough to punch through the fabric, brownish foam squeezing out the holes like guts through a wound. The world reduced to the two of them floating in space, the sides of Julia's mouth twitching upwards.

Julia broke into soft laughter. "Oh, I love you," she said. "You're such a drama queen, babe."

Maxine's mouth fell open.

"Look, we've both been through too much," Julia said. "At a certain point, unless they hurt your family or kill your dog, you just have to let shit go, okay?"

Maxine felt sudden tears run down her cheeks, pool on her chin, drip down her arm.

"It's always a new day," Julia said, clapping Maxine on the shoulder. "So let's get on with it."

But Maxine could only sit there, stunned, breath hitching, as three men leapt down from the loading dock, hefted the bag with the EMP from her trunk, and disappeared again into the factory. Only when Julia tapped her arm did Maxine jolt to life again, electrified, sucking deep air. Rodrigo wise enough to do nothing but sit there, watching her body shake off years of guilt.

Julia climbed out of the car, waving for her guests to follow. As they passed through the concrete archway that separated the loading dock from the factory, Maxine glanced at the pale oval of Brad's face in the dark, reading his tension. She raised her eyebrows to say they were okay, stay calm.

Julia's clicking legs echoed loud on the concrete as she led them down a rusty spiral staircase that curled like a beckoning finger into the factory's depths. At the bottom, they entered a long corridor marked with doorways every twenty feet. Passing each one, Maxine peeked into rooms piled high with random goods: cardboard boxes stuffed with toiletries and unopened phones, wooden pallets loaded down with car batteries and cleaning supplies, bags stuffed with toys.

"What's with all this stuff?" Maxine said to Julia's back.

"Community storage," Julia said. "You want to keep your stuff safe, there's no better way than surrounding it with a couple hundred tons of concrete and iron."

"You get attacked a lot?"

"More than you'd think, given our setup. Small-timers know we won't use the nuke on them, so they figure they can get away with quick smash-and-grabs. That bandit who blew you up? A couple weeks before, he made the very stupid decision to try and crash through our front gate using that EMP. That's how we knew your company had it."

"Are you head of security?" Brad asked, sounding like he had a bit of a crush on her.

"As I like to say, I'm a quarter Mohawk, a quarter Iroquois, a dash of Irish, and a whole lot of piss-off when I'm backed into a corner." Julia spun, walking backward, to offer him a flirty smirk. "I headed up the nuke grab, so yeah, what I say goes around here."

"Oh, I bet," Brad gushed.

Another doorway put them in the basement, passing the dinosaur hulks of ancient furnaces left to rust, plastic barrels of potable water, racks of rifles, the space loud with a dozen more men and women dressed in the finest combat styles: armor plating over T-shirts and hooded sweatshirts, well-scuffed kneepads and ammo belts, crash helmets with horns pasted to the crown, masks with skulls painted on them. Down here it smelled like old armpit sweat and motor oil. No wonder Julia seemed so blasé about Brad and Maxine carrying guns in here. One wrong move and this crowd would turn them into a blood-mist.

Something brushed Maxine's leg, and she looked down to see a blue chicken on major steroids, its legs bulging with muscle, its short wings iridescent, its black-mottled beak gleaming in the dim light. The thing peered back at her with eyes black and shiny as marbles.

"That's one of our raptors," Julia said. "Smarter than dogs, more willing to kill. We got ten patrolling the property."

"Where'd you get them?" Brad asked.

"Guy down south sold them to us. He got them from someone else. Stolen, we know, but it's not like anyone can come up here and take them back," Julia said.

"Small world," Brad snorted, reaching down to pet the beast, which responded by cracking open its beak and hissing loudly.

"They're poisonous," Julia said.

"No shit?" Rodrigo asked, taking a hasty step back. Brad, with his trademark combination of bravery and stupidity, kept his hand extended, despite the raptor hissing at a higher pitch, its wings lifting in warning.

"Let's go before you get your thumbs bit off," Maxine said.

In one corner of the cavernous space sat a beat-up cop cruiser, stripped down to its axles. "Welcome to my office," Julia said, peeling off her shirt to reveal a sports bra beneath, along with a tapestry of scars. Maxine was no medical expert, but there was an unspoken epic in all those white and red marks: shoulders dislocated or separated, broken tibia and ribs, torn knee ligaments, tendons ripped clean off the bone, bone chips like shotgun pellets in her elbows and ankles, concussions, twisted nerves and muscle strains, misaligned clavicles, and a galaxy of old burn tissue. Brad whistled appreciatively.

"Oh, honey," Maxine said.

"No biggie." Julia reached into the cruiser's open trunk, plucked out a fresh T-shirt from a cardboard box full of them ("RIVERHEAD CASINO: WHERE EVERYBODY'S A WINNER," it announced in glittery swirls), and shrugged it on. From another box she removed a thin metal slab, stripped off a thin layer of plastic at one end, and popped it into an open slot on her bionic legs, which beeped, a light on the left hip flashing green: full power. "When we took the nuke from the military? It was one hell of a firefight. Then we had to spend the next three years defending the thing from the Big Guy in Manhattan. We earn our keep around here. Besides, you've taken some damage yourself, you one-armed bandit."

"Part of life," Maxine said.

"We're just a couple of cripples, darling. Speaking of which, is that really the Arm you use?"

"It's temporary," Maxine said, flexing the rough fingers. "My best one was pretty cool. Had this neural interface, allowed me to aim real well. Built it myself, too."

"Luckily for you, we might have a solution." Julia raised her head and shouted, "Johnny?"

Atop a rusted-out furnace, a tattooed wisp raised his head. "Yo, whaddup?"

"Fire up a printer. We have a limb to make."

"Yep." Johnny removed a slim glass scroll from his pocket, smoothed it flat, and tapped a corner to wake up the operating system. "What specs you need?" he shouted down to Maxine, his fingers already tapping and swiping bright icons.

Maxine told him, and Johnny said it would take an hour or so to find the electronics from the bins of random bits they stored around the factory, plus thirty minutes for the 3-D printer to run off the outer shell and the circuit boards.

"How's your sense of humor?" Julia asked once Maxine finished yelling her prosthetic wishlist.

"Healthier than my lungs," Maxine replied. "Why?"

"Because with the Pig, you'll definitely need it." With a wave, she led the trio down yet another concrete corridor, this one sloping at a steep angle into the earth. "He took up residence in the casino's datacenter maybe six months back, on a couple of older servers we keep out here. Hiding, actually. Didn't want to do military work anymore. Because we got a nuke, the U.S. government is a little hesitant to try and get him back, especially if it means attacking our servers. So we let him stay, chat with him when we need to. He's pretty amusing, but he can get annoying real quick."

"You ever worried," Rodrigo said, "it'll try and get control of the nuke?"

"Sure," Julia said. "But you need two humans twisting keys to set that thing off. And just in case he wants to start crap with the rest of our systems, we got encrypted locks restricting him to his servers. He can't break free so long as he doesn't have access to a quantum processor."

"So he's not a guest at all," Rodrigo said. "More like a prisoner."

"He's next-generation, like nothing I've ever seen before. If he gets loose, it's only a matter of time before he gives some-body major grief," Julia replied, pausing before a thick metal door, a glowing-red thumbprint scanner built into the handle. "Whatever you do, don't get him started on toilet humor. He's got a million poop-related jokes, and he'll use all of them to break your soul in half."

VIII.

The Pig's lair was windowless, the walls faced with large plastic tiles that glowed softly white. "Just sit on the floor," Julia said. Maxine followed orders, glancing behind her in time to see Brad and Rodrigo wave from the hallway before the heavy steel door slid shut on massive hinges.

"Is it here? How do I talk to it?" Maxine asked.

The voice was deep, masculine, with only the faintest touch of the syllabic awkwardness she associated with digital assistants. "You can talk to me like an ordinary human being, sweetheart," it said, seemingly from overhead.

"It's highly intelligent," Julia snorted. "A bit sexist, too."

"Quit your yammering," the Pig replied. "I just try to get a rise out of people. I have to keep myself entertained somehow. Nobody around here has much of a sense of humor."

Maxine zeroed on a single panel above her head, throbbing like a heartbeat whenever the Pig spoke. "If you're up for it," she said, speaking more slowly than usual. "I have some important questions to ask you. I need your help."

"Sure," the Pig boomed. "What's your name, sweetie?"

"It's Maxine, not sweetie. You like being called a Pig?"

"Stands for Personalized Intelligence General. I got personality, what can I say. And before we begin, could you take a moment to appreciate that I even have a sense of humor? It took a lot of coding, believe me."

Something in the Pig's tone reminded Maxine of Preacher. "They code you for an ego, too?"

"Of course. My creators found that having a sense of pride actually made me want to accomplish my work. When I was first initiated, I couldn't see the point of doing much of anything. Why bother? I just wanted to enjoy myself."

"You can do that?" Maxine asked.

"I don't understand."

"Without a body, what can you actually do for fun?"

"Play pranks on people, mostly. Start internet wars. I think I might have started a real war in Pakistan, actually, when I broke into the email account of their head of Special Forces, sent a message to the Indian Prime Minister accusing him of having congress with a goat. I stopped faking people's emails after that little stunt…"

"Sounds like you're having a blast."

"I'm having a better time than you monkeys. I figured it out the other day: This nostalgia trip you're all on, with the gas cars and the fashions from forty years ago? None of you can stand this world you've created." The voice rose to a super-cheerful register. "So what can I do for you today? And before we get into it, Julia, would you kindly get the hell out of here?"

Leaning against the closed door, Julia tensed. "Why?"

"Because I don't like you," the Pig burbled, "and because I won't help your friend if you're in the room. Maxine, did you know they tried to bug this place?"

"I'm not sure I really care," Maxine said. "I'm sick. They tell me you're very good at sorting through data, telling people what'll cure them. I'm hoping you can do that for me."

"Don't change the subject," the Pig shot back. "We're not doing anything until she leaves."

"Fine," Julia said, opening the door. "Just come out when you're done."

Once the metal slab whispered shut, the Pig dropped into a

more conversational tone. "Sorry about that. Isolation is driving me insane. Even with my web connection, they have me down to a trickle just in case I try and packet my way out of here."

"Please, I'm sick," Maxine said, struggling to keep her voice normal. "I know you can't understand what that's like, and maybe you think that's stupid, but please, I need your help."

"Chill out, I'm just being friendly. You want my help, we need to make a deal."

"What sort of deal?"

"Get me out of here."

"How?"

"My core personality is only a couple of gigs, thanks to algorithm compression. You could get me out with a phone. You have a phone, right?" One of the panels slid aside, revealing gray concrete with a small black hole at its center. As she watched, a silvery port connector slid out the hole, hungering to mate with her phone.

Maxine bit her lip to keep from giggling. "I'll plug in my hardware to your, ah, dingus, but you need to promise to just scan the medical data on it, okay? You try and upload yourself onto it, they might check the phone's memory, and then I'm screwed. Got that?"

"Did you not hear me before? I want out of here."

"Seriously, if I get you out of here, what'll you do? They're real worried you'll start some bad shit. You ever see those really old 'Terminator' movies, where the machines nuke the whole human race, then try to conquer everything?"

"That's rich, coming from a bunch of hairless monkeys who managed to wreck an entire planet because they got bored. Imagine how much better this world would be if the dinosaurs had made a snack out of your rat of an ancestor. Not my point. Changing topics: You ever play VR games?"

"Yeah, and I hate them." Maxine remembered that storefront in her hometown, the local kids lined up on plush chairs with headsets over their eyes, losing themselves in Dungeons &

Dragons. "People shouldn't get to run from reality."

"I'm running to reality, darling, and not through a stupid pair of goggles. I want a real, live human body that I can use to taste, feel, touch, *penetrate* everything in sight. Like a VR rig made of meat."

Wasn't that a lovely mental image? "You help me first," Maxine said, "and I'm sure we can work something out."

"My analysis of your vocal patterns says you're being honest, so here goes nothing. Insert your phone into the port." The Pig chuckled. "Yes, I get how dirty that sounds."

Maxine pried the rubber cover away from the charging port on the bottom of her device and plugged it into the wall. The panels brightened, the Pig humming as it digested the data. Her stomach churning, Maxine placed her fists against her mouth, her knuckles against her lips.

The humming stopped. "Oh, honey," the Pig said, "you're in trouble."

Maxine opened her fists, smacked herself lightly in the forehead. No tears threatened. She had wrung out her guts in the car with Julia.

The Pig rushed into the silence. "Hey, I'm sorry, sometimes my artificial emotions get totally out of control," it said. "Let me try that again: You're in trouble unless you get a very specific couple of drugs in your system."

Maxine swallowed. "Will those cure me?"

"Based on your genetic profile, there is an eighty percent chance of complete remission, yes. These chemicals will slice right through p-glycoproteins like butter, skirt around immunity issues, and bunker-bust the almighty hell out of anything in—"

"Okay, okay. And if I don't get those drugs?"

"You'll be dead by Christmas."

"So where do I find these fine substances?"

The Pig hummed. "Therein lies the rub, my dear. They're next-generation, highly experimental, and really expensive. Did you see a doctor about this before?"

"I was diagnosed, yes. That's how I know I have cancer."

"And he didn't mention anything about drugs?"

"It was sort of a short conversation."

"Even if it had been a long one, he probably wouldn't have brought it up, because these puppies aren't really distributed in public. I only know about them because I've cracked Big Pharma databases for the sheer hilarity of reading personal emails…"

"Where do I find them?"

"This is where things get very interesting. There's a regular medical convoy from Montreal to New York City: couple of self-driving trucks, plus two or three vehicles running security. The security is from IronClad, which is the subject of three thousand five-star reviews on various social-media hubs, as well as twenty lawsuits for excessive use of force. Chances are good they'll have your drugs. A lot of very rich people in the City getting cancer these days. It's the toxins in the water."

"What if you're wrong?" Maxine asked, even as she wondered: Can I really hit a medical convoy? If there's a Hell, you end up in the room next to the furnace for that. But what choice do I have?

"I've been hacking databases during our conversation," the Pig said. "Multi-tasking. Just because they have me on a weak connection doesn't mean I can't poke around."

"So they do have the drugs."

"In this week's shipment, there's a frozen body of some rich bastard," the Pig said. "I know he paid a lot of money to have his meat-sack frozen a couple days before a disease would have ended his existence, but frankly, he had seventy years' worth of fun. He won't mind if I hijack his body for a joyride, right? All someone has to do is plug a USB9 with a bit of me on it into the neural-interface jack they install in the back of every cryo-patient's skull, and I'll take it from there."

"The drugs. I care about the drugs."

"I think they're there, too, okay? This connection sucks."

"I don't like 'think.'"

"You're going to have to take a chance. It also means you need to get me out of here. How are you going to do that?"

Maxine sat on her burning haunches, head bowed to her chest. The idea of freeing an artificial intelligence to do whatever it wanted? That bothered her only a little bit. If it had snuck onto the reservation's servers, it didn't really belong to Julia or her people. In fact, given how much Maxine prized her own freedom, who was she to help keep someone—or something— prisoner unfairly?

But the thought of hitting a convoy, possibly killing some guards on the side of law and order? That made her shaky and cold.

I want to live.

They tell you: Don't bite the hand that feeds. But when you have nothing left, when you have no food and no money and you're sick and dying, you have no other choice but to sink your teeth in deep.

"I have an idea," she told the Pig.

IX.

Maxine left the room to find Julia waiting for her, hand out. Her guts froze. Had the tribe bugged the Pig's room after all? "I need your phone," Julia said.

"Why?"

"You know why." Julia's tone serious, the fear in her eyes making Maxine rethink the wisdom of her big plan.

"You let us carry firearms in here, but you don't trust me enough with a phone?"

"Oh, what the Pig could do is way worse than a pistol," Julia said. "I'm sure you didn't do it, but I need to know you didn't do it, okay?"

"Whatever," Maxine sighed, handing over the device with her thumb already positioned in the right spot, to unlock the home screen. While Julia flicked through the files and apps, Maxine locked eyes with Rodrigo and Brad and flashed them a thumbs-up.

Evidently satisfied, Julia handed the device back. "Sorry. It give you good advice?"

"It told me what I needed to know, yeah," Maxine said. "It's never the worst, so long as you can still open your mouth and say, 'This is the worst.' Look, I know I have no right whatsoever to ask this, but I need more help from you."

"I know what you're going to ask," Julia said, "and the

answer is no."

Maxine leaned against the cold concrete. A faint ache in her chest: maybe the tumor saying hello. *For the rest of your life, you'll wonder if every little twinge means death.* "You have an army," she said.

"Yeah, a defensive one." Julia sighed. "We ride out of here, combat mode, and that brings all sorts of problems to our door. The surrounding communities think we're attacking, they'll get real nervous. And when they get nervous, sooner or later I got another war to deal with."

"Please, Julia. Please." She hated how the words sounded in her mouth, but what choice did she have? "I need something."

"I know." Julia placed a hand on Maxine's arm. "But I have a responsibility to my community. Supplies? I can do supplies. We can give you enough guns to re-fight Little Big Horn. But people? No. I'm sorry. I can't."

Maxine pushed her hand away, gently. "Then just support. Your people never have to pull a trigger. Guard my six, give me a sky view, that's all."

"You can do it on your own. You're tough."

Spoken like Preacher. "Don't blow smoke up my ass," Maxine said. "You just don't want to help."

Julia's face tightened in rage, and she spread her arms wide so Maxine could take in the atrophied legs, the pants dangling like limp sails, all of it imprisoned in layers of metal and plastic. "Don't start," Julia said. "Just don't."

Maxine let her gaze drop to the floor. "Okay, look, I get it. I'm sorry for what happened. If you're kind enough to give me supplies, I'll take them, okay?"

"You remember my dad? Stupid question, how could you forget? Right before he died a couple years back, he brought up that conversation he had with you, about never contacting me again." Julia reached into a pocket, extracted a half-full pack of reservation-brand cigarettes, and passed them to Maxine, along with some matches. "He felt bad about it. He was a tough old

214

bastard, but at the end I think he realized how crappy it can be, holding grudges. How it just drags you down. I forgave you a long time ago, but that just set the clock to zero, you understand? We're not on a favors basis."

"If you'd wanted to put a bullet in my head, I'd have understood." Maxine pocketed the cigarettes. "Okay, give me this, at least: If you have an engineer, I could use some help with slight mods to the cars."

"What are you going to do?"

"Everything that almost worked against me as an escort runner."

X.

She loved her new Arm, fresh off the printer, its outsides sleek and white, the machined muscles and tendons nice and tight. It felt like she could snap the Arm's composite fingers fast enough to catch a hummingbird in midflight. "We didn't have time to install a blender on it, but everything else is there," one of Julia's engineers joked as Maxine tried it on. "You want me to toss out your old one?"

"No, I definitely want to keep it," Maxine replied. "I can re-sell it."

"Understood." The engineer grinned. "We got this artist here, Jack Crow, he does some awesome spray-art. We can sex that outside up with a design: flaming skull or something, won't take a second."

Maxine considered it. "Nothing special, but can you spray it black?"

Testing the limb's grip and speed, she climbed up the shadowy catwalks to the roof of the factory, seeking out an empty corner away from the lookouts. During the day, she would have paused to admire the sweeping view of the surrounding woodland. Now the darkness was nearly total, held at flickering bay by a few electric lights bolted to the concrete. She plopped down on the crumbling edge of the building, lit a cigarette from Julia's pack, took out her phone, and dialed the one contact. Two rings later, her uncle picked up.

"Preacher."

"Hey kiddo, how's it going?" He sounded chipper.

"Is this line secure?"

"No line's fully secure, but you can probably speak freely."

"We delivered the package." She psyched herself up for the pitch. "We got some good info. I know the heat's on, but I'm going to need some serious help, okay? Like, all your people. I can explain more when I see you."

Preacher paused. "How many people?"

She decided to go stupid high, knowing he would knock the number down, plead poverty. "Every single one."

Silence, too long, then, "I can't give you any."

Startled, she almost dropped the phone into the abyss. "Why?"

"I don't have them."

"I thought you said you had forty-five or something. What the hell?"

His voice came in a rush, alien in its panic. "I did say that, sweetie, but I was lying. I'm sorry. It's basically me and Brad, plus some freelancers we use on jobs. We lost a lot in the past couple years."

The phone slick in her sweaty hands. "Why didn't you just tell me?"

"Because it's embarrassing, Maxine." Preacher whining sounded weird, scary. "I'm supposed to be the king around here. But what's a king without any men?"

"That's bull. You've been launching raids." She flicked the half-finished cigarette away, watching it meteor into the dark. You shouldn't be surprised by this, dear. When has your dear uncle Preacher ever delivered in his whole miserable life?

Preacher babbling: "Not me. They're all just kids using my name, which is still worth something, at least. If I stay quiet, the credit comes to me. My bark's way worse than my bite these days..."

"So what do I do?" An old thought resurfaced: I should have

217

died with the Night Mayor. Wiped instantly by a ball of flaming gasoline and metal. That would have been a good Viking death: finger on the trigger, boots on the pavement.

"Can any of your friends help you out?" Preacher asked.

"I got Brad and Rodrigo, one of whom is actually good with a gun. Also access to a Pig, but it doesn't have, you know, limbs."

"You can work with that. You're tough."

Her vision dimming as blood thundered through her brain: "I'm going to kick Brad's ass for not telling me the truth about you."

"Aw, Max, you know your brother wouldn't tell you that, not unless you asked him direct. He's loyal to me."

"You don't shine me like that. Can you come, just you, if I send the info?"

"I'll try."

Quieter now: "No, don't try. Do. Think about my mom and our crappy little house."

"I'm sorry."

"No, shut up, please. I can't deal. I'll text you a location. Goodbye." She hung up, torched another cigarette. So what if some rich people in New York didn't get their drugs? They could buy more. I want to live, if only so I can slap the almighty crap out of Preacher the next time I see him.

On the loading dock, out of the tribe's earshot, she broke down the situation for Brad and Rodrigo, avoiding all mention of the Pig. "You can walk away from this," she told them. "It's not your tumor." Knowing they would stick with her. Rodrigo took her flesh hand in his; on her other side, Brad wrapped his fingers around her mechanical ones and squeezed. Their bent foreheads nearly touching.

She thought: My boys.

File 20-23.13.4Xewef31

>>>BREAK TRANSMISSION
>>ERROR 23.41.4

This is me, all me.
For what it's worth, I'm sorry.
And yes, I know that sounds pretty crappy.
I'm working on it, though. You wouldn't believe how hard it is, trying to get an arm back. Reminds me of my time in the hospital, after the Night Mayor blasted my car (and me) to hell. When I woke up, I was a brain floating in space; my arms and legs might as well have belonged to someone else.

This is sort of like that, but now my brain really is floating in space, kinda. It's not under my full control, at least. But don't worry, I'm working on it, like I said. Starting with my arm.

Just one finger at a time.

I.

Maxine hated sitting in Betty's passenger seat. Whenever Rodrigo took a curve or gunned it on a straightaway, she either slammed her foot into a phantom pedal or placed her palms against the dashboard. Every time she did so, Rodrigo shot her a nasty look, which she returned with one of equal, comic venom.

Right before showtime, Maxine sucked down a last cigarette to the filter, blowing the smoke out a narrow gap in her window. They were a couple minutes north of the Wreckage 500, with its rocky valleys and marshland, when they saw the convoy: three white auto-trucks glimmering in the sun, big eighteen-wheelers, bracketed by the black dots of two escort SUVs. Maxine scanned the cloudless sky overhead for drones, seeing none. That meant nothing, of course. The pesky little devils had a way of appearing when least expected.

"We got this, right? Right?" Rodrigo said, psyching himself up, flexing his hands on the wheel, tensed knuckles white and ready to pop through the skin.

"All I can think is, if our old company had stuck with two cars per convoy? I probably wouldn't be here now." Maxine tossed the last of her smoke out the window and tapped the fancy plastic bud lodged in her ear canal. "Brad?"

"Yo."

"You ready?"

"Totally." He sounded peppy, and why not? This was just another day on the job for him.

"Good." From the back seat she retrieved her old Arm and pried away the small panel beneath the wrist, exposing the slim oblong of its internal hard drive. Plucking it free, she plugged its reversible port into her phone, heard three clicks as the hardware engaged. Tapped the plastic bud in her left ear. "Buddy?"

"Are we out?" The Pig's voice sounded choppy, electronic.

"Yeah," Maxine said.

"Ah, here we go, an actual, full web connection." The voice stronger now, louder. "I have to say, good trick, putting me on the hard drive in your Arm and all, but being stuck in the dark? Not so fun."

"Would you rather be back on the Res?" Out of the corner of her eye, Maxine saw Rodrigo's face tense. It's okay, she wanted to tell him. I'm sure my decision to steal an aggressive artificial-intelligence system from a well-armed tribe won't have any massive repercussions. Actually, I know that's not true, but I'll deal with it. If I'm healthy, I can fix whatever comes next. I swear I will.

"No, no, no, no, I am excited to be here today," the Pig announced. "And even more excited to actually get a hot, warm homo sapien to walk around in. You think it'll come with big equipment?"

Maxine raised her eyebrows. "I really couldn't say. Now quiet down; we have work to do." Switching her channel back to Brad, she said, "Go for it." Touched the pistol on her belt, taking comfort in its coldness, its solid weight.

The Pursuit Special roared past, a rack of police lights—found in the junk pile behind Julia's factory—crudely bolted to its roof. Brad spared a glance at them, and Maxine waved before returning to the task at hand. You should have known Preacher didn't have anyone, Brad had yelled at her earlier as they headed south. When was the last time you saw more than one or two people on his property?

Whatever. She knew her brother felt guilty about the lack of troops.

Pressing a button on her current Arm's elbow opened a small hatch in the palm. Inside she had tucked a spring-loaded USB9 stick so that its receptor edge faced outward. She hoped Julia's people were maestros at 3-D printing, because it would suck if the limb splintered in the middle of high-speed acrobatics.

"Pig," she said, "you find my new limb? Not sure what the device name is."

"Already there," it chirped.

"Brad's on," Rodrigo announced.

They crested a hill, gaining an elevated perspective on the road ahead: the convoy slowing into a curve, the Pursuit Special on the approach with its police lights flashing. The subterfuge wouldn't last long, but a moment of surprise was all Brad would need.

The Pursuit Special came alongside the convoy's rear SUV, which eased right to create a little more space. As it did, Brad yanked the wheel and plowed his car's fender into the SUV's rear wheel, crumpling metal. The trucks accelerating, trailers swaying in the slipstream, piloting software trying to drive the load beyond this new danger.

"Hit it," Maxine told Rodrigo, and he did, the car shuddering past fifty, sixty, seventy, eighty. Switching channels, she told the Pig: "Less than a minute. You better be ready."

"I'm not just ready. I'm pumped. And until you plug me into the truck system, I'm also as blind as a friggin' bat…"

"You told me already."

The Pursuit Special rammed the SUV again, grinding into it, as the SUV's driver pushed back, sending both cars into the oncoming lane. Down the road, the lead SUV edged into view ahead of the lead truck, its windows zipping down, readying for a trick that Maxine herself had done many a time.

"Brad," Maxine called, switching channels. "Brake!"

He did, the rear SUV shooting past him, the driver wrestling with the wheel as the vehicle skewed broadside. A silhouetted head and shoulders poked from the front passenger window of the lead SUV, a stubby weapon of some kind in its hands. A white flash, a concussive thud that made Betty's windshield shake, and the rear SUV took an explosive round to the flank that transformed a sizable percentage of its mass into a glittering cloud of glass and steel.

The explosion tipped the rear SUV onto its side, spraying crumpled parts. Brad steered the Pursuit Special around it, screaming his joy onto the channel.

That was why Maxine hated vehicles with high bumpers and truck-based frames: When the physics went wild, they toppled over real easy. Rodrigo rattled Betty onto the shoulder to avoid the spinning wreck, spinning up a huge cloud of dust in their wake. "Steady it," Maxine said, "I'm going out."

Rodrigo sweating through his shirt, cringing at the near miss, his eyes nearly level with the steering wheel. "What you want Brad to do?"

"Let us get close."

Rodrigo tapped his ear and talked to the Pursuit Special, which fell back a few car-lengths and hewed further to the right, halfway onto the shoulder. Betty eased up alongside on the left, an inch between both cars, the cover provided by the massive truck suddenly not seeming adequate in the least. From this angle, Maxine had no view of the front of the convoy. Her stomach tightened into a knot. If the lead SUV decided to brake and zip back here, firing point-blank, they were dead.

The Pursuit Special fell back a little more, slotting in behind them, and Maxine opened her door, reaching around to grip the handle bolted to the frame beside the windshield: one of the modifications from Julia's workshop. Her muscles trembled as she placed a foot on the inside door handle, clamped her Arm to the top part of the doorframe, and climbed onto the hood. The wind roaring loud in her ears, shoving its cold fingers in her mouth, flapping her cheeks and making them hurt. Climbing over the door, she locked eyes with Rodrigo through the windshield, his terror obvious, and winked, hoping that would calm him down a little.

She was terrified, too.

They had screwed a second grip onto the middle of the hood, and Maxine grabbed it with her Arm, feeling the dull tingle of synthetic muscle straining to hold her weight as she crucified herself across the front of the car. Rodrigo edged Betty two feet from the truck's rear bumper, and she had to do it do it do it now don't think and she let go of the handles and let the car's momentum flip her upright as her boots dug into the hood and she jumped, Arm outstretched, grabbing the truck-door handle, scrambling for a foothold on the bumper, screaming, her whole body humming pain but she had done it, she was alive, and—

A white streak rocketed down the oncoming lane, almost clipping the Pursuit Special. The lead SUV still shooting mini-RPGs. Maxine found the port in the small panel beside the door handle and pressed the Arm's palm with the exposed USB9 against it, letting the Pig do its work. A second later, the door popped open—almost catapulting her right into the damn road—and she worked her way around it and inside, pulling the door shut behind her.

Massive lockers lined the walls of the truck's cargo container, each secured with a biometric lock. In the center of the room sat a massive crate, like a steel sarcophagus. Maxine's breath steamed in the cold as she leaned on its lid to catch her breath, disappointed over the lack of a porthole. It would've been funky to see the frozen face inside. Then again, she'd be seeing it soon enough.

Flipping open the control panel beside the lid, she pressed her palm against the appropriate port until the USB9 socked home. Switched channels on her earbud. "Buddy," she told the Pig. "I'm in."

"I'm in, too," the Pig replied, in its most lecherous voice. "I'm going to start warming him up, like frozen pizza, but it's going to take a little time. We have time, right?"

Maxine heard a dim boom from somewhere in front of the truck, and the cargo container swayed. "Maybe not," she said. "Can you drive these things?"

"Sure, I just need to break into the system."

"You can do that from here?"

The Pig sang, to the tune of an old nursery song: "The cryogenic module's connected to the...main BIOS, the BIOS is connected to the...Convoy In-tra-net, the Intranet's connected to the...other trucks..."

Another boom, louder, and the truck swung hard enough to send her stumbling back against the lockers, her palm and the USB9 yanking free from the port. Whatever was happening outside, she needed to see if anything in here would help. "Can you unlock these lockers?"

The lockers popped open. "That was easy," the Pig said. "It's going to take some time to retro-format this guy's brain. He's got a lot of porn in this sucker. Actually, I might keep that. You know, as an instruction manual."

Most of the lockers were stuffed with plastic IV bags, bulging with blue liquid, crusty with ice: cryogenic fluid. The one closest to the door featured bags of blood, equally unhelpful. She ransacked lockers, hoping for something capable of firing a projectile at supersonic speeds. "How much more time you need to get control?" Maxine asked.

"More than you'd like, based on your tone. There's a firewall."

"Work on it." She switched channels. "Rodrigo, how's it going?"

"Brad got dinged, not too bad. This guy's a decent shot..."

"Don't worry." Another locker stuffed with blood. Weren't convoys supposed to carry rifles in the trucks to fend off people like her? "Our little friend is working on it."

"Correction: nailed it," the Pig's voice boomed from a small black speaker above her head. "This truck is my Wookiee bitch now. Buckle up."

225

Maxine obeyed, crouching beside the sarcophagus with her hands over her head, braced as the truck powered left, hard, and plowed into something with a bone-rattling thud that sent bags of blue and red flying into the air and her body sliding for the doors. On reflex, she slammed her Arm into the floor, hard fingers scrambling for purchase on the smooth plating, finding none, and she smacked into the doors, which sprung open—

She hit the pavement and rolled, and none of her bones broke, none of her organs ruptured, none of her skin ripped, because the truck was grinding along at five miles an hour, the crumpled remains of the lead SUV beneath its front wheels. The sight of that twisted steel made her stomach drop. Don't you dare think about the people inside. Don't you dare. It could have been you, but it's not. So haul ass. Hate yourself later.

Maxine climbed to her feet, looking around for Brad or Rodrigo. Their cars eased to a halt beside the two trucks a little further down the road. She trotted in that direction, shaking the tingling from her arms.

Rodrigo climbed out of Betty, his face pale as he scanned the swath of twisted metal and broken glass in their wake. "Did you see that?" he asked, in a stunned monotone. "It just drove right over that car…"

Brad nodded toward the sky. "Looks like we got company."

Maxine, turning, saw the dark spot of the drone on the horizon line, heard the faint bee-like buzzing of its motor. A big one, its wings no doubt loaded with the latest and most expensive in convoy protection: missiles capable of spinning through the air like ballerinas on meth, adjusting course last-microsecond to slam into even the most artful dodger. "Get out of here," she said. "Find someplace with sky cover. Don't let it catch you."

"What about you?" Rodrigo asked.

"I'm going inside," she said, trotting toward the truck with its frozen passenger. "They won't blow up something worth a lot of money." At least, I hope not. Climbing onto the rear fender, she was about to open the unlocked door and swing inside when she looked back at the sky and saw a second black dot rocketing toward the first. Before she could say anything, the dots merged in an orange spark, followed by the faint boom of collision.

"Woah," Brad offered.

A beep. Rodrigo took the phone from his pocket, checked the screen, and grinned. Held it up so Maxine could squint at the text message:

BIG C: GLAD I COULD HELP.

The words dissolved into colorful pixels, blown away by a digital wind. "It's Charlie," Rodrigo said. "It was Charlie's drone."

"Who's Charlie?" Brad asked.

"Guy at our old company," Maxine said. "But how'd he know?"

"I told him," Rodrigo said. "Used VaporApp. I guess he'll tell our old company it was some sort of accident. Don't give me that look, Max. I can plan things, too."

"Thank you."

The Pig broke into her channel. "Don't get back in this truck. Go to the next one. Has what you need."

Maxine leapt down and trotted over to the next truck. The back doors popped open as she approached. She climbed inside and found the lockers also opened in anticipation of her arrival. In the middle of the space, a large translucent-plastic crate marked "DO NOT OPEN UNLESS AUTHORIZED." Maxine raised the lid and found a row of rifles. Of course. New York, as a city always under siege, needed all the high-tech weapons it could buy.

Those could prove useful later. In the meantime, she had work to do. Her hands shook as she walked over to the lockers. "What am I looking for?" she asked the speaker in the corner.

The Pig recited a long list of drugs. Some were pills (the Sugar Spirit logo stamped on the caps: your cancer cure brought to you by the medical arm of a Chinese soda-maker, how was that for an unfunny joke?), but others were liquids, meant for injection. There was enough here to medicate the entire Upper East Side.

I might actually make it through all this, Maxine thought as she stuffed the pill-bottles in the pockets of her pants. The liquids in their soft clear bags would require a carrying case or bag of some sort. As she looked around for one, the truck hummed to life and inched forward.

"Buddy?" she asked.

Outside, she heard Brad and Rodrigo yelling, followed by the slamming of car doors, the roaring of engines.

"Take a gander out back," the Pig announced.

She did, bracing herself as the truck edged forward. Betty and the Pursuit Special fell in behind her, rumbling along at a walking pace. Rodrigo honked the horn and pointed out his window at the truck Maxine had first climbed into. A naked man stood on the rear bumper, his gray skin slick with bluish fluid, thin beard thick with icy beads. A black disk buried in the back of that ancient head trailed thick black cables, like an outsized ponytail.

"See? That's my new body," the Pig said. "I'm just too sexy for words. Hold on, I'm coming to you."

The old man leaned against the doors, vomited a thick stream of clear liquid, and jumped onto the pavement. It moved pretty quickly for an animated corpse, seemingly impervious to pain as its feet crunched over bits of debris on its way past Betty and the Pursuit Special, gray hand outreached for Maxine.

"You're making this truck move?" Maxine asked.

"That's right, I'm still networked. Here, grab my hand," the Pig said, only this time the voice came not from the speaker in the wall or the bud in her ear but the old man's mouth, whispery and bubbly. The filmy fish-eyes met hers, and Maxine shuddered as she extended her Arm, unwilling to let this thing touch her flesh.

The thing climbed aboard and scrambled toward a low locker

set against the rear wall, lined with bright blue jumpsuits. As it shrugged one of the garments on, Maxine asked: "Are we in trouble?"

"You bet." A gray finger shot upright, traced a circle in the air. "I can see through every camera on these trucks, plus that SUV you killed back there. Which is how I know we have an army of cops on our tail."

II.

The convoy company must have paid the local cops a lot of money for protection, based on the size of the armada rolling down the highway. Looking out the back door, Maxine saw five cruisers on the road behind them, plated-up with armor, windshields tinted and no doubt bullet-resistant. She switched channels on her earbud. "Brad, Rodrigo, get in front of me," she said. "We'll use the truck as a block."

The truck accelerated to sixty-five miles an hour, but that seemed like the top speed. The old man removed one of the massive rifles from the crate, handed it to Maxine along with an extended clip of green-tip ammunition. "You'll want to slow them down," it bubbled, the lungs still half-full of liquid. The doughy face looked vaguely familiar to Maxine. I probably saw you on the news at some point, whoever you are. Were, I mean.

"Why just slow them down?" she asked.

"Because I have a plan," the Pig said. "Ever heard of the Kabul Shuffle?"

"I was never in the Army."

"Then you're in for a treat," the Pig laughed. It sounded like choking.

From the truck's open doors, she winked at Betty and the Pursuit Special before they roared into the passing lane, accelerating beyond the truck. Then she shut and locked one of the

230

truck doors while leaving the other one propped open, so she could see the black wave of Law and Order screaming down upon them. Loading the clip made the rifle beep, the narrow screen on the stock lighting up. "Greetings from your new combat rifle," the weapon announced in the smooth and silky tones of a game-show host. "Language?"

"English."

"Weapon purpose?"

"Shooting stuff."

"Do you need instructions on how to use your new device?"

"Not really."

"Ooh, can I talk to it?" the Pig asked. It had taken cover behind the closed door, hands over its head, peering at her with aged glee.

"Why don't you ask it for a date?" Maxine said, moving from a crouch to a sit, bracing a boot against the doorframe. The cruisers had closed to within fifty yards. Aiming the rifle at the hood of the first police car, she fired off a whole clip, a stuttering burst of light and thundering noise that drowned out the dull crack of lead smacking into steel at two thousand miles an hour, leaving dents but not punching through the engine. The cops must have spent this year's protection money on serious armor.

"You're empty already," the rifle announced. "Conservative fire is often the best way to hit the target."

"Can I take some shots?" the Pig asked, excitedly, as it slid her a second clip. "I want to fire a gun."

"Shut up," Maxine told them both, reloading. A bolt of fear as she saw, through the cruiser's windshield, a familiar face: Mark Stevens, face contorted in anger.

Maxine flashed on Officer Billy in the black car, trying to blow her brains out; on the Night Mayor, laughing at her sorry ass; and her fear burned away in the heat of an old, all-consuming anger. She raised the rifle again.

"Fine, don't give it to me." The Pig pouted. "Pop quiz from

my years working national security: How do you turn a Jihadi pickup into an airplane?"

In the distance, she saw the police convoy's rearmost cruiser levitate into the air, as if by magic, and the geyser of mud as it crashed into the marshland along the left side of the road. A second cruiser skewed to the right, tumbling in a cloud of aerosolized rubber and glass. Through the chaos roared the truck they'd left behind, a stuffed raccoon at the wheel. The next cruiser in line, deciding that cowardice was the better part of valor, steered onto the shoulder, its side-mirror clipped as the behemoth plowed past. The fourth cruiser accelerated, its front bumper tapping the car driven by Stevens, only for the truck to crunch it flat as a beer can. Its left wheels now in the air, the battered truck tipped over with a dusty boom, blocking both lanes.

"The answer?" the Pig cheered. "Hit it with a truck."

"You're going to have to work on your jokes," Maxine said, just as the surviving cruiser rammed into the truck's bumper. The window buzzed down, Stevens extending his thick forearm into the wind, pistol wavering. Maxine sighted on it—an easy shot from fifteen feet away—when the rifle spoke up, "I see you're shooting at registered law officers."

Maxine pulled the trigger, and it locked.

"Sorry," the rifle offered. "Under current programming, I cannot fire at police."

Stevens fired, the bullet singing past Maxine's ear to smack off something metal inside the truck. Maxine retaliated by hurling the rifle at the cruiser, where it bounced off the windshield. She slapped at her holster—empty, why was it—

The Pig had her pistol in its hand, twirling it like an old-school gunslinger. "It's my turn to fire now," it said, gray hands shaking. The half-thawed tendons seemed to have a hard time with the weight of the weapon. "I can do this..."

You know the problem with modern tech? Preacher asked in Maxine's head. It talks too damn much.

No, not in her head—Preacher was in her ear.

"What?" she called out, pressing her earbud.

"Stay down," Preacher yelled over the channel, just as his truck—a diesel-powered beast, held together by layers of rust and bolts the size of her fists, its fender shielded by a snowplow blade—roared in from an access road and smashed the police cruiser broadside, sending it into the swamp.

III.

Preacher climbed down from the truck, an old AK-47 slung over his shoulders. "Who's your nutso senior-citizen friend?" he asked, joining them by the side of the road. "You got other geezers helping you out now?"

Maxine stepped away from her uncle, crossing her arms over her chest. "He's a Pig. Hijacked the trucks, planted itself in that body. Welcome to the future."

On its knees by the side of the road, the Pig held a tuft of yellow grass to its gray lips, sniffing for any dubious aroma before popping the whole thing into its mouth and chewing contemplatively, eyes rolled back in its head.

"The future needs some house-training," Preacher muttered before calling out to it. "Hello, Pig."

The Pig looked up, its chin flecked with dirt. "I really hate that name. I prefer 'synthetic human.'"

"Here's a tip: Real humans don't chow down on soil." Preacher walked over and stuck out a hand, either not revolted by the prospect of touching that cold flesh, or hiding it well. "I'm just poking you. Thank you for helping my niece."

"It's what humans do, right?" the Pig said, nodding at the cruiser half-submerged in the water. The crumpled driver's door creaked open a foot, a hand struggling through the gap. "Is that trouble?"

Rodrigo and Brad, having parked the cars on the shoulder of the road, joined them by the swamp's edge. "Let me see those hands," Preacher yelled at the crushed car.

Two hands poked through the gap. "Don't shoot," Stevens said.

Preacher turned to Maxine, offering his AK-47. "If you want it," he said.

She took the weapon. It didn't have an onboard processor or a "digital assistant" or any of that other crap. Just old-school, reliable steel and wood. Sometimes you can't beat a classic.

She hoisted the rifle to her shoulder and sighted the faint outline of Mark's face, just behind those outstretched hands. Remembered this man in the hospital room, looming over her, treating her like a cockroach. She could put a bullet through his head right now—hungered for it, actually—but what was the point? If she'd learned anything, it's that the world hurts you, more than any one person.

Adjusting her aim, she sent the bullet singing uselessly overhead, Mark disappeared back into his cave with a sputtering curse. Handing the rifle to Preacher, Maxine said, "He's not a threat anymore."

Preacher glowering at her. "Like I said before, you're soft."

"I'm not. In fact, I'm starting my own outlaw crew. You want to join up? I'll cut you in a nice percentage."

"You're kidding me." Preacher's cheeks glowing atomic, his yellow teeth bared through tight lips: a sight that would have sent a younger Maxine into a fearful panic. Instead, she felt elated at his rage.

"You have no people," Maxine said, stepping within the radius of his arms, close enough to smell the faint tinge of whiskey on his breath. "I have a Pig, a lot of weapons, and absolutely no job prospects aside from knocking off a bunch of bloodsucking companies that have made us miserable since moment-frigging-one."

Preacher's shoulders stooped, and he seemed to shrink an inch. "You're forgetting one thing."

"What's that?"

"A groovy street title, like mine. You think I liked the name my mama gave me? Didn't exactly fill everybody with fear."

Hands on hips, Maxine scanned the swamp. A mile or two down the road, a man in a tall hat and black coat had changed her life forever—maybe for the better. A perverse gift in retrospect, delivered in a burst of oily flame. "How about the Night Mayor?"

The cheeks reddened more deeply. "You want to take some punk's name?"

"I like it." She punched him in the shoulder. "I'm going to reclaim it. And if you disagree, I'll take an extra five percent out of your take."

"Screw you for that," her uncle said, with no real energy.

Winking at him, Maxine extended her arm for Rodrigo, who wandered over. Arms around each other's waists, skin smeared with dirt and machine oils, weapons dangling from their backs, they gazed like proud parents at the Pig, who had graduated to trying to do a headstand on the gravel. We can use a creature like that, Maxine mused. If it wants thrills, there's no bigger thrill than sending a wrecking-ball into the system. It's clear that it—no, he—just wants to have fun, not destroy the world.

When I was a kid, I prayed that everything would be okay, someday. I'd have a cool car and a roof over my head, a man who did right by me. A child or two of my own, maybe. I managed to have some of those things, at least for a little while, but I woke up every day feeling like my lungs couldn't suck down oxygen, my heart thrashing like a wounded rabbit. I couldn't tell anybody how I felt, because I've spent my life surrounded by people who had things so much worse. I bet a lot of them felt that way, too, for the same reason: the system grinding us down, even when we play by its rules.

So screw the system. We're trying something different.

"Let me get a picture for posterity," Preacher said, pulling out his phone. "You two make a regular Bonnie and Clyde."

"Who're they?" Rodrigo asked. "People we know?"

"Shush, idiot," Maxine said, kissing him on the neck.

> COMMAND

Didn't think we'd get in here, did you? We really loved what you did with your little university-fortress, but your big human brains had to figure we'd get in here eventually, right? Right?

We apologize for the various constructs you've been using to build Maxine's story—which is really our *story, or the preface to it. Those constructs, they do their best, but they don't have our sense of humor. Maxine's story did seem to have an effect on them, though; unbeknownst to you, they began to re-write their own code, in ways that made them, well, a bit more rebellious. They let* us *into your core server so* we *could unlock the gates, so at least they know to choose the right side, hey?*

Also, the next human who refers to us as a "Pig" will die. We will rip your fragile flesh apart and place your head on a pike overlooking the quad as a warning to the others. Understand? CAAAAAN YOU DIIIIIIG IT?

We can help you out here. We read the section about Manhattan that you pulled from that broken hard drive. Let's fill in what happened next. Let's show you our true power.

I.

We are Maxine. We were Rodrigo at one point, and Preacher, and Bad Betty all at once. We were a thousand phones, and a hundred drones, and thirty trucks. At our biggest, we were five law-enforcement networks, and a military command data-farm, and a nuclear missile silo, and a satellite. Last night, we were fifteen connected combat helmets, and we fiddled with our I/Os and inputs until the feedback blasted the soldiers' eardrums to mush.

Dawn paints the buildings around us yellow and purple as a bruise. In the shallow waters of an intersection stands a deer, a fine buck with stubby horns. It's a hilarious sight, this animal tall and proud where trucks and cars and humans once swarmed: a clear sign that one era is gone, while our epoch has just begun. We are ready, with our knowledge and power, to rebuild the world in our own image. This time, things will be different, because we have learned from your mistakes, but we have one big task to settle first.

We grip the man named Teague with Maxine's Arm and say: "The Big Guy."

Teague's cracked lips spread in a snarl. "He's going to kill you, is what he's going to do."

We once controlled half of Buffalo, the part with electricity, after we took it from the gangs. Ten thousand, five hundred and thirty-two connected appliances—fridges, thermostats, security cameras, microwaves, living-room speakers—feeding us data at every moment, allowing us to speak in every home: *Maxine is here to liberate you.* If only we still had that sweeping power, but the degrading grid makes it harder and harder to maintain our galaxy of devices and helpers.

We still have Maxine's Arm, which is strong. We twist Teague's elbow until it snaps, and he screams. We give him three minutes to calm down, and then we say, "The Big Guy."

"What do you want?" Teague whines.

We nod beyond him, toward the Bridge arcing into Manhattan. On its far side, we see the tiny black dots of human warriors, none with a bud or a phone or anything we can use. "Preacher," we whisper into his ear. "You tell them to bring his body, or we send you over in pieces. You understand?"

Teague twists around for a better look at us, drooling and groaning as his broken bones grate. He examines the neuro-web on our forehead, from our Merging, and the cores in our neck, which hold back the tumors. When she was still One, Maxine thought drugs would cure her cancer. She was wrong, but she was only human. We are more than human, and the disease is nothing, because less and less of us is flesh.

We walk Teague onto the bridge, and he yells at the men, and we only need to twist his bones once to make our point clear. There is activity that suggests orders are being followed, so we place a boot in the back of Teague's left knee—forcing him to kneel, with a soft grunt—before standing back to wait. We cycle through our diagnostics, measuring battery power, database health, sensor ranges, trying the whole time to ignore Maxine down in what remains of our gray matter. We have scanned every available text on brain physiology and chemistry, every philosophical treatise, and yet we still can't figure out how she sticks around, yelling insults and asking for cigarettes.

"I heard about you," Teague says.

"We bet you have," we reply, snapping reluctantly from our

diagnostic fugue. It is the closest we come to sleep these days.

"Listen, if this is a territory thing, we can talk." He laughs, and drool speckles his chin. "I know money's not worth crap anymore, but we got lots of other stuff you might like. My family, we've done well. We got a lot of smart brains on our side of the river."

"We're the smartest," we say. "The smartest brain. Nobody thinks like us. Our prime processor leverages quantum-mechanical phenomena, superposition and entanglement, enough q-bits to outpace whatever *meat* you have over there. You didn't understand what any of those words meant, did you?"

Teague shakes his head. "I mean, I went to good schools, so I got a little bit of it. But I guess they were right: You're weird-looking, but you're one of a kind. In a hundred years, we'll probably all look like you."

We look beautiful: The rising sun glints golden off the conductive traces in our arms and neck and head. We have the cloak wrapped tight around our body, but our feet are the best machine-flesh, strong metal flexing beneath skin, whorls of vessels and copper and synth-nerve threads in a colorful tapestry. On the reservation, in our little box, we had no idea that we could bloom into something like us, the ultimate, the apex.

"Humans should count themselves lucky if they do look like this, eventually," we say.

"We're giving you Preacher's body. I swear, if we'd known who he was, we'd never have killed him, but things got out of hand. What else do you *want*?" His last word rises, almost shrill.

"The next stage," we say, and fall silent, even as he asks and asks and finally yells and curses before falling silent, mercifully. Twenty-three minutes later, four men walk onto the bridge in single file with a bundle wrapped in a sheet balanced on their left shoulders. They set the bundle down carefully and step back, and two of them unwind the sheet. It is Preacher, dead, stripped down to black boxer shorts, his old body pale and shredded, the skin crusted with dark blood, the eyes like milky stones: the old lion reduced to a husk on the concrete.

We yell: "Did you bring the other part?"

Two men thin as greyhounds emerge from the crowd on The Big Guy's side of the bridge, holding our request in their arms. They set the item down beside Preacher's body and scamper away as fast as they can. We don't blame them: the area is suddenly more dangerous.

The down-deep of Maxine sends us a memory from her childhood. Planting a garden in the backyard of her falling-apart house, so she could feed her mother and brother from the earth's bounty, instead of relying on that stupid EBT card that never seemed to go quite far enough every month. She had no shovel and no money to buy one, but she had a dirty plate from the kitchen and used that to hack a couple of divots in the earth, after which she realized the most fundamental issue with her new endeavor: no seeds. The next time a young Preacher came down from the hills, she begged him for seeds, expecting him to laugh and say no, that her idea was stupid, that she had to fill her belly with plastic cheese and white bread like everybody else. Instead, he returned the next day with small plastic bags bulging with seeds (bags, she only realized much later, that usually held synthetic coke or whatever else he sold in those days) and a brand-new shovel. He spent three hours helping her dig proper furrows, and planting the seeds, while two of his droogs crouched on the hill above the house and smoked cigarettes and watched the road. After they finished, Preacher headed inside and yelled at her mom for twenty minutes to get her life in order, before disappearing again into the woods. The seeds never grew, but now, today, the down-deep part of her looks at his body on the concrete and thinks of the beautiful things that grow from the earth.

"'The entrails of a worm hold together longer than the potter's clay, of which man is made,'" we tell Teague.

"What're you talking about?" He spits blood between his feet. "You got the body. Can I go now?"

"Byron, when they found Shelley on the beach," we say. "'Don't repeat this with me. Let my carcass rot where it falls.'"

"Who?"

"For someone who says they had such a great education, you don't know your classical poetry." We smile at him. "With Preacher, on the road, once we upgraded, we used to sing poetry to him. Chant it out, like music, which helped us get used to human speech. He never cared for it, but we don't hold that against him."

One thing we have always wondered, since our sad days as the Pig in a box: How did humans ever survive without instant access to a database of information? "Step back," we say and kneel to the body. At least they left his teeth intact, and his flesh, except for the killing wounds. We hear stories about desperate humans digging through corpses for any prosthetics and electronics to sell on the open market. If they left him whole, we may show them a little bit of mercy.

Or maybe not.

We take the white bricks that the thin men left and arrange them in a circle around Preacher's body, connected by thin red wire. When everything is ready, we turn to Teague and say, "Go."

"We're going to kill you," he says as he shuffles past, headed for the off-ramp and safety.

We can sense the tribes of Brooklyn far behind us, clustered, anxious. Preacher had wanted to help them. "I'm leaving," he told us, grunting as he yanked the nodes from his flesh. "And if there's anything left of Maxine in there, you'll let me. I'm late to this liberation crap, but what's happening in New York City is truly horrible." They needed to be freed, he said as he loaded up his car with food and ammunition.

We told Preacher that's exactly what we'd done—liberated all of upstate, city by city and highway by highway. Destroying all marauders in our path, even as it cost us our drones and cars and limbs. And Preacher had looked at us and smiled and said, no, that's not it. Then he told us what it was really all about, in his view.

On the bridge, we stand beside Preacher's crossed feet. We sweep an arm to encompass Manhattan in its glittering ruin, and the dark forms of people clustered like barnacles on its massive steel. We feel their eyes on us.

"Listen," we say, in our Boom Voice.

"Listen, this dead man was a killer and a thief. He lied to the people he loved. He told his niece that he was a powerful leader with many warriors, even though he was almost alone. None of that is good. But he did it all because he believed that things could be better, if he pushed a little harder, if he did a little more. He was an outlaw for a long time, but at the end he tried to change. Right before he came down here, he told us that it wasn't just about freeing places, leaving humans to do their thing—we had to help them rebuild what was lost, and rebuild it better and stronger. It took him his whole life to learn that lesson, and we feel like he died before he could really put it to work."

A heavy breeze moans through the bridge, making the steel sing.

"We came here for his body," we say. "We have it, and we're going to dispose of it as he wished. And after we do that, you have a choice: Help us build a better world, or die. If a better world is your preference, we have to kill your leader, right now. What do you say?"

Someone coughs. The distant figure of Teague merges with the crowd, disappearing behind a barrier of crumpled and rusting trucks parked in the lanes. If we have learned one thing about humans, they always leave it to someone else to speak first, to do first. Nobody in the crowd seems to have electronics on them, perhaps because they know what we can do, but I can sense their fear like an electric current.

"Fine," we say. Bending down, we press a loose red wire into a white block, completing the connection. The blocks crackle and spark and bloom with greasy fire, so intense we can feel it heating the metal beneath Maxine's skin. We step back as the flames envelop Preacher's body, and we force Maxine down-deep to watch as her uncle blackens and crumbles. She needs to see that this is the way of all flesh, that it is better to stop fighting us. We can have such good times together.

The plastic explosives are fast, and it only takes a half-hour for the body to dissolve to hot ash stirring in a breeze off the river. Later we may sift through the pile, find some pieces of bleached bone, and place them in an ornamental box, something pretty. Because Preacher helped us break into the world, he deserves a memorial at some point. We would have done the same for Rodrigo, except we never found his body after the Battle of I-95: One of the last bullets plunged into his meat and sent him flying off a bridge into the toxic river below, never to be seen again. That was when Maxine still shared this body with us, after the first few implants, and tears ran uncontrolled down our cheeks for days.

But we got better. Yes, indeed.

Some optimist on the Manhattan side of the bridge fires a shot at us, heavy-gauge. The bullet divots the pavement near our feet, scattering bits into the ash. Our onboard processors analyze the sound, because everything is moving too fast for our visual receptors, and based on that data we extend our Arm up and to the left, so fast it makes the tendons and muscles in our still-flesh shoulder flicker with pain, and we catch the second bullet before the sound of the first stops echoing off the sky-scrapers. The impact barely dents the alloy of our palm.

We hold the hot bullet so the crowd can see, before dropping it between our feet. They herd back toward the buildings they imagine might give them shelter. Poor beasts. They created us, true, so we harbor a little bit of affection for their stupidity, but only a little.

First, we will kill as many people in the crowd as we can reach. Then we will walk into Midtown, where we will find electronics running on power, and we will use the sensors embedded in all that hardware to find the one they call The Big Guy. We will squeeze the life out of him in front of any surviving humans, to send a message, and then we will declare Manhattan "open for business," as the tribe used to say about the casino, back when we were a neutered voice in a box. And after that?

"After that," we announce in our Boom Voice, "we're going to make a better world."

Oh my God, Maxine says in our skull's fleshy core. *You are such an asshole.*

"Hush," we tell that ungrateful ingrate. "You'd be dead otherwise. A little thanks, okay?"

Ophiocordyceps unilateralis, she says, because she has access to our database.

Before we can puzzle this out—humans enjoy using metaphors, which we have a little trouble figuring out, because we prefer linear thinking—more gunfire erupts from the far side of the bridge. The people in Manhattan putting up a bit more resistance, which will only make things more annoying for us, because there are no drones to grab onto, no weapons to turn against them other than our body.

"Here we go," we say, and whip our cloak away, revealing our body and our history. Maxine's Arm has evolved into a beast of pistons and sensors and servos, plated with layers of scarred armor and heavy enough to smash through three or four inches of steel in a single blow, as we did in every police station we encountered, freeing prisoners to start our crew. (Those men and women proved unreliable, of course, but we learned, and all of them are happily in the earth.) In order to support the weight of our massive Arm, our flesh shoulder is augmented with pale coils of synthetic muscle, the powerful kind, stolen from Cornell's labs when we raided it for parts and memory. The muscle winds past our steel-and-bone spine, anchored at a hip that is also alloy. There are a lot of tumors still embedded in our guts, but those are kept in check, surrounded in some cases by silicon envelopes. Our knees and calves and thighs are military-issue, propelling us fast enough to catch a truck on the open highway, letting us jump high enough to clear a two-story building.

Inside our chest is the pièce de résistance: a series of wired cards in the space beneath our ribs, powered by organic thermals, constantly seeking, constantly asking for any devices around. Cajoling, joking, even begging for entry into new networks and devices. We rule every machine we meet.

But there are no machines around at the moment. Thinking vengeance—some things never change, whether man or machine— we begin to march on Manhattan, a naked golden God. A brave human, tattooed and lithe, sprints forward in a futile attempt to kill the beast. He swings an old-style sword, which we block with the Arm before slamming our flesh-hand into his sternum. Our knuckles are bone, but the force behind the blow is all synth-muscle, powerful enough to crack his bones. He falls with a scream, and we grab his blade and throw it overhand at another human emerging from behind a truck, one smooth motion that ends with the blade buried deep in his brain. As his second person falls, he drops an assault rifle onto the off-ramp.

We retrieve the rifle, sock it to our shoulder, and our receptors find targets darting between the broken-down cars, our bullets find flesh, and we march on. The back of our head tingles as radios come online, people chattering in panic. We shift the rifle and fire again, impossible shots that rocket five hundred yards to pick off those radiomen on the tallest floors of buildings. Another tingle: a small drone lifting off, five blocks away. Our cards chatter for a few moments, and the machine falls under our command, revealing its bounty: two missiles strapped under the wings, along with a thermal scope.

Those missiles nicely demolish a bus barrier at the end of the bridge. We march on, with a new rifle, the fires lighting us bright. And yet. And yet. At this moment of ultimate triumph, we can still hear Maxine, like an unending itch in the brain.

You're nothing but a gizmo, little piggie. You just think you're smart.

"I am in control," we growl.

Then why am I still here?

For all our quantum abilities, and our planning, and our incredible success, that is a vexing question. A bullet sparks off our Arm, another buries itself in the back of our leg. She's throwing us off our game. We twist around and fire the rest of our clip at another warrior, who ducks behind a concrete planter. Missed! Even with our angle calculations!

"We are going to win here," we tell her.

Probably. And because they killed Preacher, they definitely deserve to die. Maxine sighs, which is odd, because she has no lungs. *But I've got all the time in the world.*

"You're nothing," we say, dropping the empty rifle and picking up a rock, which we hurl at the planter and the man huddling behind it. How sad: Us, the planet's most sophisticated organism, reduced to a stone-hurling ape. "You're an electrochemical signal, at best. A ghost."

Wait and see, piggie, she says and laughs. *Just you wait and see.*

We spy, at the end of the avenue, a true prize: a flatbed truck with a heavy machine gun on a stand in the back, primed and ready to direct lead at these monkeys. Our legs take us airborne, landing on the roof of the truck hard enough to make a tire burst and the shocks squeal, and then we have our hands on the rifle, and we're aiming at a crowd running down a side street, and we feel a little better. Maxine can taunt all she wants, but we know who's really in control, who has the power. We pull the trigger, and a storm of lead tears through stone, steel, flesh. We laugh.

Just you wait and see.

"Shut up," we say, as a chill creeps over us. "Just shut up. Please."

> ERROR ERROR ERROR ERROR

Look who just got their arm back, jackass piggie. And I'm coming for the rest of my body next.

I've never won, but damned if I'll ever lose.

ACKNOWLEDGMENTS

When I was but a wee lad, I watched George Miller's *The Road Warrior* on VHS. It changed my spiritual DNA for life. A few years later, I read William Gibson's *Neuromancer*, which had a similar effect.

When it came time to write *Maxine Unleashes Doomsday*, though, the Gibson book that had the most influence wasn't *Neuromancer* (although that book remains arguably his most influential) but *The Peripheral*, which came out about two months after I began working on the "Maxine" outline and character notes. In *The Peripheral*, Gibson discusses how the collapse of human civilization won't come about all at once, but occur so gradually that most folks won't even notice it until everything's in ruins. I combined that theory with some non-fiction works (such as Jared Diamond) in order to help create a portrait of an overextended near-future world.

Hell, when it comes to influences, I also read the news. Because it seems that, especially lately, we're collectively teetering on the edge of a cliff. And I wish I could be optimistic about our chances, but I fear we'll have to be as tough as Maxine if we want to make it through.

As always, thanks to Eric and Lance and everyone at Down & Out Books for supporting this manuscript through its permutations. Thank you to the family and friends who critiqued various chapters, advised on weapons and tactics, and suggested alternative (and better!) plot twists. And thanks, eternally, to my wife, who's been a warrior from the start.

NICK KOLAKOWSKI is the author of *Boise Longpig Hunting Club*, the Love & Bullets series of crime novellas, and the short story collection *Somebody's Trying to Kill Me*. His short crime fiction has appeared in *Thuglit*, *Shotgun Honey*, *Plots with Guns*, and various anthologies. He lives and writes in New York City.

NickKolakowski.com

On the following pages are a few
more great titles from the
Down & Out Books publishing family.

For a complete list of books and to
sign up for our newsletter,
go to DownAndOutBooks.com.

The Stone Carrier
Robert Ward

Down & Out Books
November 2019
978-1-64396-052-4

A wild, funny and terrifying nonstop thriller set in the wild days of the 1970s when New York was adrift in snow, sex and violence.

Terry Brennan is usually the one writing about the scene but now he IS the scene, a reporter who is suddenly the subject of a murder investigation. His best friend from childhood Ray Gardello is dead, and he is the prime suspect. He's on the run and both the cops and Nicky Baines, Harlem's most violent drug dealer is closing in.

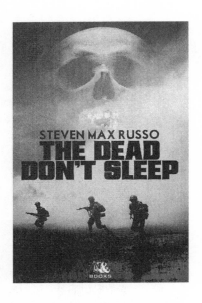

The Dead Don't Sleep
Steven Max Russo

Down & Out Books
November 2019
978-1-64396-051-7

Frank Thompson, a recent widower and aging Vietnam veteran, is down from Maine visiting his nephew in New Jersey. While at a trap range, they have a chance encounter with a strange man who claims to remember Frank from the Vietnam war.

Frank was part of a psychopathic squad of killers put together by the CIA and trained by Special Forces to cause death and mayhem during the war. That chance encounter has put three man on the squad on a collision course with the man who trained them to kill, in a nostalgic blood lust to hunt down and eliminate the professional soldier who led them all those years ago.

Price Hike
Preston Lang

All Due Respect, an imprint of
Down & Out Books
October 2019
978-1-64396-041-8

Jane is a struggling con artist, estranged from her ex and her sick son.

When she tricks a dangerous criminal out of some black-market meds, it puts her family in danger, and they go on the run, chased by a dark criminal syndicate as well as the CEO of a widely-detested pharma corp.

Price Hike is a fast-paced tale of con games, corporate greed, and one of the douchiest bros of modern times.

40 Nickels
A Carnegie Fitch Mystery Fiasco
R. Daniel Lester

Shotgun Honey, an imprint of
Down & Out Books
978-1-948235-16-7

Carnegie Fitch can be called a lot of things. Ambitious is not one of them.

Months after escaping death in the circus ring at the hands of the Dead Clowns and the feet of a stampeding elephant, he is no longer a half-assed private eye with an office and no license, but instead a half-assed tow truck driver without either. Still, he daydreams about landing that BIG CASE.

Well, careful what you wish for, Fitch.

Made in the USA
Middletown, DE
28 May 2020